12

WOMEN
DETECTIVE
STORIES

LAURA MARCUS lectures in English and Humanities at Birkbeck College, University of London. She has written and taught on popular and detective fiction for several years.

D0907507

WOMEN
DETECTIVE
STORIES

Selected and introduced by

LAURA MARCUS

with

CHRIS WILLIS

Oxford   New York

OXFORD UNIVERSITY PRESS

1997

Oxford University Press, Great Clarendon Street, Oxford OX2 6DP

Oxford New York

Athens Auckland Bangkok Bogota Bombay Buenos Aires
Calcutta Cape Town Dar es Salaam Delhi Florence Hong Kong Istanbul
Karachi Kuala Lumpur Madras Madrid Melbourne Mexico City
Nairobi Paris Singapore Taipei Tokyo Toronto Warsaw

and associated companies in
Berlin Ibadan

Oxford is a trade mark of Oxford University Press

© Introduction and selection
Laura Marcus 1997

First published as an Oxford University Press Paperback 1997

All rights reserved. No part of this publication may be reproduced,
stored in a retrieval system, or transmitted, in any form or by any means,
without the prior permission in writing of Oxford University Press.
Within the UK, exceptions are allowed in respect of any fair dealing for the
purpose of research or private study, or criticism or review, as permitted
under the Copyright, Designs and Patents Act, 1988, or in the case of
reprographic reproduction in accordance with the terms of the licences
issued by the Copyright Licensing Agency. Enquiries concerning
reproduction outside these terms and in other countries should be
sent to the Rights Department, Oxford University Press,
at the address above

This book is sold subject to the condition that it shall not, by way
of trade or otherwise, be lent, re-sold, hired out or otherwise circulated
without the publisher's prior consent in any form of binding or cover
other than that in which it is published and without a similar condition
including this condition being imposed on the subsequent purchaser

British Library Cataloguing in Publication Data
Data available

Library of Congress Cataloging in Publication Data
Data available

ISBN 0–19–288036–5

1 3 5 7 9 10 8 6 4 2

Typeset by Jayvee, Trivandrum, India
Printed in Great Britain by
Caledonian International Book Manufacturing Ltd.
Glasgow

CONTENTS

Introduction

1

ANON. (ATTRIB. W. S. HAYWARD)
The Mysterious Countess (c.1861)

I

2

CATHERINE LOUISA PIRKIS (1839–1910)
Drawn Daggers (1893)

25

3

FERGUS HUME (1859–1932)
The First Customer and the Florentine Dante (1897)

46

4

GRANT ALLEN (1848–99)
The Adventure of the Cantankerous Old Lady (1898)

63

5

L. T. MEADE (1854–1914) AND ROBERT EUSTACE (1868–1943)
Mr Bovey's Unexpected Will (1899)

81

6

BARONESS ORCZY (1865–1947)
The Man in the Inverness Cape (1910)

96

Contents

7

HUGH C. WEIR (1884–1934)
The Man With Nine Lives (1914)
114

8

ANNA KATHARINE GREEN (1846–1935)
An Intangible Clue (1915)
147

9

ARTHUR B. REEVE (1880–1936)
The Clairvoyants (1916)
167

10

F. TENNYSON JESSE (1888–1958)
Lot's Wife (1931)
182

11

GLADYS MITCHELL (1901–1983)
A Light on Murder (1950)
214

12

HENRY CECIL (1902–1976)
On Principle (1948)
222

Notes
227

Acknowledgements
230

INTRODUCTION

Aficionados of the detective novel will be familiar with the female 'private eyes' created in the last two decades by Sara Paretsky, Katherine V. Forrest, and Mary Wings, and with the reworkings of 'Golden Age' detective fiction (notably the novels of Dorothy L. Sayers) by writers such as Valerie Miner, Amanda Cross, and Joan Smith. The revival of crime fiction is closely related to the revival of women's fiction and contemporary women writers have revitalized the genre, transforming many of its scripts and stereotypes. The female 'private eye' works outside the law to uncover corruption and cruelty, and criminality is often corporate and political rather than the province of the lone killer. The spate of feminist detective and crime fiction from the 1970s onwards is not represented in this collection, however, because it has found its form in the novel rather than in the short story. The stories in this volume span nearly a century, and not only reveal accomplished play with character, plot, and narrative technique; they also use the structure of the short story with superb confidence.

Many of the stories in this collection appeared in the last decades of the nineteenth century and the early decades of the twentieth. This is not coincidental. First, popular fiction of the kind represented here often first appeared in the periodical press; this form of publication shaped the genre of the short story in the nineteenth century. Secondly, and most crucially, the end of the century saw the mythologizing of the 'New Woman', a term which entered the language in the 1890s to describe a generation of women who rebelled against restrictive Victorian norms of femininity and were often committed to women's suffrage and women's rights. The concept of the 'new' suggests an evolutionary model of womanhood, in which women are seen as standing at the dawn of a new century and of a new age in which 'the future is female'. In popular imagery, positive and negative, the 'New Woman' is often represented as college-educated, independent, and physically, if not sexually, liberated. She finds her exemplar in this collection in Grant Allen's Lois Cayley, a Girton girl noted for her bicycling skills, who turns detective to earn a living when she is left alone and unsupported in the world.

The first women detectives in British fiction, however, made their appearance in the mid- rather than late nineteenth century. In 1861 an anonymously authored book appeared entitled *The Revelations of a Lady Detective*; one of the adventures of its heroine, Mrs Paschal, opens this collection. *The Revelations of a Lady Detective* set the tone for much of the female sleuthing that was to follow. Mrs Paschal is a mistress of reticence and disguise, notable not for those quirks and idiosyncrasies that characterize so many of her male counterparts, but for her ability, compared to that of 'an accomplished actress', to 'play my part in any drama in which I was instructed to play a part'. In 'The Mysterious Countess' she is Nemesis acting as third lady's maid. Mrs Paschal played her part in the developing conventions of the detective story, a relatively new genre whose father is often held to be Edgar Allen Poe, writing in the 1840s. The stories in which she appears also call heavily, however, on the motifs and conventions of Gothic and sensation fiction; at the close of 'The Mysterious Countess' one of the technologies of modernity, the railway, speeds Mrs Paschal to the archaic, Gothic gloom of a Yorkshire abbey. The anachronism is surely deliberate; the railway, intimately bound up with the new form of the detective novel, will cut through the conventions of the most popular fiction of the late eighteenth and early nineteenth centuries, the Gothic novel.

The 1860s were the age of the sensation novel, a genre in which women, as authors and as characters—victims, criminals, and amateur detectives—played a central role. The genre helped to shape the conventions of detective fiction and contributed to the creation of the woman detective, who appeared in fiction some twenty years before women were allowed any form of employment with the Metropolitan Police. (In the 1880s women began to be employed as guards to female prisoners, but they were not given full police status by the Metropolitan Police until 1918, and by the CID until the early 1920s.) The 'nature' of woman was strongly debated and contested in this period and the sensation fiction of Wilkie Collins and Mary Braddon depicted women at the extremes of strength and passivity, transgression and virtue. Wilkie Collins's Valeria Woodville, heroine of *The Law and the Lady* (1875), turns sleuth in order to clear the name of her husband, suspected of having poisoned his first wife. Unlike Mrs Paschal, Valeria is driven to detection not to earn a living but to defend her husband's reputation. Such altruism, becoming a 'lady', is shared by a number of fictional women detectives, many of whom are revealed, early or late in their narratives, to be working for the benefit of male relatives. Valeria is also guided less by reason and science than by intuition. 'Feminine intuition' was outlawed in the rules for 'fair play' in detection drawn up by the Detection Club (a group of detective writers which included Dorothy L. Sayers) in 1930, but it has always hovered at the edges of women's detective fiction, to be embraced or satirized. Hugh Weir's Miss Madelyn Mack, who appears in this collection and is a fine representative of the tradition of American detective heroines, is firmly stated to employ 'hard work and common sense' and not mystical forms of knowing.

The creators of women detectives were all, none the less, confronting the question of women's particular relationships to crime and its detection. That so many male writers (a number of whom are included here) created women sleuths may say something about their feminist sympathies, but it also suggests that female characters allowed for quite specific kinds of detective work and detective narrative. Such particularities arise from entrenched cultural images of femininity, which work both for and against women. Summarized, these would include adeptness at disguise, including the 'disguises' of an only seemingly bedimmed old age or of an appealing, helpless femininity which conceals a ruthless intelligence; an acute eye for those telling details which appear to others as trivia; a driving curiosity in which the stereotype of women's 'nosiness' is turned to good advantage; an 'outsider' status which gives knowledge of the motives and means of social transgressors.

Opinions divide over the question of whether the detective genre is inherently conservative—crime is uncovered and punished and the community is made safe; or inherently subversive—criminality is the focus of interest and even sympathy. There is no simple answer to this question but the reader of the stories that follow may well note ambiguous and ambivalent attitudes towards crime and its punishment. F. Tennyson Jesse's Solange allows a murderous hus-band to live in the shadow of his guilt. And Henry Cecil's unnamed detective narrator, who closes this collection of women detective sto-ries, is one of literature's finest examples of the good bad girl.

LAURA MARCUS, BIRKBECK COLLEGE, LONDON.

1

ANON.

The Mysterious Countess

I

THE CHIEF OF THE DETECTIVE POLICE

I TURNED a familiar corner, and was soon threading the well-known avenues of Whitehall. It was in a small street, the houses in which cover the site of the once splendid palace of the Stuarts, where one king was born and another lost his head, that the headquarters of the London Detective Police were situated. I stopped at a door of modest pretensions, and knocked three times. I was instantly admitted. The porter bowed when he saw who I was, and at once conducted me into a room of limited dimensions. I had not to wait long. Coming from an inner room, a man of spare build, but with keen searching eyes, like those of a ferret, shook me, in a cold, businesslike way, by the hand, and desired me to be seated. His forehead bulged out a little, indicating the talent of which he was the undoubted possessor. All who knew him personally, or by reputation, admired him; he performed the difficult duties of an arduous position with untiring industry and the most praiseworthy skill and perseverance. He left nothing to others, except, of course, the bare execution. This man with the stern demeanour and the penetrating glance was Colonel Warner—at the time of which I am writing, head of the Detective Department of the Metropolitan Police. It was through his instigation that women were first of all employed as detectives. It must be confessed that the idea was not original, but it showed him to be a clever adapter, and not above imitating those whose talent led them to take the initiative in works of progress. Fouché, the great Frenchman, was constantly in the habit of employing women to assist him in discovering the various political intrigues which disturbed the peace of the first empire. His petticoated police were as successful as the most sanguine innovator could wish; and Colonel Warner, having this fact before his eyes, determined to imitate the example of a man who united the courage of a lion with the cunning of a fox, culminating his acquisitions with the sagacity of a dog.

'Sit down, Mrs Paschal,' exclaimed the colonel, handing me a chair.

I did so immediately, with that prompt and passive obedience which always pleased him. I was particularly desirous at all times of conciliating Colonel Warner, because I had not long been employed as a female detective, and now having given up my time and attention to what I may call a new profession, I was anxious to acquit myself as well and favourably as I could, and gain the goodwill and approbation of my superior. It is hardly necessary to refer to the circumstances which led me to embark in a career at once strange, exciting, and mysterious, but I may say that my husband died suddenly, leaving me badly off. An offer was made me through a peculiar channel. I accepted it without hesitation, and became one of the much-dreaded, but little-known people called Female Detectives, at the time I was verging upon forty. My brain was vigorous and subtle, and I concentrated all my energies upon the proper fulfilment and execution of those duties which devolved upon me. I met the glance of Colonel Warner and returned it unflinchingly; he liked people to stare back again at him, because it betokened confidence in themselves, and evidenced that they would not shrink in the hour of peril, when danger encompassed them and lurked in front and rear. I was well born and well educated, so that, like an accomplished actress, I could play my part in any drama in which I was instructed to take a part. My dramas, however, were dramas of real life, not the mimetic representations which obtain on the stage. For the parts I had to play, it was necessary to have nerve and strength, cunning and confidence, resources unlimited, confidence and numerous other qualities of which actors are totally ignorant. They strut, and talk, and give expression to the thoughts of others, but it is such as I who really create the incidents upon which their dialogue is based and grounded.

'I have sent for you,' exclaimed the colonel, 'to entrust a serious case to your care and judgement. I do not know a woman more fitted for the task than yourself. Your services, if successful, will be hand-somely rewarded, and you shall have no reason to complain of my parsimony in the matter of your daily expenses. Let me caution you about hasting—take time—elaborate and mature your plans; for although the hare is swift, the slow and sure tortoise more often wins the race than its fleet opponent. I need hardly talk to you in this way, but advice is never prejudicial to anyone's interests.'

'I am very glad, I am sure,' I replied, 'to hear any suggestions you are good enough to throw out for my guidance.'

'Quite so,' he said; 'I am aware that you possess an unusual amount of common sense, and consequently are not at all likely to take umbrage at what is kindly meant.'

'Of what nature is the business?' I asked.

'Of a very delicate one,' answered Colonel Warner; 'you have heard of the Countess of Vervaine?'

'Frequently; you mean the lady who is dazzling all London at the present moment by the splendour of her equipage and her diamonds, and the magnificent way in which she spends what must be a colossal fortune.'

'That's her,' said the colonel. 'But I have taken great pains to ascer-tain what her fortune actually consists of. Now, I have been unable to identify any property as belonging to her, nor can I discern that she has a large balance in the hands of any banker. From what source, then, is her income derived?'

I acknowledged that I was at a loss to conjecture.

'Very well,' cried Colonel Warner, 'the task I propose for you is to discover where, and in what way, Lady Vervaine obtains the funds which enable her to carry on a career, the splendour and the profuse-ness of which exceed that of a prince of the blood royal during the Augustan age of France, when Louis XIV set an example of extrava-gance which was pursued to ruination by the dissolute nobility, who surrounded the avenues of his palaces, and thronged the drawing-rooms of his country seats. Will it be an occupation to your mind, do you think? If not, pray decline it at once. It is always bad to undertake a commission when it involves a duty which is repugnant to you.'

'Not at all,' I replied; 'I should like above all things to unravel the secrets of the mysterious countess, and I not only undertake to do so, but promise to bring you the tidings and information you wish for within six weeks.'

'Take your own time,' said the colonel; 'anyone will tell you her ladyship's residence; let me see or hear from you occasionally, for I shall be anxious to know how you are getting on. Once more, do not be precipitate. Take this cheque for your expenses. If you should require more, send to me. And now, good morning, Mrs Paschal. I hope sincerely that your endeavours may be crowned with the success they are sure to merit.'

I took the draft, wished Colonel Warner goodbye, and returned to my own lodgings to ruminate over the task which had just been confided to me.

II

THE BLACK MASK

I IMAGINED that the best and surest way of penetrating the veil of secrecy which surrounded the Countess of Vervaine would be to obtain a footing in her household, either as a domestic servant, or in some capacity such as would enable me to play the spy upon her actions, and watch all her movements with the greatest care and closeness. I felt confident that Colonel Warner had some excellent motive for having the countess unmasked; but he was a man who always made you find your own tools, and do your work with as little assistance as possible from him. He told you what he wanted done, and nothing remained but for you to go and do it. The Countess of Vervaine was the young and lovely widow of the old earl of that name. She was on the stage when the notorious and imbecile nobleman made her his wife. His extravagance and unsuccessful speculations in railway shares, in the days when Hudson was king, ruined him, and it was well known that, when he died broken-hearted, his income was very much reduced—so much so, that when his relict began to lead the gay and luxurious life she did, more than one head was gravely shaken, and people wondered how she did it. She thought nothing of giving a thousand pounds for a pair of carriage horses, and all enterprising tradesmen were only too rejoiced when anything rare came in their way, for the Countess of Vervaine was sure to buy it. A rare picture, or a precious stone of great and peculiar value, were things that she would buy without a murmur, and pay the price demanded for them without endeavouring to abate the proprietor's price the value of a penny piece. Personally, she was a rare combination of loveliness and accomplishments. Even the women admitted that she was beautiful, and the men raved about her. She went into the best society, and those of the highest rank and the most exalted social position in London were very glad to be asked to her magnificent and exclusive parties. Fanny, Countess of Vervaine, knew very well that if you wish to become celebrated in the gay and giddy world of fashion, you must be very careful who you admit into your house. It may be convenient, and even necessary, to ask your attorney to dine with you occasionally; but forbear to ask a ducal friend on the same day, because his grace would never forgive you for making so great a blunder. The attorney would go about amongst his friends and tell them all in what company he had been. Your house would acquire the reputation of being an 'easy' one, and your acquaintances who were really worth knowing would not any more visit at a house where 'anybody' was received with the same cordiality that they had themselves met with. The Countess of Vervaine lived in a large mansion in one of the new, but aristocratic squares in Belgravia. A huge towering erection it was to look at—a corner house with many windows and balconies and verandahs and conservatories. It had belonged to the earl, and he bequeathed it to her with all its wealth of furniture, rare pictures, and valuable books. It was pretty well all he had to leave her, for his lands were all sold, and the amount of ready money standing to his credit at his banker's was lamentably small—so small, indeed, as to be almost insignificant. The earl had been dead a year and a half now. She had mourned six months for him, and at the expiration of that time she cast off her widow's weeds—disdaining the example of royalty to wear them for an indefinite period—and launched into all the gaiety and dissipation that the Babylon of the moderns could supply her with. Very clever and versatile was her ladyship, as well able to talk upon abstruse subjects with a member of a scientific society as to converse with one of her patrician friends upon the merits of the latest fashions which the Parisians had with their usual taste designed.

I dressed myself one morning, after having gained the information I have just detailed, and put on the simplest things I could find in my wardrobe, which was as extensive and as full of disguises as that of a costumier's shop. I wished to appear like a servant out of place. My idea was to represent myself as a lady's-maid or under housekeeper. I did not care what situation I took as long as I obtained a footing in the household. When I approached Lady Vervaine's house, I was very much struck by its majestic and imposing appearance. I liked to see the porcelain boxes in the windows filled with the choicest flowers, which a market gardener and floriculturist undertook by contract to change twice a week, so that they should never appear shabby or out of season. I took a delight in gazing at the trailing creepers running in a wild, luxuriant, tropical manner, all over the spacious balconies, and I derived especial pleasure from the contemplation of the orange trees growing in large wooden tubs, loaded with their yellow fruit, the sheen and glimmer of which I could faintly see through the well-cleaned windows of the conservatory, which stood over the porch protecting the entrance to the front door.

I envied this successful actress all the beautiful things she appeared to have in her possession, and wondered why she should be so much more fortunate than myself; but a moment afterwards, I congratulated myself that I was not, like her, an object of suspicion and mistrust to the police, and that a female detective, like Nemesis, was not already upon my track. I vowed that all her splendour should be short-lived, and that in those gilded saloons and lofty halls, where now all was mirth and song and gladness, there should soon be nothing but weeping and gnashing of teeth. I descended the area steps, and even here there was a trace of refinement and good taste, for a small box of mignonette was placed on the sill of each window, and a large Virginia creeper reared its slender limbs against the stuccoed wall.

A request to see the housekeeper brought me into the presence of that worthy. I stated my business to her, and asked her favourable consideration of my case. She shook her head, and said she was afraid that there was no vacancy just at present, but if I would call again, she might perhaps be able to give me a more encouraging reply. I knew perfectly well how to treat a lady of her calibre. Servants in gentlemen's families are generally engaged in making a purse, upon the proceeds of which they are enabled to retire when the domestic harness begins to gall their necks, and they sigh for rest after years of hard work and toil. They either patronize savings' banks, where they get their two and a half per cent, on the principle that every little helps, although they could at the same time obtain six per cent in foreign guaranteed government stock; but those who work hard, know how to take care of their money, because they understand its value, and they distrust speculative undertakings, as it is the duty of all prudent people to do; or if they distrust the parochial banks, they have a stocking which they keep carefully concealed, the contents of which are to help their possessors to furnish a lodging-house, or take a tavern, when the time arrives at which they think fit to assert their independence and retire from the servitude which they have all along tolerated for a purpose. Armed with a thorough knowledge of the class, I produced a five-pound note, and said that it was part of my savings from my last place, and that I should be happy to make her a present of it, if she would use the influence I was sure she possessed to procure me the situation I was so desirous of obtaining.

This offer produced a relaxation of the housekeeper's sternness. She asked for a reference, which I gave her; we always knew how to arrange those little matters, which were managed without any difficulty; and the result of our interview was, that I was engaged as third lady's-maid at a salary of fifteen pounds a year, and to find myself in tea and sugar. I entered my new place in less than a week, and soon had an opportunity of observing the demeanour of the Countess of Vervaine; at times it was restless and excited. Her manner was frequently preoccupied, and she was then what is called absent. You might speak to her three or four times before you obtained an answer. She did not appear to hear you. Some weighty matter was occupying her attention, and she was so engrossed by its contemplation that she could not bestow a single thought on external objects. She was very young—scarcely five-and-twenty, and not giving evidence of being so old as that. She was not one of those proud, stern, and haughty aristocrats whom you see in the Park, leaning back in their open carriages as if they were casting their mantle of despisal and scorn to those who are walking. She was not pale, and fagged, and bilious-looking; on the contrary, she was fat and chubby, with just the smallest tinge of rose-colour on her cheek—natural colour, I mean, not the artificial hue which pernicious compounds impart to a pallid cheek.

Now and then there was an air of positive joyousness about her, as if she was enamoured of life and derived the most intense pleasure from existence in this world below, where most of us experience more blows and buffets than we do occurrences of a more gratifying nature. Although not pretending to do so, I studied her with great care, and the result of my observations was, that I could have sworn before any court of justice in the world that to the best of my belief, she had a secret—a secret which weighed her down and crushed her young, elastic spirit, sitting on her chest like a nightmare, and spoiling her rest by hideous visions. In society she showed nothing of this. It was in the company of others that she shone; at home, in her bed-room, with her attendant satellites about her, whom she regarded as nobodies, she gave way to her fits of melancholy, and showed that every shining mirror has its dull side and its leaden reverse. There are some people who are constituted in such a manner by nature, that though they may be standing upon the crater of a volcano given to chronic eruptions, and though they are perfectly cognizant of the per-ilous position in which they are, will not trouble themselves much about it. It was my private opinion that the ground under the feet of the Countess of Vervaine was mined, and that she knew it, but that she had adopted that fallacious motto which has for its burden 'a short life and a merry one'. There was something very mysterious about her, and I made the strongest resolution that I ever made in my life that I would discover the nature of the mystery before many days had passed over my head. The countess had not the remotest idea that I was in any way inimical to her. She regarded me as something for which she paid, and which was useful to her on certain occasions. I believe she looked upon me very much as a lady in the Southern States of America looks upon a slave—a thing to minister to her van-ity and obey her commands. Lady Vervaine was one of those fascin-ating little women who charm you by their simple, winning ways, and you do not dream for a moment that they are not terrestrial angels; did you know them intimately, however, you would discover that they have a will and a temper of their own, such as would render the life of a husband miserable and unhappy if he did succumb to her slightest wish and put up with her most frivolous caprice. She was frequently tyrannical with her servants, and would have her most trivial command obeyed to the letter, under pain of her sovereign displeasure. One day she struck me on the knuckles with a hairbrush, because I ran a hairpin into her head by the merest accident in the world. I said nothing, but I cherished an idea of retaliation nevertheless. We had dressed her on a particular evening for the Opera. She looked very charming; but so graceful was her manner, so pleasant was her bearing, and so unexceptionable her taste, that she could never look anything else.

'Paschal,' she said to me.

'Yes, my lady,' I replied.

'I shall come home a little before twelve; wait up for me.'

'Yes, my lady,' I replied again, in the monotonous, parrot-like tone that servants are supposed to make use of when talking to those who have authority over them.

It was a long, dreary evening; there was not much to do, so I took up a book and tried to read; but although I tried to bring my attention upon the printed page, I was unable to succeed in doing so. I was animated with a conviction that I should make some important discovery that night. It is a singular thing, but in my mind coming events always cast their shadows before they actually occurred. I invariably had an intuition that such and such a thing would happen before it actually took place. It was considerably past twelve when the mysterious countess came home; the charms of the Opera and the Floral Hall must have detained her until the last moment, unless she had met with some entertaining companion who beguiled the hours by soft speeches and tender phrases, such as lovers alone know how to invent and utter. I began to unrobe her, but after I had divested her of her cloak, she called for her dressing-gown, and told me to go and bring her some coffee. The cook was gone to bed, and I found some difficulty in making the water boil, but at last I succeeded in brewing the desired beverage, and took it upstairs. The countess was, on my return, industriously making calculations, at least so it seemed to me, in a little book bound in morocco leather, and smelling very much like a stationer's shop. She might have been making poetry, or concerting the plot of a drama, but she stopped every now and then, as if to 'carry' something, after the manner of mathematicians who do not keep a calculating machine on the premises.

After I had put down the coffee, she exclaimed—

'You can go. Goodnight.'

I replied in suitable terms, and left her, but not to go to my room or to sleep. I hung about the corridor in a stealthy way, for I knew very well that no one else was likely to be about, and I wanted to watch my lady that night, which I felt convinced was going to be prolific of events of a startling nature. The night was a little chilly, but I did not care for that. Sheltering myself as well as I could in the shadow of a doorway, I waited with the amount of resignation and patience that the occasion required. In about half an hour's time the door of the Countess of Vervaine's apartment opened. I listened breathlessly, never daring to move a muscle, lest my proximity to her should be discovered. What was my surprise and astonishment to see a man issue from the room! He held a light in his hand, and began to descend a flight of stairs by its aid.

I rubbed my eyes to see whether I had not fallen asleep and dreamed a dream; but no, I was wide awake. The man must, I imagined, have been concealed somewhere about the apartment, for I saw no trace of him during the time that I was in the room. He was a person of small size, and dressed in an odd way, as if he was not a gentleman, but a servant out of livery. This puzzled me more than ever, but I had seen a few things in my life which appeared scarcely susceptible of explanation at first, but which, when eliminated by the calm light of reason and dissected by the keen knife of judgement, were in a short time as plain as the sun at noonday. I thought for a brief space, and then I flattered myself that I had penetrated the mystery. I said to myself, *It is a disguise*. The Countess of Vervaine was a little woman. She would consequently make a very small man. The one before me, slowly and with careful tread going down the staircase, was a man of unusually small stature. You would call him decidedly undersized. There was a flabbiness about the clothes he wore which seemed to indicate that they had not been made for him. The coat-sleeves were especially long. This gave strength to the supposition that the countess had assumed male attire for purposes of her own. She could not possibly have had herself measured for a suit of clothes. No tailor in

London would have done such a thing. She had probably bought the things somewhere—picking them up at random without being very particular as to their size or fit. I allowed the man to reach the bottom of the staircase before I followed in pursuit. Gliding stealthily along with a care and precision I had often practised in the dead of night at home in order that I might become well versed and experienced in an art so useful to a detective, I went down step by step and caught sight of the man turning an angle which hid him from my view, but as he did so I contrived to glance at his features. I started and felt inclined to shriek. Every lineament of his face was concealed by a hideous black mask. My sensations were not enviable for many a long night afterwards; that dark funereal face-covering was imprinted in an almost indelible manner upon my mind, and once or twice I awoke in bed shivering all over in a cold perspiration, fancying that the Black Mask was standing over me, holding a loaded pistol at my head, and threatening my life if I did not comply with some importunate demand which I felt I could not pay the slightest attention to. Recovering myself as best I could, I raised my dress, and stepping on my toes, followed the Black Mask. He descended to the lower regions. He held the light before him, occasionally looking around to see if any one were behind him. I contrived whenever he did this to vanish into some corner or fall in a heap so that the rays of the lamp should not fall upon my erect form. We passed the kitchens, from which the stale cabbage-watery smell arose which always infests those interesting domestic offices after their occupants have retired to rest. I could hear the head cook snoring. He slept in a small room on the basement, and was, I have no doubt, glad to go to bed after the various onerous duties that he had to perform during the day, for the office of cook in a good family is by no means a sinecure. Aristocratic birth does not prevent the possessor from nourishing a somewhat plebeian appetite, which must be satisfied at least four or five times a day. A plain joint is not sufficient, a dozen messes called *entrées* must accompany it, composed of truffles and other evil-smelling abominations, such as are to be met with at the shop of a Parisian *épicier*. I had not searched the rooms on the basement very closely, but during the cursory investigation I had made, I noticed that there was one which was always kept locked. No one ever entered it. Some said the key was lost, but none of the servants seemed to trouble themselves much about it. It was an empty room, or it was a lumber room. They did not know, neither did they care. This being the state of things existent respecting that room, I was astonished to see the man in the black mask produce a key well oiled so as to make it facile of turning, put it in the lock, turn it, open the door, enter and disappear, shutting the door after him. It did not take me long to reach the keyhole, to which I applied my eye. The key was not in it, but whether the Black Mask had secured the door inside or not, I could not tell. The time had not then arrived at which it was either necessary or prudent to solve the riddle. I could see inside the room with the greatest ease. The lamp was on the floor, and the Black Mask was on his knees engaged in scrutinizing the flooring. The apartment was utterly destitute of furniture, not even a chair or a common deal table adorned the vacant space, but a few bricks piled on the top of one another lay in one corner. Near them was a little mound of dry mortar, which, from its appearance, had been made and brought there months ago. A trowel such as bricklayers use was not far off. While I was noticing these things the man in the black mask had succeeded in raising a couple of planks from the floor. These he laid in a gentle way on one side. I could perceive that he had revealed a black yawning gulf such as the entrance to a sewer might be. After hesitating a moment to see if his lamp was burning brightly and well, he essayed the chasm and disappeared in its murky depths, as if he had done the same thing before and knew very well where he was going. Perfectly amazed at the discoveries I was making, I looked on in passive wonderment. I was, as may be supposed, much pleased at what I saw, because I felt that I had discovered the way to unravel a tangled skein. Queen Eleanor, when she found out the clue which led her through the maze to the bower of fair Rosamond, was not more delighted than myself, when I saw the strange and mystic proceeding on the part of the Black Mask. When I had allowed what I considered a sufficient time to elapse, I tried the handle of the door—it turned. A slight push and the door began to revolve on its hinges; another one, and that more vigorous, admitted me to the room. All was in darkness. Sinking on my hands and knees, I crawled with the utmost caution in the direction of the hole in the floor. Half a minute's search brought me to it. My hand sank down as I endeavoured to find a resting-place for it. I then made it my business to feel the sides of the pit to discover if there was any ladder, through the instrumentality of whose friendly steps I could follow the Black Mask. There was. Having satisfied myself of this fact, I with as much rapidity as possible took off the small crinoline I wore, for I considered that it would very much impede my movements. When I had divested myself of the obnoxious garment, and thrown it on the floor, I lowered myself into the hole and went down the ladder. Four or five feet, I should think, brought me to the end of the flight of steps. As well as I could judge I was in a stone passage. The air was damp and cold. The sudden chill made me shudder. It was evidently a long way underground, and the terrestrial warmth was wanting. It had succumbed to the subterraneous vapours, which were more searching than pleasant. A faint glimmer of light some distance up the passage showed me that the Black Mask had not so much the best of the chase. My heart palpitated, and I hastened on at the quickest pace I considered consistent with prudence.

III

BARS OF GOLD AND INGOTS

I COULD see that the passage I was traversing had been built for some purpose to connect two houses together. What the object of such a connection was it was difficult to conceive. But rich people are frequently eccentric, and do things that those poorer and simpler than themselves would never dream of. The Black Mask had discovered the underground communication, and was making use of it for the furtherance of some clandestine operation. The passage was not of great length. The Black Mask stopped and set the light upon the ground. I also halted, lest the noise of my footsteps might alarm the mysterious individual I was pursuing. I had been in many perplexities and exciting situations before, and I had taken a prominent part in more than one extremely perilous adventure, but I do not think that I was ever, during the whole course of my life, actuated by so strong a curiosity, or animated with so firm a desire to know what the end would be, as I was on the present occasion. In moments such as those which were flitting with the proverbial velocity of time, but which seemed to me very slow and sluggish, the blood flows more quickly through your veins, your heart beats with a more rapid motion, and the tension of the nerves becomes positively painful. I watched the movements of the Black Mask with the greatest care and minuteness. He removed, by some means with which he was acquainted, half a dozen good-sized bricks from the wall, revealing an aperture of sufficient dimensions to permit the passage of a human body. He was not slow in passing through the hole. The light he took with him. I was in darkness. Crawling along like a cat about to commit an act of feline ferocity upon some musipular abortion, I reached the cavity and raised my eyes to the edge, so as to be able to scrutinize the interior of the apartment into which the Black Mask had gone. It was a small place, and more like a vault than anything else. The light had been placed upon a chest, and its flickering rays fell around, affording a sickly glare very much like that produced on a dark afternoon in a shrine situated in a Roman Catholic Continental church. The sacred edifice is full of darkening shadows, but through the bronzed railings which shut off egress to the shrine, you can see the long wax tapers burning, emitting their fiery tribute to the manes of the dead. The Black Mask had fallen on his knees before a chest of a peculiar shape and make; it was long and narrow. Shooting back some bolts, the lid flew open and disclosed a large glittering pile of gold to my wondering gaze. There was the precious metal, not coined and mixed with alloy, but shining in all the splendour of its native purity. There were bars of gold and ingots, such as Cortez and Pizarro, together with their bold followers, found in Peru, when the last of the Incas was driven from his home, his kingdom, and his friends, after many a sanguinary battle, after many a hard-fought fray. The bars were heavy and valuable, for they were pure and unadulterated. There were many chests, safes, and cases, in the vault. Were they all full of gold? If so, what a prize had this audacious robber acquired! He carefully selected five of the largest and heaviest ingots. Each must have been worth at least a thousand pounds. It was virgin gold, such as nuggets are formed of, and, of course, worth a great deal of money. After having made his choice, it was necessary to place the bars in some receptacle. He was evidently a man of resources, for he drew a stout canvas bag from his pocket, and, opening it, placed them inside; but, as he was doing so, the mask fell from his face. Before he could replace the hideous facial covering,

14

I made a discovery, one I was not altogether unprepared for. The black mask—ungainly and repulsive as it was—had hitherto concealed the lovely features of the Countess of Vervaine. With a tiny exclamation of annoyance she replaced the mask and continued her task. I smiled grimly as I saw who the midnight robber was, whose footsteps I had tracked so well, whose movements I had watched so unerringly. It would take but few visits to this treasure vault, I thought to myself, to bring in a magnificent income; and then I marvelled much what the vault might be, and how the vast and almost countless treasure got there. Questions easy to propound, but by no means so facile of reply. At present my attention was concentrated wholly and solely upon the countess. It would be quite time enough next morning to speculate upon the causes which brought about effects of which I was the exultant witness. Having stowed away the ingots in the canvas bag, the mysterious countess rose to her feet, and made a motion indicative of retiring. At this juncture I was somewhat troubled in my mind. Would it be better for me to raise an alarm or to remain quiet? Supposing I were to cry out, who was there to hear my exclamation or respond to my earnest entreaty for help and assistance. Perhaps the countess was armed. So desperate an adventuress as she seemed to be would very probably carry some offensive weapon about her, which it was a fair presumption she would not hesitate to use if hard pressed, and that lonely passage, the intricacies of which were in all probability known but to herself and me, would for ever hide from prying eyes my blanching bones and whitening skeleton. This was not a particularly pleasant reflection, and I saw that it behoved me to be cautious. I fancied that I could regain the lumber room before the countess could overtake me, because it would be necessary for her to shut down and fasten the chest, and when she had done that she would be obliged to replace the bricks she had removed from the wall, which proceeding would take her some little time and occupy her attention while I made my escape. I had gained as much information as I wished, and I was perfectly satisfied with the discovery I had made. The countess was undoubtedly a robber, but it required some skill to succeed in bringing her to justice. In just that species of skill and cunning I flattered myself I was a proficient. Hastily retreating, I walked some distance, but to my surprise did not meet with the ladder. Could I have gone wrong? Was it possible that I had taken the wrong turning? I was totally unacquainted with the ramifications of these subterranean corridors. I trembled violently, for a suspicion arose in my breast that I might be shut in the vault. I stopped a moment to think, and leaned against the damp and slimy wall in a pensive attitude.

IV

IN THE VAULT

WITHOUT a light I could not tell where I was, or in which direction it would be best for me to go. I was in doubt whether it would be better to go steadily on or stay where I was, or retrace my steps. I had a strong inclination to do the latter. Whilst I was ruminating a light appeared to the left of me. It was that borne by the Countess of Vervaine. I had then gone wrong. The passage prolonged itself, and I had not taken the right turning. The countess was replacing the bricks, so that it was incumbent upon me to remain perfectly still, which I did. Having accomplished her task, she once more took up her bag, the valuable contents of which were almost as much as she could carry. I was in the most critical position. She would unquestionably replace the planks, and perhaps fasten them in some way so as to prevent my escaping as she had done. My only chance lay in reaching the ladder before her, but how was it possible to do so when she was between myself and the ladder? I should have to make a sudden attack upon her, throw her down, and pass over her prostrate body,—all very desirable, but totally impossible. I was defenceless. I believed her to be armed. I should run the risk of having a couple of inches of cold steel plunged into my body, or else an ounce of lead would make a passage for itself through the ventricles of my heart, which were not at all desirous of the honour of being pierced by a lady of rank. I sighed for a Colt's revolver, and blamed myself for not having taken the precaution of being armed. Although I wished to capture Lady Vervaine above all things, I was not tired of my life. Once above ground again and in the house I should feel myself more of a free agent than I did in those dreary vaults, where I felt sure I should fall an easy prey to the attacks of an unscrupulous woman. Lady Vervaine pursued her way with a quick step, which showed that she had accomplished her object, and was anxious to get to her own room again, and reach a haven of safety. As for me, I resigned myself to my fate. What could I do? To attack her ladyship would, I thought, be the forerunner of instant death. It would be like running upon a sword, or firing a pistol in one's own mouth. She would turn upon me like a tiger, and in order to save herself from the dreadful consequences of her crime, she would not hesitate a moment to kill me. Serpents without fangs are harmless, but when they have those obnoxious weapons it is just as well to put your iron heel upon their heads and crush them, so as to render them harmless and subservient to your sovereign and conquering will. I followed the Countess of Vervaine slowly, and at a distance, but I dared not approach her. I was usually fertile in expedients, and I thought I should be able to find my way out of the dilemma in some way. I was not a woman of one idea, and if one dart did not hit the mark I always had another feathered shaft ready for action in my well-stocked quiver. Yet it was not without a sickening feeling of uncertainty and doubt that I saw her ladyship ascend the ladder and vanish through the opening in the flooring. I was alone in the vault, and abandoned to my own resources. I waited in the black darkness in no enviable frame of mind, until I thought the countess had had sufficient time to evacuate the premises, then I groped my way to the ladder and mounted it. I reached the planks and pushed against them with all my might, but the strength I possessed was not sufficient to move them. My efforts were futile. Tired and exhausted, I once more tried the flags which paved the passage, and cast about in my mind for some means of escape from my unpleasant position. If I could find no way of extrication it was clear that I should languish horribly for a time, and ultimately perish of starvation. This was not an alluring prospect, nor did I consider it so. I had satisfied myself that it was impossible to escape through the flooring, as the Countess of Vervaine had in some manner securely fastened the boards. Suddenly an idea shot through my mind with the vivid quickness of a flash of lightning. I could work my way back through the passage, and by feeling every brick as I went, discover those which gave her ladyship admittance into the vault where the massive ingots of solid bullion were kept. I had no doubt whatever that so precious a hoard was visited occasionally by those it belonged to, and I should not only be liberated from my captivity, but I should discover the mystery which was at present perplexing me. Both of these were things I was desirous of accomplishing, so I put my shoulder to the wheel, and once more threaded the circumscribed dimensions of the corridor which led to the place in which such a vast quantity of gold was concealed. I took an immense deal of trouble, for I felt every brick singly, and after passing my fingers over its rough surface gave it a push to see if it yielded. At last, to my inexpressible joy, I reached one which 'gave', another vigorous thrust and it fell through with a harsh crash upon the floor inside. The others I took out more carefully. When I had succeeded in removing them all I entered the bullion vault in the same way in which her ladyship had, and stopped to congratulate myself upon having achieved so much. The falling brick had made a loud noise, which had reverberated through the vault, producing cavernous echoes; but I had not surmised that this would be productive of the consequences that followed it. Whilst I was considering what I should do or how I should dispose myself to sleep for an hour or so—for, in nursery parlance, the miller had been throwing dust in my eyes, and I was weary—I heard a noise in one corner of the vault, where I afterwards found the door was situated. A moment of breathless expectation followed, and then dazzling blinding lights flashed before me and made me close my shrinking eyes involuntarily. Harsh voices rang in my ears, rude hands grasped me tightly, and I was a prisoner. When I recovered my power of vision, I was surrounded by three watchmen, and as many policemen. They manacled me. I protested against such an indignity, but appearances were against me.

'I am willing to come with you,' I exclaimed, in a calm voice, because I knew I had nothing to fear in the long run. 'But why treat me so badly?'

'Only doing my duty,' replied one of the police, who seemed to have the command of the others.

'Why do you take me in custody?' I demanded.

'Why? Come, that's a good joke,' he replied.

'Answer my question.'

'Well, if you don't know, I'll tell you,' he answered, with a grin.

'I have an idea, but I want to be satisfied about the matter.'

'We arrest you for *robbing the bank*,' he replied, solemnly.

My face brightened. So it was a bank, and the place we were in was the bullion vault of the house. The mystery was now explained. The Countess of Vervaine had by some means discovered her proximity to so rich a place, and had either had the passage built, or had been fortunate enough to find it ready-made to her hand. This was a matter for subsequent explanation.

'I am ready to go with you,' I said; 'when we arrive at the station-house I shall speak to the inspector on duty.'

The man replied in a gruff voice, and I was led from the vault, happy in the reflection that I had escaped from the gloom and darkness of the treasure house.

V

HUNTED DOWN

'GLAD to see you, Mrs Paschal,' exclaimed Colonel Warner when I was ushered into his presence. 'I must congratulate you upon your tact, discrimination, and perseverance, in running the Countess of Vervaine to earth as cleverly as you did. Rather an unpleasant affair, though, that of the subterranean passage.'

'I am accustomed to those little dramatic episodes,' I replied: 'when I was taken to the station-house by the exultant policeman, the inspector quickly released me on finding who I was. I always carry my credentials in my pocket, and your name is a tower of strength with the executive.'

'We must consider now what is to be done,' said the colonel; 'there is no doubt whatever that the South Belgrave Bank has been plundered to a great extent, and that it is from that source that our mysterious countess has managed to supply her extravagant habits and keep up her transitory magnificence, which she ought to have seen would, from its nature, be evanescent. I am only surprised to think that her depredations were not discovered before; she must have managed everything in a skilful manner, so skilful indeed as to be worthy of the expertest burglar of modern times. I have had the manager of the bank with me this morning, and he is desirous of having the matter hushed up if possible; but I told him frankly that I could consent to nothing of the kind. One of the watchmen or policemen who took you into custody must have gone directly to a newspaper office, and have apprised the editor of the fact, because here is a statement of the circumstance in a daily paper, which seems to have escaped the manager's notice. Newspapers pay a small sum for information, and that must have induced the man to do as he apparently has done. The astute Countess of Vervaine has, I may tell you, taken advantage of this hint, and gone away from London, for I sent to her house this morning, which was shut up. The only reply my messengers could get was that her ladyship had gone out of town, owing to the illness of a near relation; which is, of course, a ruse.'

'Clearly,' I replied, 'she has taken the alarm, and wishes to throw dust in our eyes.'

'What do you advise?' asked Colonel Warner, walking up and down the room.

'I should say, leave her alone until her fears die away and she returns to town. It is now the height of the season, and she will not like to be away for any great length of time.'

'I don't agree with you, Mrs Paschal,' returned the colonel, testily.

'Indeed, and why not?'

'For many reasons. In the first place, she may escape from the country with the plunder. What is to prevent her from letting her house and furniture in London, and going abroad with the proceeds?'

'There is some truth in that,' I said, more than half convinced that the colonel took the correct view of the case.

'Very well; my second reason is, that a bird in the hand is worth two in the bush.'

Proverbial, but true, I thought to myself.

'Thirdly, I wish to recover as much of the stolen property as I can. A criminal with full hands is worth more than one whose digits are empty.'

'Do you propose that I shall follow her up?' I demanded.

'Most certainly I do.'

'In that case, the sooner I start the better it will be.'

'Start at once, if your arrangements will permit you to do so. Servants are not immaculate, and by dint of enquiry at her ladyship's mansion, I have little doubt you will learn something which you will find of use to you.'

'In less than a week, colonel,' I replied, confidently, 'the Countess of Vervaine shall be in the hands of the police.'

'In the hands of the police!' What a terrible phrase!—full of significance and awful import—redolent of prisons and solitary confinement—replete with visions of hard-labour and a long and weary imprisonment—expressive of a life of labour, disgrace, and pain—perhaps indicative of summary annihilation by the hands of the hangman.

'I rely upon you,' said Colonel Warner, shaking my hand. 'In seven days from this time I shall expect the fulfilment of your promise.'

I assented, and left the office in which affairs of so much importance to the community at large were daily conducted, and in nine cases out of ten brought to a successful issue.

Yet the salary this man received from a grateful nation, or more strictly speaking from its Government, was a bare one thousand a year, while many sinecurists get treble that sum for doing nothing at all. My first care was to return to the Countess of Vervaine's house. It was shut up, but that merely meant that the blinds were down and the shutters closed in the front part. The larger portion of the servants were still there and glad to see me. They imagined that I had been allowed a holiday, or that I had been somewhere on business for her ladyship. I at once sought the housekeeper.

'Well, Paschal,' she said, 'what do you want?'

'I have been to get some money for the countess, who sent me into the City for that purpose, ma'am,' I boldly replied, 'and she told me I was to come to you, give you ten pounds, and you would give me her address, for she wished me to follow her into the country.'

'Oh! indeed. Where is the money?'

I gave the housekeeper ten sovereigns, saying—

'You can have five more if you like, I dare say she wont miss it.'

'Not she. She has plenty.'

The five additional portraits of Her Majesty were eagerly taken possession of by the housekeeper, who blandly told me that the countess would be found at Blinton Abbey, in Yorkshire, whither she had gone to spend a fortnight with some aristocratic acquaintance. I always made a point of being very quiet, civil, and obliging when in the presence of the housekeeper, who looked upon me as remarkably

21

innocent, simple, and hardworking. After obtaining the information I was in search of I remained chatting in an amicable and agreeable manner for a short time, after which I took my leave. When, ho! for the night mail, north. I was accompanied by a superintendent, to whom I invariably intrusted the consummation of arduous enterprises which required masculine strength. He was a sociable man, and we might between us have proved a match for the cleverest thieves in Christendom. In fact we frequently were so, as they discovered to their cost. There is to me always something very exhilarating in the quickly rushing motion of a railway carriage. It is typical of progress, and raises my spirits in proportion to the speed at which we career along, now through meadow and now through woodland, at one time cutting through a defile and afterwards steaming through a dark and sombre tunnel. What can equal such magical travelling? It was night when we reached Blinton. The Abbey was about a mile and a half from the railway station. Neither the superintendent or myself felt inclined to go to rest, for we had indulged in a nap during the journey, from which we awoke very much invigorated. We left our carpet bags in the care of a sleepy railway porter who had only awaited the arrival of the night mail north, and at half-past one o'clock set out to reconnoitre the position of Blinton Abbey. The moon was shining brightly. We pursued a bridle path and found little difficulty in finding the Abbey as we followed the porter's instructions to the letter. All was still as we gazed undisturbed upon the venerable pile which had withstood the blasts of many a winter and reflected the burning rays of innumerable summer suns. I was particularly struck with the chapel, which was grey and sombre before us; the darkened roof, the lofty buttresses, the clustered shafts, all spoke of former grandeur. The scene forcibly recalled Sir Walter Scott's lines,

> 'If thou would'st view fair Melrose aright,
> Go visit it by the pale moonlight;
> For the gay beams of lightsome day
> Gild but to flout the ruins grey.
> When the broken arches are black in night,
> And each shafted oriel glimmers white;
> When the cold light's uncertain shower
> Streams on the ruined central tower;

When buttress and buttress alternately
Seem framed of ebon and ivory—
Then go, but go alone the while,
And view St David's sacred pile.'

We halted, inspired with a sort of sacred awe. The chapel, the tur-
reted castle, the pale and silvery moonlight, the still and witching time
of night, the deep castellated windows, the embrasures on the roof
from which, in days gone by, many a sharp-speaking culverin was
pointed against the firm and lawless invader, all conspired to inspire
me with sadness and melancholy. I was aroused from my reverie by
the hand of the Superintendent which sought my arm. Without
speaking a word he drew me within the shadow of a recess, and having safely ensconced me together with himself, he whispered the
single word, 'Look!' in my ear. I did as he directed me, and following
the direction indicated by his outstretched finger saw a dark figure
stealing out of a side door of Blinton Abbey. Stealthily and with cat-
like tread did that sombre figure advance until it reached the base of
a spreading cedar tree whose funereal branches afforded a deathlike
shade like that of yew trees in a churchyard, when the figure produced
a sharp-pointed instrument and made a hole as if about to bury something. I could scarcely refrain a hoarse cry of delight, for it seemed
palpable to me that the Countess of Vervaine was about to dispose of
her ill-gotten booty. I blessed the instinct which prompted me to propose a visit to the Abbey in the night-time, although I invariably selected
the small hours for making voyages of discovery. I have generally found
that criminals shun the light of day and seek the friendly shelter of a too
often treacherous night. In a low voice I communicated my suspicions
to the superintendent, and he concurred with me. I suggested the
instant arrest of the dark figure. The lady was so intently engaged that
she did not notice our approach; had she done so she might have
escaped into the Abbey. The strong hand of the superintendent was
upon her white throat before she could utter a sound. He dragged her
remorselessly into the moonlight, and the well-known features of the
Countess of Vervaine were revealed indisputably.

'What do you want of me, and why am I attacked in this way?' she
demanded in a tremulous voice as soon as the grasp upon her throat
was relaxed.

I had meanwhile seized a bag, the same canvas bag which had contained the ingots on the night of the robbery. They were still there. When I heard her ladyship's enquiry, I replied to it. 'The directors of the South Belgravia Bank are very anxious to have an interview with your ladyship,' I said.

She raised her eyes to mine, and an expression of anguish ran down her beautiful countenance. She knew me, and the act of recognition informed her that she was hunted down. With a rapid motion, so swift, so quick, that it resembled a sleight-of-hand, the Countess of Vervaine raised something to her mouth; in another moment her hand was by her side again, as if nothing had happened. Something glittering in the moonlight attracted my attention. I stooped down and picked it up. It was a gold ring of exquisite workmanship. A spring lid revealing a cavity was open. I raised it to my face. A strong smell of bitter almonds arose. I turned round with a flushed countenance to her ladyship. She was very pale. The superintendent was preparing to place handcuffs around her slender wrists; he held the manacles in his hand and was adjusting them. But she was by her own daring act spared this indignity. A subtle poison was contained in the secret top of her ring, and she had with a boldness peculiar to herself swallowed it before we could anticipate or prevent her rash act. The action of the virulent drug was as quick as it was deadly She tottered. A smile which seemed to say, the battle is over, and I soon shall be at rest, sat upon her lips. Then she fell heavily to the ground with her features convulsed with a hard spasm, a final pain; her eyes were fixed, her lips parted, and Fanny, the accomplished, lovely, and versatile Countess of Vervaine was no more. I did not regret that so young and fair a creature had escaped the felon's dock, the burglar's doom. The affair created much excitement at the time, and the illustrated papers were full of pictures of Blinton Abbey, but it has long since passed from the public mind, and hundreds of more sensations have cropped up since then. The South Belgravian Bank recovered its ingots, but it was nevertheless a heavy loser through the former depredations of the famous Countess of Vervaine.

2

CATHERINE LOUISA PIRKIS

Drawn Daggers

'I ADMIT that the dagger business is something of a puzzle to me, but as for the lost necklace—well, I should have thought a child would have understood that,' said Mr Dyer irritably. 'When a young lady loses a valuable article of jewellery and wishes to hush the matter up, the explanation is obvious.'

'Sometimes,' answered Miss Brooke calmly, 'the explanation that is obvious is the one to be rejected, not accepted.'

Off and on these two had been, so to speak, 'jangling' a good deal that morning. Perhaps the fact was in part to be attributed to the biting east wind which had set Loveday's eyes watering with the gritty dust, as she had made her way to Lynch Court, and which was, at the present moment, sending the smoke, in aggravating gusts, down the chimney into Mr Dyer's face. Thus it was, however. On the various topics that had chanced to come up for discussion that morning between Mr Dyer and his colleague, they had each taken up, as if by design, diametrically opposite points of view.

His temper altogether gave way now.

'If,' he said, bringing his hand down with emphasis on his writing-table, 'you lay it down as a principle that the obvious is to be rejected in favour of the abstruse, you'll soon find yourself launched in the predicament of having to prove that two apples added to two other apples do not make four. But there, if you don't choose to see things from my point of view, that is no reason why you should lose your temper!'

'Mr Hawke wishes to see you, sir,' said a clerk, at that moment entering the room.

It was a fortunate diversion. Whatever might be the differences of opinion in which these two might indulge in private, they were careful never to parade those differences before their clients.

Mr Dyer's irritability vanished in a moment.

'Show the gentleman in,' he said to the clerk. Then he turned to Loveday. 'This is the Revd Anthony Hawke, the gentleman at whose house I told you that Miss Monroe is staying temporarily. He is a clergyman of the Church of England, but gave up his living some twenty years ago when he married a wealthy lady. Miss Monroe has been sent over to his guardianship from Pekin by her father, Sir George Monroe, in order to get her out of the way of a troublesome and undesirable suitor.'

The last sentence was added in a low and hurried tone, for Mr Hawke was at that moment entering the room.

He was a man close upon sixty years of age, white-haired, clean shaven, with a full, round face, to which a small nose imparted a somewhat infantine expression. His manner of greeting was urbane but slightly flurried and nervous. He gave Loveday the impression of being an easy-going, happy-tempered man who, for the moment, was unusually disturbed and perplexed.

He glanced uneasily at Loveday. Mr Dyer hastened to explain that this was the lady by whose aid he hoped to get to the bottom of the matter now under consideration.

'In that case there can be no objection to my showing you this,' said Mr Hawke; 'it came by post this morning. You see my enemy still pursues me.'

As he spoke he took from his pocket a big, square envelope, from which he drew a large-sized sheet of paper.

On this sheet of paper were roughly drawn, in ink, two daggers, about six inches in length, with remarkably pointed blades.

Mr Dyer looked at the sketch with interest.

'We will compare this drawing and its envelope with those you previously received,' he said, opening a drawer of his writing-table and taking thence a precisely similar envelope. On the sheet of paper, however, that this envelope enclosed, there was drawn one dagger only.

He placed both envelopes and their enclosures side by side, and in silence compared them. Then, without a word, he handed them to

Miss Brooke, who, taking a glass from her pocket, subjected them to a similar careful and minute scrutiny.

Both envelopes were of precisely the same make, and were each addressed to Mr Hawke's London address in a round, schoolboyish, copy-book sort of hand—the hand so easy to write and so difficult to bring home to any writer on account of its want of individuality. Each envelope likewise bore a Cork and a London postmark.

The sheet of paper, however, that the first envelope enclosed bore the sketch of one dagger only.

Loveday laid down her glass.

'The envelopes,' she said, 'have, undoubtedly, been addressed by the same person, but these last two daggers have not been drawn by the hand that drew the first. Dagger number one was, evidently, drawn by a timid, uncertain, and inartistic hand—see how the lines wave and how they have been patched here and there. The person who drew the other daggers, I should say, could do better work: the outline, though rugged, is bold and free. I should like to take these sketches home with me and compare them again at my leisure.'

'Ah, I felt sure what your opinion would be!' said Mr Dyer complacently.

Mr Hawke seemed much disturbed.

'Good gracious!' he ejaculated; 'you don't mean to say I have two enemies pursuing me in this fashion! What does it mean? Can it be—is it possible, do you think, that these things have been sent to me by the members of some Secret Society in Ireland—under error, of course—mistaking me for someone else? They can't be meant for me; I have never, in my whole life, been mixed up with any political agitation of any sort.'

Mr Dyer shook his head. 'Members of secret societies generally make pretty sure of their ground before they send out missives of this kind,' he said. 'I have never heard of such an error being made. I think, too, we mustn't build any theories on the Irish postmark: the letters may have been posted in Cork for the whole and sole purpose of drawing off attention from some other quarter.'

'Will you mind telling me a little about the loss of the necklace?' here said Loveday, bringing the conversation suddenly round from the daggers to the diamonds.

'I think,' interposed Mr Dyer, turning towards her, 'that the episode of the drawn daggers—drawn in a double sense—should be treated entirely on its own merits, considered as a thing apart from the loss of the necklace. I am inclined to believe that when we have gone a little further into the matter we shall find that each circumstance belongs to a different group of facts. After all, it is possible that these daggers may have been sent by way of a joke—a rather foolish one, I admit—by some harum-scarum fellow bent on causing a sensation.'

Mr Hawke's face brightened. 'Ah! now, do you think so—really think so?' he ejaculated. 'It would lift such a load from my mind if you could bring the thing home, in this way, to some practical joker. There are a lot of such fellows knocking about the world. Why, now I come to think of it, my nephew, Jack, who is a good deal with us just now, and is not quite so steady a fellow as I should like him to be, must have a good many such scamps among his acquaintances.'

'A good many such scamps among his acquaintances,' echoed Loveday; 'that certainly gives plausibility to Mr Dyer's supposition. At the same time, I think we are bound to look at the other side of the case, and admit the possibility of these daggers being sent in right-down sober earnest by persons concerned in the robbery, with the intention of intimidating you and preventing full investigation of the matter. If this be so, it will not signify which thread we take up and follow. If we find the sender of the daggers we are safe to come upon the thief; or, if we follow up and find the thief, the sender of the daggers will not be far off.'

Mr Hawke's face fell once more.

'It's an uncomfortable position to be in,' he said slowly. 'I suppose, whoever they are, they will do the regulation thing, and next time will send an instalment of three daggers, in which case I may consider myself a doomed man. It did not occur to me before, but I remember now that I did not receive the first dagger until after I had spoken very strongly to Mrs Hawke, before the servants, about my wish to set the police to work. I told her I felt bound, in honour to Sir George, to do so, as the necklace had been lost under my roof.'

'Did Mrs Hawke object to your calling in the aid of the police?' asked Loveday.

'Yes, most strongly. She entirely supported Miss Monroe in her wish to take no steps in the matter. Indeed, I should not have come round as I did last night to Mr Dyer, if my wife had not been suddenly summoned from home by the serious illness of her sister. At least,' he corrected himself with a little attempt at self-assertion, 'my coming to him might have been a little delayed. I hope you understand, Mr Dyer; I do not mean to imply that I am not master in my own house.'

'Oh, quite so, quite so,' responded Mr Dyer. 'Did Mrs Hawke or Miss Monroe give any reasons for not wishing you to move in the matter?'

'All told, I should think they gave about a hundred reasons—I can't remember them all. For one thing, Miss Monroe said it might necessitate her appearing in the police courts, a thing she would not consent to do; and she certainly did not consider the necklace was worth the fuss I was making over it. And that necklace, sir, has been valued at over nine hundred pounds, and has come down to the young lady from her mother.'

'And Mrs Hawke?'

'Mrs Hawke supported Miss Monroe in her views in her presence. But privately to me afterwards, she gave other reasons for not wishing the police called in. Girls, she said, were always careless with their jewellery, she might have lost the necklace in Pekin, and never have brought it to England at all.'

'Quite so,' said Mr Dyer. 'I think I understood you to say that no one had seen the necklace since Miss Monroe's arrival in England. Also, I believe it was she who first discovered it to be missing?'

'Yes. Sir George, when he wrote apprising me of his daughter's visit, added a postscript to his letter, saying that his daughter was bringing her necklace with her and that he would feel greatly obliged if I would have it deposited with as little delay as possible at my bankers', where it could be easily got at if required. I spoke to Miss Monroe about doing this two or three times, but she did not seem at all inclined to comply with her father's wishes. Then my wife took the matter in hand—Mrs Hawke, I must tell you, has a very firm, resolute manner—she told Miss Monroe plainly that she would not have the responsibility of those diamonds in the house, and insisted that there and then they should be sent off to the bankers. Upon this

Miss Monroe went up to her room, and presently returned, saying that her necklace had disappeared. She herself, she said, had placed it in her jewel-case and the jewel-case in her wardrobe, when her boxes were unpacked. The jewel-case was in the wardrobe right enough, and no other article of jewellery appeared to have been disturbed, but the little padded niche in which the necklace had been deposited was empty. My wife and her maid went upstairs immediately, and searched every corner of the room, but, I'm sorry to say, without any result.'

'Miss Monroe, I suppose, has her own maid?'

'No, she has not. The maid—an elderly native woman—who left Pekin with her, suffered so terribly from sea-sickness that, when they reached Malta, Miss Monroe allowed her to land and remain there in charge of an agent of the P. and O. Company till an outward bound packet could take her back to China. It seems the poor woman thought she was going to die, and was in a terrible state of mind because she hadn't brought her coffin with her. I dare say you know the terror these Chinese have of being buried in foreign soil. After her departure, Miss Monroe engaged one of the steerage passengers to act as her maid for the remainder of the voyage.'

'Did Miss Monroe make the long journey from Pekin accompanied only by this native woman?'

'No; friends escorted her to Hong Kong—by far the roughest part of the journey. From Hong Kong she came on in *The Colombo*, accompanied only by her maid. I wrote and told her father I would meet her at the docks in London; the young lady, however, preferred landing at Plymouth, and telegraphed to me from there that she was coming on by rail to Waterloo, where, if I liked, I might meet her.'

'She seems to be a young lady of independent habits. Was she brought up and educated in China?'

'Yes; by a succession of French and American governesses. After her mother's death, when she was little more than a baby, Sir George could not make up his mind to part with her, as she was his only child.'

'I suppose you and Sir George Monroe are old friends?'

'Yes; he and I were great chums before he went out to China—now about twenty years ago—and it was only natural, when he wished to get his daughter out of the way of young Danvers's impertinent attentions, that he should ask me to take charge of her till he could claim his retiring pension and set up his tent in England.'

'What was the chief objection to Mr Danvers's attentions?'

'Well, he is only a boy of one-and-twenty, and has no money into the bargain. He has been sent out to Pekin by his father to study the language, in order to qualify for a billet in the customs, and it may be a dozen years before he is in a position to keep a wife. Now, Miss Monroe is an heiress—will come into her mother's large fortune when she is of age—and Sir George, naturally, would like her to make a good match.'

'I suppose Miss Monroe came to England very reluctantly?'

'I imagine so. No doubt it was a great wrench for her to leave her home and friends in that sudden fashion and come to us, who are, one and all, utter strangers to her. She is very quiet, very shy and reserved. She goes nowhere, sees no one. When some old China friends of her father's called to see her the other day, she immediately found she had a headache and went to bed. I think, on the whole, she gets on better with my nephew than with anyone else.'

'Will you kindly tell me of how many persons your household consists at the present moment?'

'At the present moment we are one more than usual, for my nephew, Jack, is home with his regiment from India, and is staying with us. As a rule, my household consists of my wife and myself, butler, cook, housemaid, and my wife's maid, who just now is doing double duty as Miss Monroe's maid also.'

Mr Dyer looked at his watch.

'I have an important engagement in ten minutes' time,' he said, 'so I must leave you and Miss Brooke to arrange details as to how and when she is to begin her work inside your house, for, of course, in a case of this sort we must, in the first instance at any rate, concentrate attention within your four walls.'

'The less delay the better,' said Loveday. 'I should like to attack the mystery at once—this afternoon.'

Mr Hawke thought for a moment.

'According to present arrangements,' he said, with a little hesitation, 'Mrs Hawke will return next Friday, that is the day after tomorrow, so I can only ask you to remain in the house till the morning of that day. I'm sure you will understand that there might be some—some little awkwardness in ——'

'Oh, quite so,' interrupted Loveday. 'I don't see at present that there will be any necessity for me to sleep in the house at all. How would it be for me to assume the part of a lady house decorator in the employment of a West-end firm, and sent by them to survey your house and advise upon its redecoration? All I should have to do, would be to walk about your rooms with my head on one side, and a pencil and notebook in my hand. I should interfere with no one, your family life would go on as usual, and I could make my work as short or as long as necessity might dictate.'

Mr Hawke had no objection to offer to this. He had, however, a request to make as he rose to depart, and he made it a little nervously.

'If,' he said, 'by any chance there should come to telegram from Mrs Hawke, saying she will return by an earlier train, I suppose—I hope, that is, you will make some excuse, and—and not get me into hot water, I mean.'

To this, Loveday answered a little evasively that she trusted no such telegram would be forthcoming, but that, in any case, he might rely upon her discretion.

Four o'clock was striking from a neighbouring church clock as Loveday lifted the old-fashioned brass knocker of Mr Hawke's house in Tavistock Square. An elderly butler admitted her and showed her into the drawing-room on the first floor. A single glance round showed Loveday that if her role had been real instead of assumed, she would have found plenty of scope for her talents. Although the house was in all respects comfortably furnished, it bore unmistakably the impress of those early Victorian days when aesthetic surroundings were not deemed a necessity of existence; an impress which people past middle age, and growing increasingly indifferent to the accessories of life, are frequently careless to remove.

'Young life here is evidently an excrescence, not part of the home; a troop of daughters turned into this room would speedily set going a different condition of things,' thought Loveday, taking stock of the faded white and gold wallpaper, the chairs covered with lilies and roses in cross-stitch, and the knick-knacks of a past generation that were scattered about on tables and mantelpiece.

A yellow damask curtain, half-festooned, divided the back drawing-room from the front in which she was seated. From the other side of this curtain there came to her the sound of voices—those of a man and a girl.

'Cut the cards again, please,' said the man's voice. 'Thank you. There you are again—the queen of hearts, surrounded with diamonds, and turning her back on a knave. Miss Monroe, you can't do better than make that fortune come true. Turn your back on the man who let you go without a word and——'

'Hush!' interrupted the girl with a little laugh; 'I heard the next room door open—I'm sure someone came in.'

The girl's laugh seemed to Loveday utterly destitute of that echo of heartache that in the circumstances might have been expected.

At this moment Mr Hawke entered the room, and almost simultaneously the two young people came from the other side of the yellow curtain and crossed towards the door.

Loveday took a survey of them as they passed.

The young man—evidently 'my nephew, Jack'—was a good-looking young fellow, with dark eyes and hair. The girl was small, slight, and fair. She was perceptibly less at home with Jack's uncle than she was with Jack, for her manner changed and grew formal and reserved as she came face to face with him.

'We're going downstairs to have a game of billiards,' said Jack, addressing Mr Hawke, and throwing a look of curiosity at Loveday.

'Jack,' said the old gentleman, 'what would you say if I told you I was going to have the house redecorated from top to bottom, and that this lady had come to advise on the matter.'

This was the nearest (and most Anglicé) approach to a fabrication that Mr Hawke would allow to pass his lips.

'Well,' answered Jack promptly, 'I should say, "not before its time". That would cover a good deal.'

Then the two young people departed in company.

Loveday went straight to her work.

'I'll begin my surveying at the top of the house, and at once, if you please,' she said. 'Will you kindly tell one of your maids to show me through the bedrooms? If it is possible, let that maid be the one who waits on Miss Monroe and Mrs Hawke.'

The maid who responded to Mr Hawke's summons was in perfect harmony with the general appearance of the house. In addition, however, to being elderly and faded, she was also remarkably sourvisaged, and carried herself as if she thought that Mr Hawke had taken a great liberty in thus commanding her attendance.

In dignified silence she showed Loveday over the topmost storey, where the servants' bedrooms were situated, and with a somewhat supercilious expression of countenance, watched her making various entries in her notebook.

In dignified silence, also, she led the way down to the second floor, where were the principal bedrooms of the house.

'This is Miss Monroe's room,' she said, as she threw back a door of one of these rooms, and then shut her lips with a snap, as if they were never going to open again.

The room that Loveday entered was, like the rest of the house, furnished in the style that prevailed in the early Victorian period. The bedstead was elaborately curtained with pink lined upholstery; the toilet-table was befrilled with muslin and tarlatan out of all likeness to a table. The one point, however, that chiefly attracted Loveday's attention was the extreme neatness that prevailed throughout the apartment—a neatness, however, that was carried out with so strict an eye to comfort and convenience that it seemed to proclaim the hand of a first-class maid. Everything in the room was, so to speak, squared to the quarter of an inch, and yet everything that a lady could require in dressing lay ready to hand. The dressing-gown lying on the back of a chair had footstool and slippers beside it. A chair stood in front of the toilet table, and on a small Japanese table to the right of the chair were placed hairpin box, comb and brush, and hand mirror.

'This room will want money spent upon it,' said Loveday, letting her eyes roam critically in all directions. 'Nothing but Moorish woodwork will take off the squareness of those corners. But what a maid Miss Monroe must have. I never before saw a room so orderly and, at the same time, so comfortable.'

This was so direct an appeal to conversation that the sour-visaged maid felt compelled to open her lips.

'I wait on Miss Monroe, for the present,' she said snappishly;

'but, to speak the truth, she scarcely requires a maid. I never before in my life had dealings with such a young lady.'

'She does so much for herself, you mean—declines much assistance.'

'She's like no one else I ever had to do with.' (This was said even more snappishly than before.) 'She not only won't be helped in dressing, but she arranges her room every day before leaving it, even to placing the chair in front of the looking glass.'

'And to opening the lid of the hairpin box, so that she may have the pins ready to her hand,' added Loveday, for a moment bending over the Japanese table, with its toilet accessories.

Another five minutes were all that Loveday accorded to the inspection of this room. Then, a little to the surprise of the dignified maid, she announced her intention of completing her survey of the bedrooms some other time, and dismissed her at the drawing-room door, to tell Mr Hawke that she wished to see him before leaving.

Mr Hawke, looking much disturbed and with a telegram in his hand, quickly made his appearance.

'From my wife, to say she'll be back tonight. She'll be at Waterloo in about half an hour from now,' he said, holding up the brown envelope. 'Now, Miss Brooke, what are we to do? I told you how much Mrs Hawke objected to the investigation of this matter, and she is very— well—firm when she once says a thing, and—and——'

'Set your mind at rest,' interrupted Loveday; 'I have done all I wished to do within your walls, and the remainder of my investigation can be carried on just as well at Lynch Court or at my own private rooms.'

'Done all you wished to do!' echoed Mr Hawke in amazement; 'why, you've not been an hour in the house, and do you mean to tell me you've found out anything about the necklace or the daggers?'

'Don't ask me any questions just yet; I want you to answer one or two instead. Now, can you tell me anything about any letters Miss Monroe may have written or received since she has been in your house?'

'Yes, certainly. Sir George wrote to me very strongly about her correspondence, and begged me to keep a sharp eye on it, so as to nip in the bud any attempt to communicate with Danvers. So far, however, she does not appear to have made any such attempt. She is frankness itself over her correspondence. Every letter that has come addressed to her, she has shown either to me or to my wife, and they have one and all been letters from old friends of her father's, wishing to make her acquaintance now that she is in England. With regard to letter-writing, I am sorry to say she has a marked and most peculiar objection to it. Every one of the letters she has received, my wife tells me, remain unanswered still. She has never once been seen, since she came to the house, with a pen in her hand. And if she wrote on the sly, I don't know how she would get her letters posted—she never goes outside the door by herself, and she would have no opportunity of giving them to any of the servants to post except Mrs Hawke's maid, and she is beyond suspicion in such a matter. She has been well cautioned, and, in addition, is not the sort of person who would assist a young lady in carrying on a clandestine correspondence.'

'I should imagine not! I suppose Miss Monroe has been present at the breakfast table each time that you have received your daggers through the post—you told me, I think, that they had come by the first post in the morning?'

'Yes; Miss Monroe is very punctual at meals, and has been present each time. Naturally, when I received such unpleasant missives, I made some sort of exclamation and then handed the thing round the table for inspection, and Miss Monroe was very much concerned to know who my secret enemy could be.'

'No doubt. Now, Mr Hawke, I have a very special request to make to you, and I hope you will be most exact in carrying it out.'

'You may rely upon my doing so to the very letter.'

'Thank you. If, then, you should receive by post tomorrow morning one of those big envelopes you already know the look of, and find that it contains a sketch of three, not two, drawn daggers——'

'Good gracious! what makes you think such a thing likely?' exclaimed Mr Hawke, greatly disturbed. 'Why am I to be persecuted in this way? Am I to take it for granted that I am a doomed man?'

He began to pace the room in a state of great excitement.

'I don't think I would if I were you,' answered Loveday calmly. 'Pray let me finish. I want you to open the big envelope that may come to you by post tomorrow morning just as you have opened the others—

in full view of your family at the breakfast-table—and to hand round the sketch it may contain for inspection to your wife, your nephew, and to Miss Monroe. Now, will you promise me to do this?'

'Oh, certainly; I should most likely have done so without any promising. But—but—I'm sure you'll understand that I feel myself to be in a peculiarly uncomfortable position, and I shall feel so very much obliged to you if you'll tell me—that is if you'll enter a little more fully into an explanation.'

Loveday looked at her watch. 'I should think Mrs Hawke would be just at this moment arriving at Waterloo; I'm sure you'll be glad to see the last of me. Please come to me at my rooms in Gower Street tomorrow at twelve—here is my card. I shall then be able to enter into fuller explanations I hope. Goodbye.'

The old gentleman showed her politely downstairs, and, as he shook hands with her at the front door, again asked, in a most emphatic manner, if she did not consider him to be placed in a 'peculiarly unpleasant position'.

Those last words at parting were to be the first with which he greeted her on the following morning when he presented himself at her rooms in Gower Street. They were, however, repeated in considerably more agitated a manner.

'Was there ever a man in a more miserable position!' he exclaimed, as he took the chair that Loveday indicated. 'I not only received the three daggers for which you prepared me, but I got an additional worry, for which I was totally unprepared. This morning, immediately after breakfast, Miss Monroe walked out of the house all by herself, and no one knows where she has gone. And the girl has never before been outside the door alone. It seems the servants saw her go out, but did not think it necessary to tell either me or Mrs Hawke, feeling sure we must have been aware of the fact.'

'So Mrs Hawke has returned,' said Loveday. 'Well, I suppose you will be greatly surprised if I inform you that the young lady, who has so unceremoniously left your house, is at the present moment to be found at the Charing Cross Hotel, where she has engaged a private room in her real name of Miss Mary O'Grady.'

'Eh! What! Private room! Real name O'Grady! I'm all bewildered!'

'It is a little bewildering; let me explain. The young lady whom you received into your house as the daughter of your old friend, was in reality the person engaged by Miss Monroe to fulfil the duties of her maid on board ship, after her native attendant had been landed at Malta. Her real name, as I have told you, is Mary O'Grady, and she has proved herself a valuable coadjutor to Miss Monroe in assisting her to carry out a programme, which she must have arranged with her lover, Mr Danvers, before she left Pekin.'

'Eh! what!' again ejaculated Mr Hawke; 'how do you know all this? Tell me the whole story.'

'I will tell you the whole story first, and then explain to you how I came to know it. From what has followed, it seems to me that Miss Monroe must have arranged with Mr Danvers that he was to leave Pekin within ten days of her so doing, travel by the route by which she came, and land at Plymouth, where he was to receive a note from her, apprising him of her whereabouts. So soon as she was on board ship, Miss Monroe appears to have set her wits to work with great energy; every obstacle to the carrying-out of her programme she appears to have met and conquered. Step number one was to get rid of her native maid, who, perhaps, might have been faithful to her master's interests and have proved troublesome. I have no doubt the poor woman suffered terribly from sea-sickness, as it was her first voyage, and I have equally no doubt that Miss Monroe worked on her fears, and persuaded her to land at Malta, and return to China by the next packet. Step number two was to find a suitable person, who, for a consideration, would be willing to play the part of the Pekin heiress among the heiress's friends in England, while the young lady herself arranged her private affairs to her own liking. That person was quickly found among the steerage passengers of the *Colombo* in Miss Mary O'Grady, who had come on board with her mother at Ceylon, and who, from the glimpse I had of her, must, I should conjecture, have been absent many years from the land of her birth. You know how cleverly this young lady has played her part in your house—how, without attracting attention to the matter, she has shunned the society of her father's old Chinese friends, who might be likely to involve her in embarrassing conversations; how she has avoided the use of pen and ink lest——'

'Yes, yes,' interrupted Mr Hawke; 'but, my dear Miss Brooke, wouldn't it be as well for you and me to go at once to the Charing

Cross Hotel, and get all the information we can out of her respecting Miss Monroe and her movements—she may be bolting, you know?'

'I do not think she will. She is waiting there patiently for an answer to a telegram she dispatched more than two hours ago to her mother, Mrs O'Grady, at 14 Woburn Place, Cork.'

'Dear me! dear me! How is it possible for you to know all this.'

'Oh, that last little fact was simply a matter of astuteness on the part of the man whom I have deputed to watch the young lady's movements today. Other details, I assure you, in this somewhat intricate case, have been infinitely more difficult to get at. I think I have to thank those "drawn daggers", that caused you so much consternation, for having, in the first instance, put me on the right track.'

'Ah—h,' said Mr Hawke, drawing a long breath; 'now we come to the daggers! I feel sure you are going to set my mind at rest on that score.'

'I hope so. Would it surprise you very much to be told that it was I who sent to you those three daggers this morning?'

'You! Is it possible?'

'Yes; they were sent by me, and for a reason that I will presently explain to you. But let me begin at the beginning. Those roughly-drawn sketches, that to you suggested terrifying ideas of blood-shedding and violence, to my mind were open to a more peaceful and commonplace explanation. They appeared to me to suggest the herald's office rather than the armoury; the cross fitchée of the knight's shield rather than the poniard with which the members of secret societies are supposed to render their recalcitrant brethren familiar. Now, if you will look at these sketches again, you will see what I mean.' Here Loveday produced from her writing-table the missives which had so greatly disturbed Mr Hawke's peace of mind. 'To begin with, the blade of the dagger of common life is, as a rule, at least two-thirds of the weapon in length; in this sketch, what you would call the blade, does not exceed the hilt in length. Secondly, please note the absence of guard for the hand. Thirdly, let me draw your attention to the squareness of what you considered the hilt of the weapon, and what, to my mind, suggested the upper portion of a crusader's cross. No hand could grip such a hilt as the one outlined here. After your departure yesterday, I drove to the British Museum, and there consulted a certain valuable work on heraldry, which has more than once done me good service. There I found my surmise substantiated in a surprising manner. Among the illustrations of the various crosses borne on armorial shields, I found one that had been taken by Henri d'Anvers from his own armorial bearings, for his crest when he joined the Crusaders under Edward I, and which has since been handed down as the crest of the Danvers family. This was an important item of information to me. Here was someone in Cork sending to your house, on two several occasions, the crest of the Danvers family; with what object it would be difficult to say, unless it were in some sort a communication to someone in your house. With my mind full of this idea, I left the Museum and drove next to the office of the P. and O. Company, and requested to have given me the list of the passengers who arrived by the *Colombo*. I found this list to be a remarkably small one; I suppose people, if possible, avoid crossing the Bay of Biscay during the Equinoxes. The only passengers who landed at Plymouth besides Miss Monroe, I found, were a certain Mrs and Miss O'Grady, steerage passengers who had gone on board at Ceylon on their way home from Australia. Their name, together with their landing at Plymouth, suggested the possibility that Cork might be their destination. After this I asked to see the list of the passengers who arrived by the packet following the *Colombo*, telling the clerk who attended to me that I was on the look-out for the arrival of a friend. In that second list of arrivals I quickly found my friend—William Wentworth Danvers by name.'

'No! The effrontery! How dared he! In his own name, too!'

'Well, you see, a plausible pretext for leaving Pekin could easily be invented by him—the death of a relative, the illness of a father or mother. And Sir George, though he might dislike the idea of the young man going to England so soon after his daughter's departure, and may, perhaps, write to you by the next mail on the matter, was utterly powerless to prevent his so doing. This young man, like Miss Monroe and the O'Gradys, also landed at Plymouth. I had only arrived so far in my investigation when I went to your house yesterday afternoon. By chance, as I waited a few minutes in your drawing-room, another important item of information was acquired. A fragment of conversation between your nephew and the supposed

Miss Monroe fell upon my ear, and one word spoken by the young lady convinced me of her nationality. That one word was the monosyllable "Hush" '.

'No! You surprise me!'

'Have you never noted the difference between the "hush" of an Englishman and that of an Irishman? The former begins his "hush" with a distinct aspirate, the latter with as distinct a W. That W is a mark of his nationality which he never loses. The unmitigated "whist" may lapse into a "whish" when he is transplanted to another soil, and the "whish" may in course of time pass into a "whush", but to the distinct aspirate of the English "hush", he never attains. Now Miss O'Grady's was as pronounced a "whush" as it was possible for the lips of a Hibernian to utter.'

'And from that you concluded that Mary O'Grady was playing the part of Miss Monroe in my house?'

'Not immediately. My suspicions were excited, certainly; and when I went up to her room, in company with Mrs Hawke's maid, those suspicions were confirmed. The orderliness of that room was something remarkable. Now, there is the orderliness of a lady in the arrangement of her room, and the orderliness of a maid, and the two things, believe me, are widely different. A lady, who has no maid, and who has the gift of orderliness, will put things away when done with, and so leave her room a picture of neatness. I don't think, however, it would for a moment occur to her to put things so as to be conveniently ready for her to use the next time she dresses in that room. This would be what a maid, accustomed to arrange a room for her mistress's use, would do mechanically. Now the neatness I found in the supposed Miss Monroe's room was the neatness of a maid—not of a lady, and I was assured by Mrs Hawke's maid that it was a neatness accomplished by her own hands. As I stood there, looking at that room, the whole conspiracy—if I may so call it—little by little pieced itself together, and became plain to me. Possibilities quickly grew into probabilities, and these probabilities once admitted, brought other suppositions in their train. Now, supposing that Miss Monroe and Mary O'Grady had agreed to change places, the Pekin heiress, for the time being, occupying Mary O'Grady's place in the humble home at Cork and vice versa, what means of communicating with each other had they

41

arranged? How was Mary O'Grady to know when she might lay aside her assumed role and go back to her mother's house. There was no denying the necessity for such communication; the difficulties in its way must have been equally obvious to the two girls. Now, I think we must admit that we must credit these young women with having hit upon a very clever way of meeting those difficulties. An anonymous and startling missive sent to you would be bound to be mentioned in the house, and in this way a code of signals might be set up between them that could not direct suspicion to them. In this connection, the Danvers crest, which it is possible that they mistook for a dagger, suggested itself naturally, for no doubt Miss Monroe had many impressions of it on her lover's letters. As I thought over these things, it occurred to me that possibly dagger (or cross) number one was sent to notify the safe arrival of Miss Monroe and Mrs O'Grady at Cork. The two daggers or crosses you subsequently received were sent on the day of Mr Danvers's arrival at Plymouth, and were, I should say, sketched by his hand. Now, was it not within the bounds of likelihood that Miss Monroe's marriage to this young man, and the consequent release of Mary O'Grady from the onerous part she was playing, might be notified to her by the sending of three such crosses or daggers to you. The idea no sooner occurred to me than I determined to act upon it, forestall the sending of this latest communication, and watch the result. Accordingly, after I left your house yesterday, I had a sketch made of three daggers or crosses exactly similar to those you had already received, and had it posted to you so that you would get it by the first post. I told off one of our staff at Lynch Court to watch your house, and gave him special directions to follow and report on Miss O'Grady's movements throughout the day. The results I anticipated quickly came to pass. About half-past nine this morning the man sent a telegram to me saying that he had followed Miss O'Grady from your house to the Charing Cross Hotel, and furthermore had ascertained that she had since dispatched a telegram, which (possibly by following the hotel servant who carried it to the telegraph office), he had overheard was addressed to Mrs O'Grady, at Woburn Place, Cork. Since I received this information an altogether remarkable cross-firing of telegrams has been going backwards and forwards along the wires to Cork.'

'A cross-firing of telegrams! I do not understand.'

'In this way. So soon as I knew Mrs O'Grady's address I telegraphed to her, in her daughter's name, desiring her to address her reply to 115*a* Gower Street, not to Charing Cross Hotel. About three-quarters of an hour afterwards I received in reply this telegram, which I am sure you will read with interest.'

Here Loveday handed a telegram—one of several that lay on her writing table—to Mr Hawke.

He opened it and read aloud as follows:

Am puzzled. Why such hurry? Wedding took place this morning. You will receive signal as agreed tomorrow. Better return to Tavistock Square for the night.

'The wedding took place this morning,' repeated Mr Hawke blankly. 'My poor old friend! It will break his heart.'

'Now that the thing is done past recall we must hope he will make the best of it,' said Loveday. 'In reply to this telegram,' she went on, 'I sent another, asking as to the movements of the bride and bridegroom, and got in reply this:'

Here she read aloud as follows:

They will be at Plymouth tomorrow night; at Charing Cross Hotel the next day, as agreed.

'So, Mr Hawke,' she added, 'if you wish to see your old friend's daughter and tell her what you think of the part she has played, all you will have to do will be to watch the arrival of the Plymouth trains.'

'Miss O'Grady has called to see a lady and gentleman,' said a maid at that moment entering.

'Miss O'Grady!' repeated Mr Hawke in astonishment.

'Ah, yes, I telegraphed to her, just before you came in, to come here to meet a lady and gentleman, and she, no doubt thinking that she would find here the newly-married pair, has, you see, lost no time in complying with my request. Show the lady in.'

'It's all so intricate—so bewildering,' said Mr Hawke, as he lay back in his chair, 'I can scarcely get it all into my head.'

His bewilderment, however, was nothing compared with that of

Miss O'Grady, when she entered the room and found herself face to face with her late guardian, instead of the radiant bride and bridegroom whom she had expected to meet.

She stood silent in the middle of the room, looking the picture of astonishment and distress.

Mr Hawke also seemed a little at a loss for words, so Loveday took the initiative.

'Please sit down,' she said, placing a chair for the girl. 'Mr Hawke and I have sent for you in order to ask you a few questions. Before doing so, however, let me tell you that the whole of your conspiracy with Miss Monroe has been brought to light, and the best thing you can do, if you want your share in it treated leniently, will be to answer our questions as fully and truthfully as possible.'

The girl burst into tears. 'It was all Miss Monroe's fault from beginning to end,' she sobbed. 'Mother didn't want to do it—I didn't want to—to go into a gentleman's house and pretend to be what I was not. And we didn't want her hundred pounds——'

Here sobs checked her speech.

'Oh,' said Loveday contemptuously, 'so you were to have a hundred pounds for your share in this fraud, were you?'

'We didn't want to take it,' said the girl, between hysterical bursts of tears; 'but Miss Monroe said if we didn't help her someone else would, and so I agreed to——'

'I think,' interrupted Loveday, 'that you can tell us very little that we do not already know about what you agreed to do. What we want you to tell us is what has been done with Miss Monroe's diamond necklace—who has possession of it now?'

The girl's sobs and tears redoubled. 'I've had nothing to do with the necklace—it has never been in my possession,' she sobbed. 'Miss Monroe gave it to Mr Danvers two or three months before she left Pekin, and he sent it on to some people he knew in Hong Kong, diamond merchants, who lent him money on it. Decastro, Miss Monroe said, was the name of these people.'

'Decastro, diamond merchant, Hong Kong. I should think that would be sufficient address,' said Loveday, entering it in a ledger; 'and I suppose Mr Danvers retained part of that money for his own use and travelling expenses, and handed the remainder to Miss Monroe to enable her to bribe such creatures as you and your mother, to practise a fraud that ought to land both of you in jail.'

The girl grew deadly white. 'Oh, don't do that—don't send us to prison!' she implored, clasping her hands together. 'We haven't touched a penny of Miss Monroe's money yet, and we don't want to touch a penny, if you'll only let us off! Oh, pray, pray, pray be merciful!'

Loveday looked at Mr Hawke.

He rose from his chair. 'I think the best thing you can do,' he said, 'will be to get back home to your mother at Cork as quickly as possible, and advise her never to play such a risky game again. Have you any money in your purse? No—well then here's some for you, and lose no time in getting home. It will be best for Miss Monroe—Mrs Danvers I mean—to come to my house and claim her own property there. At any rate, there it will remain until she does so.'

As the girl, with incoherent expressions of gratitude, left the room, he turned to Loveday.

'I should like to have consulted Mrs Hawke before arranging matters in this way,' he said a little hesitatingly; 'but still, I don't see that I could have done otherwise.'

'I feel sure Mrs Hawke will approve what you have done when she hears all the circumstance of the case,' said Loveday.

'And,' continued the old clergyman, 'when I write to Sir George, as, of course, I must immediately, I shall advise him to make the best of a bad bargain, now that the thing is done. "Past cure should be past care;" eh, Miss Brooke? And, think! what a narrow escape my nephew, Jack, has had!'

3

FERGUS HUME

The First Customer and the Florentine Dante

It has been explained otherwhere how Hagar Stanley, against her own interests, took charge of the pawnshop and property of Jacob Dix during the absence of the rightful heir. She had full control of everything by the terms of the will. Jacob had made many good bargains in his life, but none better than that which had brought him Hagar for a slave—Hagar, with her strict sense of duty, her upright nature, and her determination to act honestly, even when her own interests were at stake. Such a character was almost unknown amongst the denizens of Carby's Crescent.

Vark, the lawyer, thought her a fool. First, because she refused to make a nest-egg for herself out of the estate; secondly, because she had surrendered a fine fortune to benefit a man she hated; thirdly, because she declined to become Mrs Vark. Otherwise she was sharp enough— too sharp, the lawyer thought; for with her keen business instinct, and her faculty for organizing and administering and understanding, he found it impossible to trick her in any way. Out of the Dix estate Vark received his due fees and no more, which position was humiliating to a man of his intelligence.

Hagar, however, minded neither Vark nor anyone else. She advertised for the absent heir, she administered the estate, and carried on the business of the pawnshop; living in the back-parlour meanwhile, after the penurious fashion of her late master. It had been a shock to her to learn that the heir of the old pawnbroker was none other than Goliath, the red-haired suitor who had forced her to leave the gypsy camp. Still, her honesty would not permit her to rob him of his heritage; and she attended to his interests as though they were those of the man she loved best in the world. When Jimmy Dix, alias Goliath, appeared to claim the property, Hagar intended to deliver up all to him, and to leave the shop as poor as when she entered it. In the meantime, as the months went by and brought not the claimant, Hagar minded the shop, transacted business, and drove bargains. Also, she became the heroine of several adventures, such as the following:

During a June twilight she was summoned to the shop by a sharp rapping, and on entering she found a young man waiting to pawn a book which he held in his hand. He was tall, slim, fair-haired and blue-eyed, with a clever and intellectual face, lighted by rather dreamy eyes. Quick at reading physiognomies, Hagar liked his appearance at the first glance, and, moreover, admired his good looks.

'I—I wish to get some money on this book,' said the stranger in a hesitating manner, a flush invading his fair complexion; 'could you—that is, will you——' He paused in confusion, and held out the book, which Hagar took in silence.

It was an old and costly book, over which a bibliomaniac would have gloated.

The date was that of the fourteenth century, the printer a famous Florentine publisher of that epoch; and the author was none other than one Dante Alighieri, a poet not unknown to fame. In short, the volume was a second edition of 'La Divina Commedia', extremely rare, and worth much money. Hagar, who had learnt many things under the able tuition of Jacob, at once recognized the value of the book; but with keen business instinct—notwithstanding her prepossession concerning the young man—she began promptly to disparage it.

'I don't care for old books,' she said, offering it back to him. 'Why not take it to a second-hand bookseller?'

'Because I don't want to part with it. At the present moment I need money, as you can see from my appearance. Let me have five pounds on the book until I can redeem it.'

Hagar, who already had noted the haggard looks of this customer, and the threadbare quality of his apparel, laid down the Dante with a bang. 'I can't give five pounds,' she said, bluntly. 'The book isn't worth it!'

'Shows how much you know of such things, my girl! It is a rare edition of a celebrated Italian poet, and it is worth over a hundred pounds.'

'Really?' said Hagar, drily. 'In that case, why not sell it?'

'Because I don't want to. Give me five pounds.'

'No; four is all that I can advance.'

'Four ten,' pleaded the customer.

'Four,' retorted the inexorable Hagar. 'Or else——'

She pushed the book towards him with one finger. Seeing that he could get nothing more out of her, the young man sighed and relented. 'Give me the four pounds,' he said, gloomily. 'I might have guessed that a foreigner would grind me down to the lowest.'

'I am a gypsy,' replied Hagar, making out the ticket.

'A gypsy!' said the other, peering into her face. 'And what is a Romany lass doing in this Levitical tabernacle?'

'That's my business!' retorted Hagar, curtly. 'Name and address?'

'Eustace Lorn, 42, Castle Road,' said the young man, giving an address near at hand. 'But I say—if you are true Romany, you can talk the calo jib.'

'I talk it with my kind, young man; not with the Gentiles.'

'But I am a Romany Rye.'

'I'm not a fool, young man! Romany Ryes don't live in cities for choice.'

'Nor do gypsy girls dwell in pawn-shops, my lass!'

'Four pounds,' said Hagar, taking no notice of this remark; 'there it is, in gold; your ticket also—number eight hundred and twenty. You can redeem the book whenever you like, on paying six per cent interest. Goodnight.'

'But I say,' cried Lorn, as he slipped money and ticket into his pocket, 'I want to speak to you, and——'

'Goodnight, sir,' said Hagar, sharply, and vanished into the darkness of the shop. Lorn was annoyed by her curt manner and his sudden dismissal; but as there was no help for it, he walked out into the street.

'What a handsome girl!' was his first thought; and 'What a spitfire!' was his second.

After his departure, Hagar put away the Dante, and, as it was late, shut up the shop. Then she retired to the back-parlour to eat her supper—dry bread-and-cheese with cold water—and to think over the young man. As a rule, Hagar was far too self-possessed to be impressionable; but there was something about Eustace Lorn—she had the name pat—which attracted her not a little. From the short interview she had not learnt much of his personality. He was poor, proud, rather absent-minded; and—from the fact of his yielding to her on the question of price—rather weak in character. Yet she liked his face, the kindly expression of his eyes, and the sweetness of his mouth. But after all he was only a chance customer; and—unless he returned to redeem the Dante—she might not see him again. On this thought occurring to her, Hagar called common-sense to her aid, and strove to banish the young man's image from her mind. The task was more difficult than she thought.

A week later, Lorn and his pawning of the book were recalled to her mind by a stranger who entered the shop shortly after midday. This man was short, stout, elderly, and vulgar. He was much excited, and spoke badly, as Hagar noted when he laid a pawn-ticket number eight hundred and twenty on the counter.

' 'Ere, girl,' said he in rough tones, 'gimme the book this ticket's for.'

'You come from Mr Lorn?' asked Hagar, remembering the Dante.

'Yes; he wants that book. There's the brass. Sharp, now, young woman!'

Hagar made no move to get the volume, or even to take the money. Instead of doing either, she asked a question. 'Is Mr Lorn ill, that he could not come himself?' she demanded, looking keenly at the man's coarse face.

'No; but I've bought the pawn-ticket off him. 'Ere, gimme the book!'

'I cannot at present,' replied Hagar, who did not trust the looks of this man, and who wished, moreover, to see Eustace again.

'Dash yer imperance! Why not?'

'Because you did not pawn the Dante; and as it is a valuable book, I might get into trouble if I gave it into other hands than Mr Lorn's.'

'Well, I'm blest! There's the ticket!'

'So I see; but how do I know the way you became possessed of it?'

'Lorn gave it me,' said the man, sulkily, 'and I want the Dante!'

'I'm sorry for that,' retorted Hagar, certain that all was not right, 'for no one but Mr Lorn shall get it. If he isn't ill, let him come and receive it from me.'

The man swore and completely lost his temper—a fact which did not disturb Hagar in the least. 'You may as well clear out,' she said, coldly. 'I have said that you shan't have the book, so that closes the question.'

'I'll call in the police!'

'Do so; there's a station five minutes' walk from here.'

Confounded by her coolness, the man snatched up the pawn-ticket, and stamped out of the shop in a rage. Hagar took down the Dante, looked at it carefully, and considered the position. Clearly there was something wrong, and Eustace was in trouble, else why should he send a stranger to redeem the book upon which he set such store? In an ordinary case, Hagar might have received the ticket and money without a qualm, so long as she was acting rightly in a legal sense; but Eustace Lorn interested her strangely—why, she could not guess—and she was anxious to guard his interests. Moreover, the emissary possessed an untrustworthy face, and looked a man capable, if not of crime, at least of treachery. How he had obtained the ticket could only be explained by its owner; so, after some cogitation, Hagar sent a message to Lorn. The gist of this was, that he should come to the pawnshop after closing time.

All the evening Hagar anxiously waited for her visitor, and—such is the inconsequence of maids—she was angered with herself for this very anxiety. She tried to think that it was sheer curiosity to know the truth of the matter that made her impatient for the arrival of Lorn; but deep in her heart there lurked a perception of the actual state of things. It was not curiosity so much as a wish to see the young man's face again, to hear him speak, and feel that he was beside her. Though without a chaperon, though not brought up under parental government, Hagar had her own social code, and that a strict one. In this instance, she thought that her mental attitude was unmaidenly and unworthy of an unmarried girl. Hence, when Eustace made his appearance at nine o'clock, she was brusque to the verge of rudeness.

'Who was that man you sent for your book?' she demanded, abruptly, when Lorn was seated in the back-parlour.

'Jabez Treadle. I could not come myself, so I sent him with the ticket. Why did you not give him the Dante?'

'Because I did not like his face, and I thought he might have stolen the ticket from you. Besides, I'—here Hagar hesitated, for she was not anxious to admit that her real reason had been a desire to see him again—'besides, I don't think he is your friend,' she finished, lamely.

'Very probably he is not,' replied Lorn, shrugging his shoulders. 'I have no friends.'

'That is a pity,' said Hagar, casting a searching glance at his irresolute face. 'I think you need friends—or, at all events, one staunch one.'

'May that staunch one be of your own sex,' said Lorn, rather surprised at the interest this strange girl displayed in his welfare—'yourself, for instance?'

'If that could be so, I might give you unpalatable advice, Mr Lorn.'

'Such as—what?'

'Don't trust the man you sent here—Mr Treadle. See, here is your Dante, young man. Pay me the money, and take it away.'

'I can't pay you the money, as I have none. I am as poor as Job, but hardly so patient.'

'But you offered the money through that Treadle creature.'

'Indeed no!' explained Eustace, frankly. 'I gave him the ticket, and he wished to redeem the book with his own money.'

'Did he really?' said Hagar, thoughtfully. 'He does not look like a student—as you do. Why did he want this book?'

'To find out a secret.'

'A secret, young man—contained in the Dante?'

'Yes. There is a secret in the book which means money.'

'To you or Mr Treadle?' demanded Hagar.

Eustace shrugged his shoulders. 'To either one of us who finds out the secret,' he said, carelessly. 'But indeed I don't think it will ever be discovered—at all events by me. Treadle may be more fortunate.'

'If crafty ways can bring fortune, your man will succeed,' said Hagar, calmly. 'He is a dangerous friend for you, that Treadle. There is evidently some story about this Dante of yours which he knows, and which he desires to turn to his own advantage. If the story means money, tell it to me, and I may be able to help you to the wealth. I am only a young girl, it is true, Mr Lorn; still, I am old in experience, and I may succeed where you fail.'

'I doubt it,' replied Lorn, gloomily; 'still, it is kind of you to take this interest in a stranger. I am much obliged to you, Miss——'

'Call me Hagar,' she interrupted, hastily. 'I am not used to fine titles.'

'Well, then, Hagar,' said he, with a kindly glance, 'I'll tell you the story of my Uncle Ben and his strange will.'

Hagar smiled to herself. It seemed to be her fate to have dealings with wills—first that of Jacob; now this of Lorn's uncle. However, she knew when to hold her tongue, and saying nothing, she waited for Eustace to explain. This he did at once.

'My uncle, Benjamin Gurth, died six months ago at the age of fifty-eight,' said he, slowly. 'In his early days he had lived a roving life, and ten years ago he came home with a fortune from the West Indies.'

'How much fortune?' demanded Hagar, always interested in financial matters.

'That is the odd part about it,' continued Eustace; 'nobody ever knew the amount of his wealth, for he was a grumpy old curmudgeon, who confided in no one. He bought a little house and garden at Woking, and there lived for the ten years he was in England. His great luxury was books, and as he knew many languages—Italian among others—he collected quite a polyglot library.'

'Where is it now.'

'It was sold after his death along with the house and land. A man in the City claimed the money and obtained it.'

'A creditor. What about the fortune?'

'I'm telling you, Hagar, if you'll only listen,' said Eustace, impatiently. 'Well, Uncle Ben, as I have said, was a miser. He hoarded up all his moneys and kept them in the house, trusting neither to banks nor investments. My mother was his sister, and very poor; but he never gave her a penny, and to me nothing but the Dante, which he presented in an unusual fit of generosity.'

'But from what you said before,' remarked Hagar, shrewdly, 'it seemed to me that he had some motive in giving you the Dante.'

'No doubt,' assented Eustace, admiring her sharpness. 'The secret of where his money is hidden is contained in that Dante.'

'Then you may be sure, Mr Lorn, that he intended to make you his heir. But what has your friend Treadle to do with the matter?'

'Oh, Treadle is a grocer in Woking,' responded Lorn. 'He is greedy for money, and knowing that Uncle Ben was rich, he tried to get the cash left to him. He wheedled and flattered the old man; he made him presents, and always tried to set him against me as his only relative.'

'Didn't I say the man was your enemy? Well, go on.'

'There is little more to tell, Hagar. Uncle Ben hid his money away, and left a will which give it all to the person who should find out where it was concealed. The testament said the secret was contained in the Dante. You may be sure that Treadle visited me at once and asked to see the book. I showed it to him, but neither of us could find any sign in its pages likely to lead us to discover the hidden treasure. The other day Treadle came to see the Dante again. I told him that I had pawned it, so he volunteered to redeem it if I gave him the ticket. I did so, and he called on you. The result you know.'

'Yes; I refused to give it to him,' said Hagar, 'and I see now that I was quite right to do so, as the man is your enemy. Well, Mr Lorn, it seems from your story that a fortune is waiting for you, if you can find it.'

'Very true; but I can't find it. There isn't a single sign in the Dante by which I can trace the hiding-place.'

'Do you know Italian?'

'Very well. Uncle Ben taught it to me.'

'That's one point gained,' said Hagar, placing the Dante on the table and lighting another candle. 'The secret may be contained in the poem itself. However, we shall see. Is there any mark in the book—a marginal mark, I mean?'

'Not one. Look for yourself.'

The two comely young heads, one so fair, the other so dark, were bent over the book in that dismal and tenebrous atmosphere. Eustace, the weaker character of the twain, yielded in all things to Hagar. She turned over page after page of the old Florentine edition, but not one pencil or pen-mark marred its pure white surface from beginning to end. From 'L'Inferno' to 'Il Paradiso' no hint betrayed the secret of the hidden money. At the last page, Eustace, with a sigh, threw himself back in his chair.

'You see, Hagar, there is nothing. What are you frowning at?'

'I am not frowning, but thinking, young man,' was her reply. 'If the secret is in this book, there must be some trace of it. Now, nothing appears at present, but later on——'

'Well,' said Eustace, impatiently, 'later on?'

'Invisible ink.'

'Invisible ink!' he repeated, vaguely. 'I don't quite understand.'

'My late master,' said Hagar, without emotion, 'was accustomed to deal with thieves, rogues, and vagabonds. Naturally, he had many secrets, and sometimes, by force of circumstances, he had to trust these secrets to the post. Naturally, also, he did not wish to risk discovery, so when he sent a letter, about stolen goods for instance, he always wrote it in lemon-juice.'

'In lemon-juice! And what good was that?'

'It was good for invisible writing. When the letter was written, it looked like a blank page. No one, you understand, could read what was set out, for to the ordinary eye there was no writing at all.'

'And to the cultured eye?' asked Eustace, in ironical tones.

'It appeared the same—a blank sheet,' retorted Hagar. 'But then the cultured mind came in, young man. The person to whom the letter was sent warmed the seeming blank page over the fire, when at once the writing appeared, black and legible.'

'The deuce!' Eustace jumped up in his excitement. 'And you think——'

'I think that your late uncle may have adopted the same plan,' interrupted Hagar, coolly, 'but I am not sure. However, we shall soon see.' She turned over a page or two of the Dante. 'It is impossible to heat these over the fire,' she added, 'as the book is valuable, and we must not spoil it; but I know of a plan.'

With a confident smile she left the room and returned with a flat iron, which she placed on the fire. While it was heating Eustace looked at this quick-witted woman with admiration. Not only had she brains, but beauty also; and, man-like, he was attracted by this last in no small degree. Shortly he began to think that this strange and unexpected friendship between himself and the pawnbroking gypsy beauty might develop into something stronger and warmer. But here he sighed; both of them were poor, so it would be impossible to——

'We will not begin at the beginning of the book,' said Hagar, taking the iron off the fire, and thereby interrupting his thoughts, 'but at the end.'

'Why?' asked Eustace, who could see no good reason for this decision.

'Well,' said Hagar, poising the heated iron over the book, 'when I search for an article I find it always at the bottom of a heap of things I don't want. As we began with the first page of this book and found nothing, let us start this time from the end, and perhaps we shall learn your uncle's secret the sooner. It is only a whim of mine, but I should like to satisfy it by way of experiment.'

Eustace nodded and laughed, while Hagar placed a sheet of brown paper over the last page of the Dante to preserve the book from being scorched. In a minute she lifted the iron and paper, but the page still showed no mark. With a cheerful air the girl shook her head, and repeated the operation on the second page from the end. This time, when she took away the brown paper, Eustace, who had been watching her actions with much interest, bent forward with an ejaculation of surprise. Hagar echoed it with one of delight; for there was a mark and date on the page, half-way down, as thus:

> Oh, abbondante grazia, ond' io presumi
> Ficcar lo viso per la luce eterna 27.12.38.
> Tanto, che la veduta vi consumi!

'There, Mr Lorn!' cried Hagar, joyously—'there is the secret! My fancy for beginning at the end was right. I was right also about the invisible ink.'

'You are a wonder!' said Eustace, with sincere admiration; 'but I am as much in the dark as ever. I see a marked line, and a date, the twenty-seventh of December, in the year, I presume, one thousand eight hundred and thirty-eight. We can't make any sense out of that simplicity.'

'Don't be in a hurry,' said Hagar, soothingly; 'we have found out so much, we may learn more. First of all, please to translate those three lines.'

'Roughly,' said Eustace, reading them, 'they run thus: "O abundant grace, with whom I tried to look through the eternal light so much that I lost my sight." ' He shrugged his shoulders. 'I don't see how that transcendentalism can help us.'

'What about the date?'

'One thousand eight hundred and thirty-eight,' said Lorn, thoughtfully; 'and this is ninety-six. Take one from the other, it leaves fifty-eight, the age at which, as I told you before, my uncle died. Evidently this is the date of his birth.'

'A date of birth—a line of Dante!' muttered Hagar. 'I must say that it is difficult to make sense out of it. Yet, in figures and letters, I am sure the place where the money is concealed is told.'

'Well,' remarked Eustace, giving up the solution of this problem in despair, 'if you can make out the riddle it is more than I can.'

'Patience, patience!' replied Hagar, with a nod. 'Sooner or later we shall find out the meaning. Could you take me to see your uncle's house at Woking?'

'Oh, yes; it is not yet let, so we can easily go over it. But will you trouble about coming all that way with me?'

'Certainly! I am anxious to know the meaning of this line and date. There may be something about your uncle's house likely to give a clue to its reading. I shall keep the Dante, and puzzle over the riddle; you can call for me on Sunday, when the shop is closed, and we shall go to Woking together.'

'O Hagar! how can I ever thank——'

'Thank me when you get the money, and rid yourself of Mr Treadle!' said Hagar, cutting him short. 'Besides, I am only doing this to satisfy my own curiosity.'

'You are an angel!'

'And you a fool, who talks nonsense!' said Hagar, sharply. 'Here is your hat and cane. Come out this way by the back. I have an ill enough name already, without desiring a fresh scandal. Goodnight.'

'But may I say——'

'Nothing, nothing!' retorted Hagar, pushing him out of the door. 'Goodnight.'

The door snapped to sharply, and Lorn went out into the hot July night with his heart beating and his blood aflame. He had seen this girl only twice, yet, with the inconsiderate rashness of youth, he was already in love with her. The beauty and kindness and brilliant mind of Hagar attracted him strongly; and she had shown him such favour that he felt certain she loved him in return. But a girl out of a pawn-shop! He had neither birth nor money, yet he drew back from mating himself with such a one. True, his mother was dead, and he was quite alone in the world—alone and poor. Still, if he found his uncle's fortune, he would be rich enough to marry. Hagar, did she aid him to get the money, might expect reward in the shape of marriage. And she was so beautiful, so clever! By the time he reached his poor lodging Eustace had put all scruples out of his head, and had settled to marry the gypsy as soon as the lost treasure came into his possession. In no other way could he thank her for the interest she was taking in him. This may seem a hasty decision; but young blood is soon heated; young hearts are soon filled with love. Youth and beauty drawn together are as flint and tinder to light the torch of Hymen.

Punctual to the appointed hour, Eustace, as smart as he could make himself with the poor means at his command, appeared at the door of the pawnshop. Hagar was already waiting for him, with the Dante in her hand. She wore a black dress, a black cloak, and a hat of the same sombre hue—such clothes being the mourning she had worn, and was wearing, for Jacob. Averse as she was to using Goliath's money, she thought he would hardly grudge her these garments of woe for his father. Besides, as manageress of the shop, she deserved some salary.

'Why are you taking the Dante?' asked Eustace, when they set out for Waterloo Station.

'It may be useful to read the riddle,' said Hagar.

'Have you solved it?'

'I don't know; I am not sure,' she said, meditatively. 'I tried by counting the lines on that page up and down. You understand—twenty-seven, twelve, thirty-eight; but the lines I lighted on gave me no clue.'

'You didn't understand them?'

'Yes I did,' replied Hagar, coolly. 'I got a second-hand copy of a translation from the old bookseller in Carby's Crescent, and by counting the lines to correspond with those in the Florentine edition I arrived at the sense.'

'And none of them point to the solution of the problem?'

'Not one. Then I tried by pages. I counted twenty-seven pages, but could find no clue; I reckoned twelve pages; also thirty-eight; still the same result. Then I took the twelfth, the twenty-seventh, and the thirty-eighth page by numbers, but found nothing. The riddle is hard to read.'

'Impossible, I should say,' said Eustace, in despair.

'No; I think I have found out the meaning.'

'How? how? Tell me quick!'

'Not now. I found a word, but it seems nonsense, as I could not find it in the Italian dictionary which I borrowed.'

'What is the word?'

'I'll tell you when I have seen the house.'

In vain Eustace tried to move her from this determination. Hagar was stubborn when she took an idea into her strong brain; so she simply declined to explain until she arrived at Woking—at the house of Uncle Ben. Weak himself, Eustace could not understand how she could hold out so long against his persuasions. Finally, he decided in his own mind that she did not care about him. In this he was wrong. Hagar liked him—loved him; but she deemed it her duty to teach him patience—a quality he lacked sadly. Hence her closed mouth.

When they arrived at Woking, Eustace led the way towards his late uncle's house, which was some distance out of the town. He addressed Hagar, after a long silence, when they were crossing a piece of waste land and saw the cottage in the distance.

'If you find this money for me,' he said, abruptly, 'what service am I to do for you in return.'

'I have thought of that,' replied Hagar, promptly. 'Find Goliath—otherwise James Dix.'

'Who is he?' asked Lorn, flushing. 'Someone you are fond of?'

'Someone I hate with all my soul!' she flashed out; 'but he is the son of my late master, and heir to the pawnshop. I look after it only because he is absent; and on the day he returns I shall walk out of it, and never set eyes on it, or him again.'

'Why don't you advertise?'

'I have done so for months; so has Vark, the lawyer; but Jimmy Dix never replies. He was with my tribe in the New Forest, and it was because I hated him that I left the Romany. Since then he has gone away, and I don't know where he is. Find him if you wish to thank me, and let me get away from the pawnshop.'

'Very good,' replied Eustace, quietly. 'I shall find him. In the meantime, here is the hermitage of my late uncle.'

It was a bare little cottage, small and shabby, set at the end of a square of ground fenced in from the barren moor. Within the quadrangle there were fruit trees—cherry, apple, plum, and pear; also a large fig-tree in the centre of the unshaven lawn facing the house. All was desolate and neglected; the fruit trees were unpruned, the grass was growing in the paths, and the flowers were straggling here and there, rich masses of ragged colour. Desolate certainly, this deserted hermitage, but not lonely, for as Hagar and her companion turned in at the little gate a figure rose from a stooping position under an apple tree. It was that of a man with a spade in his hand, who had been digging for some time, as was testified by the heap of freshly turned earth at his feet.

'Mr Treadle!' cried Lorn, indignantly. 'What are you doing here?'

'Lookin' fur the old un's cash!' retorted Mr Treadle, with a scowl directed equally at the young man and Hagar. 'An' if I gets it I keeps it. Lord! to think as 'ow I pampered that old sinner with figs and such like—to say nothing of French brandy, which he drank by the quart!'

'You have no business here!'

'No more 'ave you!' snapped the irate grocer. 'If I ain't, you ain't, fur till the 'ouse is let it's public property. I s'pose you've come 'ere with that Jezebel to look fur the money?'

Hagar, hearing herself called names, stepped promptly up to Mr Treadle, and boxed his red ears. 'Now then,' she said, when the grocer fell back in dismay at this onslaught, 'perhaps you'll be civil! Mr Lorn, sit down on this seat, and I'll explain the riddle.'

'The Dante!' cried Mr Treadle, recognizing the book which lay on Hagar's lap—'an' she'll explain the riddle—swindling me out of my rightful cash!'

'The cash belongs to Mr Lorn, as his uncle's heir!' said Hagar, wrathfully. 'Be quiet, sir, or you'll get another box on the ears!'

'Never mind him,' said Eustace, impatiently; 'tell me the riddle.'

'I don't know if I have guessed it correctly,' answered Hagar, opening the book; 'but I've tried by line and page and number, all of which revealed nothing. Now I try by letters, and you will see if the word they make is a proper Italian one.'

She read out the marked line and the date. ' "Ficcar lo viso per la luce eterna, 27th December, '38." Now,' said Hagar, slowly; 'if you run all the figures together they stand as 271238.'

'Yes, yes!' said Eustace, impatiently; 'I see. Go on, please.'

Hagar continued: 'Take the second letter of the word "Ficcar." '

' "I." '

'Also the seventh letter from the beginning of the line.'

Eustace counted. ' "L." I see,' he went on, eagerly. 'Also the first letter, "F," the second again, "i," the third and the eighth, "c" and "o." '

'Good!' said Hagar, writing these down. 'Now, the whole make up the word "Ilfico." Is that an Italian word?'

'I'm not sure,' said Eustace, thoughtfully. ' "Ilfico." No.'

'Shows what eddication 'e's got!' growled Mr Treadle, who was leaning on his spade.

Eustace raised his eyes to dart a withering glance at the grocer, and in doing so his vision passed on to the tree looming up behind the man. At once the meaning of the word flashed on his brain.

' "Il fico!" ' he cried, rising. 'Two words instead of one! You have found it, Hagar! It means the fig-tree—the one yonder. I believe the money is buried under it.'

Before he could advance a step Treadle had leaped forward, and was slashing away at the tangled grass round the fig-tree like a madman.

'If 'tis there, 'tis mine!' he shouted. 'Don't you come nigh me, young Lorn, or I'll brain you with my spade! I fed up that old uncle of yours like a fighting cock, and now I'm going to have his cash to pay me!'

Eustace leaped forward in the like manner as Treadle had done, and would have wrenched the spade out of his grip, but that Hagar laid a detaining hand on his arm.

'Let him dig,' she said, coolly. 'The money is yours; I can prove it. He'll have the work and you the fortune.'

'Hagar! Hagar! how can I thank you!'

The girl stepped back, and a blush rose in her cheeks. 'Find Goliath,' she said, 'and let me get rid of the pawnshop.'

At this moment Treadle gave a shout of glee, and with both arms wrenched a goodly sized tin box out of the hole he had dug.

'Mine! mine!' he cried, plumping this down on the grass. 'This will pay for the dinners I gave him, the presents I made him. I've bin castin' my bread on the waters, and here it's back again.'

He fell to forcing the lid of the box with the edge of the spade, all the time laughing and crying like one demented. Lorn and Hagar drew near, in the expectation of seeing a shower of gold pieces rain on the ground when the lid was opened. As Treadle gave a final wrench it flew wide, and they saw—an empty box.

'Why—what,' stammered Treadle, thunderstruck—'what does it mean?'

Eustace, equally taken aback, bent down and looked in. There was absolutely nothing in the box but a piece of folded paper. Unable to make a remark, he held it out to the amazed Hagar.

'What the d—l does it mean?' said Treadle again.

'This explains,' said Hagar, running her eye over the writing. 'It seems that this wealthy Uncle Ben was a pauper.'

'A pauper!' cried Eustace and Treadle together.

'Listen!' said Hagar, and read out from the page: 'When I returned to England I was thought wealthy, so that all my friends and relations fawned on me for the crumbs which fell from the rich man's table. But I had just enough money to rent the cottage for a term of years, and to purchase an annuity barely sufficient for the necessities of life. But, owing to the report of my wealth, the luxuries have been supplied by those who hoped for legacies. This is my legacy to one and all—these golden words, which I have proved true: "It is better to be thought rich than to be rich." '

The paper fell from the hand of Eustace, and Treadle, with a howl of rage, threw himself on the grass, loading the memory of the deceased with opprobrious names. Seeing that all was over, that the expected fortune had vanished into thin air, Hagar left the disappointed grocer weeping with rage over the deceptive tin box, and led Eustace away. He followed her as in a dream, and all the time during their sad journey back to town he spoke hardly a word. What they did say—how Eustace bewailed his fate and Hagar comforted him—is not to the point. But on arriving at the door of the pawnshop Hagar gave the copy of Dante to the young man. 'I give this back to you,' she said, pressing his hand. 'Sell it, and with the proceeds build up your own fortune.'

'But shall I not see you again?' he asked, piteously.

'Yes, Mr Lorn; you shall see me when you bring back Goliath.'

Then she entered the pawnshop and shut the door. Left alone in the deserted crescent, Eustace sighed and walked slowly away. Hugging to his breast the Florentine Dante, he went away to make his fortune, to find Goliath, and—although he did not know it at the time—to marry Hagar.

4

GRANT ALLEN

The Adventure of the Cantankerous Old Lady

On the day when I found myself with twopence in my pocket, I naturally made up my mind to go round the world.

It was my stepfather's death that drove me to it. I had never seen my stepfather. Indeed, I never thought of him as anything more than even Colonel Watts-Morgan. I owed him nothing except my poverty. He married my dear mother when I was a girl at school in Switzerland; and he proceeded to spend her little fortune, left at her sole disposal by my father's will, in paying his gambling debts. After that, he carried my dear mother off to Burma; and when he and the climate between them had succeeded in killing her, he made up for his appropriations cheaply by allowing me just enough to send me to Girton. So, when the Colonel died, in the year I was leaving college, I did not think it necessary to go into mourning for him. Especially as he chose the precise moment when my allowance was due, and bequeathed me nothing but his consolidated liabilities.

'Of course you will teach,' said Elsie Petheridge, when I explained my affairs to her. 'There is a good demand just now for high-school teachers.'

I looked at her, aghast. '*Teach*! Elsie,' I cried. (I had come up to town to settle her in at her unfurnished lodgings.) 'Did you say *teach*? That's just like you dear good schoolmistresses! You go to Cambridge, and get examined till the heart and life have been examined out of you; then you say to yourselves at the end of it all, "Let me see; what am I good for now? I'm just about fit to go away and examine other people!" That's what our Principal would call "a vicious circle"—if one could ever admit there was anything vicious at all about you, dear. No, Elsie, my child, I do *not* propose to teach. Nature did not cut me out for a high-school teacher. I couldn't swallow a poker if I tried for weeks. Pokers don't agree with me. My dear, between ourselves, I am a bit of a rebel.'

'You are, Brownie,' she answered, pausing in her papering, with her sleeves rolled up—they called me 'Brownie', partly because of my complexion, but partly because they could never understand me. 'We all knew that long ago.'

I laid down the paste-brush and mused.

'Do you remember, Elsie,' I said, staring hard at the paper-board, 'when I first went to Girton, how all you girls wore your hair quite straight, in neat smooth coils, plaited up at the back about the size of a pancake; and how of a sudden I burst in upon you, like a tropical hurricane, and demoralized you; and how, after three days of me, some of the dear innocents began with awe to cut themselves artless fringes, while others went out in fear and trembling and surreptitiously purchased a pair of curling-tongs? I was a bombshell in your midst in those days; why, you yourself were almost afraid at first to speak to me.'

'You see, you had a bicycle,' Elsie put in, smoothing the half-papered wall; 'and in those days, of course, ladies didn't yet bicycle. You must admit, Brownie, dear, it *was* a startling innovation. You terrified us so. And yet, after all, there isn't much harm in you.'

'I hope not,' I said, devoutly. 'I was before my time, that was all; at present even a curate's wife may blamelessly bicycle.'

'But if you don't teach,' Elsie went on, gazing at me with those wondering big blue eyes of hers, 'what ever will you do, Brownie?' Her horizon was bounded by the scholastic circle.

'I haven't the faintest idea,' I answered, continuing to paste. 'Only, as I can't trespass upon your elegant hospitality for life, whatever I mean to do, I must begin doing this morning, when we've finished the papering. I couldn't teach' (teaching, like mauve, is the refuge of the incompetent); 'and I don't, if possible, want to sell bonnets.'

'As a milliner's girl?' Elsie asked, with a face of red horror.

'As a milliner's girl; why not? 'Tis an honest calling. Earls' daughters do it now. But you needn't look so shocked. I tell you, just at present, I am not contemplating it.'

'Then what *do* you contemplate?'

I paused and reflected. 'I am here in London,' I answered, gazing rapt at the ceiling; 'London, whose streets are paved with gold—though it *looks* at first sight like muddy flagstones; London, the greatest and richest city in the world, where an adventurous soul ought surely to find some loophole for an adventure. (That piece is hung crooked, dear; we must take it down again.) I have a Plan, therefore. I submit myself to fate; or, if you prefer it, I leave my future in the hands of Providence, I shall go out this morning, as soon as I've "cleaned myself", and embrace the first stray enterprise that offers. Our Baghdad teems with enchanted carpets. Let one but float my way, and, hi, presto, I seize it. I go where glory or a modest competence waits me. I snatch at the first offer, the first hint of an opening.'

Elsie stared at me, more aghast and more puzzled than ever. 'But, how?' she asked. 'Where? When? You *are* so strange! What will you do to find one?'

'Put on my hat and walk out,' I answered. 'Nothing could be simpler. This city bursts with enterprises and surprises. Strangers from east and west hurry through it in all directions. Omnibuses traverse it from end to end, even, I am told, to Islington and Putney; within, folk sit face to face who never saw one another before in their lives, and who may never see one another again, or, on the contrary, may pass the rest of their days together.'

I had a lovely harangue all pat in my head, in much the same strain, on the infinite possibilities of entertaining angels unawares, in cabs, on the Underground, in the Aërated Bread shops; but Elsie's widening eyes of horror pulled me up short like a hansom in Piccadilly when the inexorable upturned hand of the policeman checks it. 'Oh, Brownie,' she cried, drawing back, 'you *don't* mean to tell me you're going to ask the first young man you meet in an omnibus to marry you?'

I shrieked with laughter. 'Elsie,' I cried, kissing her dear yellow little head; 'you are *impayable*. You never will learn what I mean. You don't understand the language. No, no; I am going out, simply in search of adventure. What adventure may come, I have not at this moment the faintest conception. The fun lies in the search, the uncertainty, the toss-up of it. What is the good of being penniless—with the trifling exception of twopence—unless you are prepared to accept your position in the spirit of a masked ball at Covent Garden?'

'I have never been to one,' Elsie put in.

'Gracious heavens, neither have I! What on earth do you take me for? But I mean to see where fate will lead me.'

'I may go with you?' Elsie pleaded.

'Certainly *not*, my child,' I answered—she was three years older than I, so I had the right to patronize her. 'That would spoil all. Your dear little face would be quite enough to scare away a timid adventure.' She knew what I meant. It was gentle and pensive, but it lacked initiative.

So, when we had finished that wall, I put on my best hat, and strolled out by myself into Kensington Gardens.

I am told I ought to have been terribly alarmed at the straits in which I found myself—a girl of twenty-one, alone in the world, and only twopence short of penniless, without a friend to protect, a relation to counsel, her. (I don't count Aunt Susan, who lurked in ladylike indigence at Blackheath, and whose counsel was given away too profusely to everybody to allow of one's placing any very high value upon it.) But, as a matter of fact, I must admit I was not in the least alarmed. Nature had endowed me with a profusion of crisp black hair, and plenty of high spirits. If my eyes had been like Elsie's—that liquid blue which looks out upon life with mingled pity and amazement—I might have felt as a girl ought to feel under such conditions: but having large dark eyes, with a bit of a twinkle in them, and being as well able to pilot a bicycle as any girl of my acquaintance, I have inherited or acquired an outlook on the world which distinctly leans rather towards cheeriness than despondency. I croak with difficulty. So I accepted my plight as an amusing experience, affording full scope for the congenial exercise of courage and ingenuity.

How boundless are the opportunities of Kensington Gardens—the Round Pond, the winding Serpentine, the mysterious seclusion of the Dutch brick Palace. Genii swarm there. It is a land of romance, bounded on the north by the Abyss of Bayswater, and on the south by the Amphitheatre of the Albert Hall. But for a centre of adventure I chose the Long Walk; it beckoned me somewhat as the North-West Passage beckoned my seafaring ancestors—the buccaneering mariners of Elizabethan Devon. I sat down on a chain at the foot of an old elm with a poetic hollow, prosaically filled by a utilitarian plate of galvanized iron. Two ancient ladies were seated on the other side already—very grand-looking dames, with the haughty and exclusive ugliness of the English aristocracy in its later stages. For frank hideousness, commend me to the noble dowager. They were talking confidentially as I sat down; the trifling episode of my approach did not suffice to stem the full stream of their conversation. The great ignore the intrusion of their inferiors.

'Yes, it's a terrible nuisance,' the eldest and ugliest of the two observed—she was a high-born lady, with a distinctly cantankerous cast of countenance. She had a Roman nose, and her skin was wrinkled like a wilted apple; she wore coffee-coloured point-lace in her bonnet, with a complexion to match. 'But what could I do, my dear? I simply *couldn't* put up with such insolence. So I looked her straight back in the face—oh, she quailed, I can tell you; and I said to her, in my iciest voice—you know how icy I can be when occasion demands it'—the second old lady nodded an ungrudging assent, as if perfectly prepared to admit her friend's gift of iciness—'I said to her, "Célestine, you can take your month's wages, and half an hour to get out of this house." And she dropped me a deep reverence, and she answered: "*Oui, madame; merci beaucoup, madame; je ne désire pas mieux, madame.*" And out she flounced. So there was the end of it.'

'Still, you go to Schlangenbad on Monday?'

'That's the point. On Monday. If it weren't for the journey, I should have been glad enough to be rid of the minx. I'm glad as it is, indeed; for a more insolent, independent, answer-you-back-again young woman, with a sneer of her own, *I* never saw, Amelia—but I *must* get to Schlangenbad. Now, there the difficulty comes in. On the one hand, if I engage a maid in London, I have the choice of two evils. I must either take a trapesing English girl—and I know by experience that an English girl on the Continent is a vast deal worse than no maid at all: *you* have to wait upon *her*, instead of her waiting upon you; she gets seasick on the crossing, and when she reaches France or Germany, she hates the meals, and she can't speak the language, so that she's always calling you in to interpret for her in her private differences with the *fille-de-chambre* and the landlord: or else I must pick up a French maid in London, and I know equally by experience that the French maids one engages in London are invariably dishonest—more dishonest than the rest even; they've come here because they have no character elsewhere, and they think you aren't likely to write and enquire of their last mistress in Toulouse or St Petersburg. Then, again, on the other hand, I can't wait to get a Gretchen, an unsophisticated little Gretchen of the Taunus at Schlangenbad—I suppose there *are* unsophisticated girls in Germany still—made in Germany—they don't make 'em any longer in England, I'm sure—like everything else, the trade in rustic innocence has been driven from the country. I can't wait to get a Gretchen, as I should like to do, of course, because I simply *daren't* undertake to cross the Channel alone and go all that long journey by Ostend or Calais, Brussels and Cologne, to Schlangenbad.'

'You could get a temporary maid,' her friend suggested, in a lull of the tornado.

The Cantankerous Old Lady flared up. 'Yes, and have my jewel-case stolen! Or find she was an English girl without one word of German. Or nurse her on the boat when I want to give my undivided attention to my own misfortunes. No, Amelia, I call it positively unkind of you to suggest such a thing. You're *so* unsympathetic! I put my foot down there. I will *not* take any temporary person.'

I saw my chance. This was a delightful idea. Why not start for Schlangenbad with the Cantankerous Old Lady?

Of course, I had not the slightest intention of taking a lady's-maid's place for a permanency. Nor even, if it comes to that, as a passing expedient. But *if* I wanted to go round the world, how could I do better than set out by the Rhine country? The Rhine leads you on to the Danube, the Danube to the Black Sea, the Black Sea to Asia; and so by way of India, China, and Japan, you reach the Pacific and San Francisco; whence one returns quite easily by New York and the White Star Liners. I began to feel like a globe-trotter already; the Cantankerous Old Lady was the thin end of the wedge—the first rung of the ladder!

I leaned around the corner of the tree and spoke. 'Excuse me,' I said, in my suavest voice, 'but I think I see a way out of your difficulty.'

My first impression was that the Cantankerous Old Lady would go off in a fit of apoplexy. She grew purple in the face with indignation and astonishment, that a casual outsider should venture to address her; so much so, indeed, that for a second I almost regretted my well-meant interposition. Then she scanned me up and down, as if I were a girl in a mantle shop, and she contemplated buying either me or the mantle. At last, catching my eye, she thought better of it, and burst out laughing.

'What do you mean by this eavesdropping?' she asked.

I flushed up in turn. 'This is a public place,' I replied, with dignity; 'and you spoke in a tone which was hardly designed for the strictest privacy. Besides, I desired to do you a service.'

The Cantankerous Old Lady regarded me once more from head to foot. I did not quail. Then she turned to her companion. 'The girl has spirit,' she remarked, in an encouraging tone, as if she were discussing some absent person. 'Upon my word, Amelia, I rather like the look of her. Well, my good woman, what do you want to suggest to me?'

'Merely this,' I replied, bridling up and crushing her. 'I am a Girton girl, an officer's daughter, and I have nothing in particular to do for the moment. I don't object to going to Schlangenbad. I would convoy you over, as companion, or lady-help, or anything else you choose to call it; I would remain with you there for a week, till you could arrange with your Gretchen, presumably unsophisticated; and then I would leave you. Salary is unimportant; my fare suffices. I accept the chance as a cheap opportunity of attaining Schlangenbad.'

The yellow-faced old lady put up her long-handled tortoise-shell eyeglasses and inspected me all over again. 'Well, I declare,' she murmured. 'What are girls coming to, I wonder? Girton, you say; Girton! That place at Cambridge! You speak Greek, of course; but how about German?'

'Like a native,' I answered, with cheerful promptitude. 'I was at school in Canton Berne; it is a mother tongue to me.'

'No, no,' the old lady went on, fixing her keen small eyes on my mouth. 'Those little lips could never frame themselves to "schlecht" or "wunderschön"; they were not cut out for it.'

'Pardon me,' I answered, in German. 'What I say, that I mean. The never-to-be-forgotten music of the Fatherland's-speech has on my infant ear from the first-beginning impressed itself.'

The old lady laughed aloud.

'Don't jabber it to me, child,' she cried. 'I hate the lingo. It's the one tongue on earth that even a pretty girl's lips fail to render attractive. You yourself make faces over it. What's your name, young woman?'

'Lois Cayley.'

'Lois! *What* a name! I never heard of any Lois in my life before, except Timothy's grandmother. *You're* not anybody's grandmother, are you?'

'Not to my knowledge,' I answered, gravely.

She burst out laughing again.

'Well, you'll do, I think,' she said, catching my arm. 'That big mill down yonder hasn't ground the originality altogether out of you. I adore originality. It was clever of you to catch at the suggestion of this arrangement. Lois Cayley, you say; any relation of a madcap Captain Cayley whom I used once to know, in the Forty-second Highlanders?'

'His daughter,' I answered, flushing. For I was proud of my father.

'Ha! I remember; he died, poor fellow; he was a good soldier—and his'—I felt she was going to say 'his fool of a widow', but a glance from me quelled her; 'his widow went and married that good-looking scape-grace, Jack Watts-Morgan. Never marry a man, my dear, with a double-barrelled name and no visible means of subsistence: above all, if he's generally known by a nickname. So you're poor Tom Cayley's daughter, are you? Well, well, we can settle this little matter between us. Mind, I'm a person who always expects to have my own way. If you come with *me* to Schlangenbad, you must do as I tell you.'

'I *think* I could manage it—for a week,' I answered, demurely.

She smiled at my audacity. We passed on to terms. They were quite satisfactory. She wanted no references. 'Do I look like a woman who cares about a reference? You take my fancy; that's the point! And poor Tom Cayley! But, mind, I will *not* be contradicted.'

'And your name and address?' I asked, after we had settled preliminaries.

A faint red spot rose quaintly in the centre of the Cantankerous Old Lady's sallow cheek. 'My dear,' she murmured, 'my name is the one thing on earth I'm really ashamed of. My parents chose to inflict upon me the most odious label that human ingenuity ever devised for a Christian soul; and I've not had courage enough to burst out and change it.'

A gleam of intuition flashed across me. 'You don't mean to say,' I exclaimed, 'that you're called Georgina?'

The Cantankerous Old Lady gripped my arm hard. 'What an unusually intelligent girl!' she broke in. 'How on earth did you guess? It *is* Georgina.'

'Fellow-feeling,' I answered. 'So is mine, Georgina Lois. But as I quite agree with you as to the atrocity of such conduct, I have suppressed the Georgina. It ought to be made penal to send innocent girls into the world so burdened.'

'My opinion to a T! You are really an exceptionally sensible young woman. There's my name and address; I start on Monday.'

I glanced at her card. The very copperplate was noisy. 'Lady Georgina Fawley, 49 Fortescue Crescent, W.'

It had taken us twenty minutes to arrange our protocols. As I walked off, well pleased, Lady Georgina's friend ran after me quickly.

'You must take care,' she said, in a warning voice. 'You've caught a Tartar.'

'So I suspect,' I answered. 'But a week in Tartary will be at least an experience.'

'She has an awful temper.'

'That's nothing. So have I. Appalling, I assure you. And if it comes to blows, I'm bigger and younger and stronger than she is.'

'Well, I wish you well out of it.'

'Thank you. It is kind of you to give me this warning. But I think I can take care of myself. I come, you see, of a military family.'

I nodded my thanks, and strolled back to Elsie's. Dear little Elsie was in transports of surprise when I related my adventure.

'Will you really go? And what will you do, my dear, when you get there?'

'I haven't a notion,' I answered; 'but, anyhow, I shall have got there.'

'Oh, Brownie, you might starve!'

'And I might starve in London. In either place, I have only two hands and one head to help me.'

'But, then, here you are among friends. You might stop with me for ever.'

I kissed her fluffy forehead. 'You good, generous little Elsie,' I cried; 'I won't stop here one moment after I have finished the painting and papering. I came here to help you. I couldn't go on eating your hard-earned bread and doing nothing. I know how sweet you are; but the last thing I want is to add to your burdens. Now let us roll up our sleeves again and get on with the dado.'

'But, Brownie, you'll want to be getting your own things ready. Remember, you're off to Germany on Monday.'

I shrugged my shoulders. 'Tis a foreign trick I picked up in Switzerland. 'What have I got to get ready?' I asked. 'I can't go out and buy a complete summer outfit in Bond Street for twopence. Now, don't look at me like that: be practical, Elsie, and let me help you paint the dado.' For unless I helped her, poor Elsie could never have finished it herself. I cut out half her clothes for her; her own ideas were almost entirely limited to differential calculus. And cutting out a blouse by differential calculus is weary, uphill work for a high-school teacher.

By Monday I had papered and furnished the rooms, and was ready to start on my voyage of exploration. I met the Cantankerous Old Lady at Charing Cross, by appointment, and proceeded to take charge of her luggage and tickets.

Oh my, how fussy she was! 'You will drop that basket! I hope you have got through tickets, *viâ* Malines, *not* by Brussels—I won't go by Brussels. You have to change there. Now, mind you notice how much the luggage weighs in English pounds, and make the man at the office give you a note of it to check those horrid Belgian porters. They'll charge you for double the weight, unless you reduce it at once to kilogrammes. *I* know their ways. Foreigners have no consciences. They just go to the priest and confess, you know, and wipe it all out, and start fresh again on a career of crime next morning. I'm sure I don't know why I *ever* go abroad. The only country in the world fit to live in is England. No mosquitoes, no passports, no—goodness gracious, child, don't let that odious man bang about my hat-box! Have you no immortal soul, porter, that you crush other people's property as if it was blackbeetles? No, I will *not* let you take this, Lois; this is my jewel-box—it contains all that remains of the Fawley family jewels. I positively decline to appear at Schlangenbad without a diamond to my back. This never leaves my hands. It's hard enough nowadays to keep body and skirt together. *Have* you secured that *coupé* at Ostend?'

We got into our first-class carriage. It was clean and comfortable;

but the Cantankerous Old Lady made the porter mop the floor, and fidgeted and worried till we slid out of the station. Fortunately, the only other occupant of the compartment was a most urbane and obliging Continental gentleman—I say Continental, because I never quite made out whether he was French, German, or Austrian—who was anxious in every way to meet Lady Georgina's wishes. Did madame desire to have the window open? Oh, certainly, with pleasure; the day was so sultry. Closed a little more? *Parfaitement*, there *was* a current of air, *il faut l'admettre*. Madame would prefer the corner? No? Then perhaps she would like this valise for a footstool? *Permettez*—just thus. A cold draught runs so often along the floor in railway carriages. This is Kent that we traverse; ah, the garden of England! As a diplomat, he knew every nook of Europe, and he echoed the *mot* he had accidentally heard drop from madame's lips on the platform: no country in the world so delightful as England!

'Monsieur is attached to the Embassy in London?' Lady Georgina enquired, growing affable.

He twirled his grey moustache: a waxed moustache of great distinction. 'No, madame; I have quitted the diplomatic service; I inhabit London now *pour mon agrément*. Some of my compatriots call it *triste*; for me, I find it the most fascinating capital in Europe. What gaiety! What movement! What poetry! What mystery!'

'If mystery means fog, it challenges the world,' I interposed.

He gazed at me with fixed eyes. 'Yes, mademoiselle,' he answered, in quite a different and markedly chilly voice. 'Whatever your great country attempts—were it only a fog—it achieves consummately.'

I have quick intuitions. I felt the foreign gentleman took an instinctive dislike to me.

To make up for it, he talked much, and with animation, to Lady Georgina. They ferreted out friends in common, and were as much surprised at it as people always are at that inevitable experience.

'Ah, yes, madame, I recollect him well in Vienna. I was there at the time, attached to our Legation. He was a charming man; you read his masterly paper on the Central Problem of the Dual Empire?'

'You were in Vienna then!' the Cantankerous Old Lady mused back. 'Lois, my child, don't stare'—she had covenanted from the first to call me Lois, as my father's daughter, and I confess I preferred it to being Miss Cayley'd. 'We must surely have met. Dare I ask your name, monsieur?'

I could see the foreign gentleman was delighted at this turn. He had played for it, and carried his point. He meant her to ask him. He had a card in his pocket, conveniently close; and he handed it across to her. She read it, and passed it on: 'M. le Comte de Laroche-sur-Loiret'.

'Oh, I remember your name well,' the Cantankerous Old Lady broke in. 'I think you knew my husband, Sir Evelyn Fawley, and my father, Lord Kynaston.'

The Count looked profoundly surprised and delighted. 'What! you are then Lady Georgina Fawley!' he cried, striking an attitude. 'Indeed, miladi, your admirable husband was one of the very first to exert his influence in my favour at Vienna. Do I recall him, *ce cher* Sir Evelyn? If I recall him! What a fortunate rencounter! I must have seen you some years ago at Vienna, miladi, though I had not then the great pleasure of making your acquaintance. But your face had impressed itself on my subconscious self!' (I did not learn till later that the esoteric doctrine of the subconscious self was Lady Georgina's favourite hobby.) 'The moment chance led me to this carriage this morning, I said to myself, "That face, those features: so vivid, so striking: I have seen them somewhere. With what do I connect them in the recesses of my memory? A high-born family; genius; rank; the diplomatic service; some unnameable charm; some faint touch of eccentricity. Ha! I have it. Vienna, a carriage with footmen in red livery, a noble presence, a crowd of wits—poets, artists, politicians—pressing eagerly round the landau." That was my mental picture as I sat and confronted you: I understand it all now; this is Lady Georgina Fawley!'

I thought the Cantankerous Old Lady, who was a shrewd person in her way, must surely see through this obvious patter; but I had underestimated the average human capacity for swallowing flattery. Instead of dismissing his fulsome nonsense with a contemptuous smile, Lady Georgina perked herself up with a conscious air of coquetry, and asked for more. 'Yes, they were delightful days in Vienna,' she said, simpering; 'I was young then, Count; I enjoyed life with a zest.'

'Persons of miladi's temperament are always young,' the Count retorted, glibly, leaning forward and gazing at her. 'Growing old is a foolish habit of the stupid and the vacant. Men and women of *esprit* are never older. One learns as one goes on in life to admire, not the obvious beauty of mere youth and health'—he glanced across at me disdainfully—'but the profounder beauty of deep character in a face—that calm and serene beauty which is imprinted on the brow by experience of the emotions.'

'I have had my moments,' Lady Georgina murmured, with her head on one side.

'I believe it, miladi,' the Count answered, and ogled her.

Thenceforward to Dover, they talked together with ceaseless animation. The Cantankerous Old Lady was capital company. She had a tang in her tongue, and in the course of ninety minutes she had flayed alive the greater part of London society, with keen wit and sprightliness. I laughed against my will at her ill-tempered sallies; they were too funny not to amuse, in spite of their vitriol. As for the Count, he was charmed. He talked well himself, too, and between them, I almost forgot the time till we arrived at Dover.

It was a very rough passage. The Count helped us to carry our nineteen hand-packages and four rugs on board; but I noticed that, fascinated as she was with him, Lady Georgina resisted his ingenious efforts to gain possession of her precious jewel-case as she descended the gangway. She clung to it like grim death, even in the chops of the Channel. Fortunately I am a good sailor, and when Lady Georgina's sallow cheek began to grow pale, I was steady enough to supply her with her shawl and her smelling-bottle. She fidgeted and worried the whole way over. She *would* be treated like a vertebrate animal. Those horrid Belgians had no right to stick their deck-chairs just in front of her. The impertinence of the hussies with the bright red hair—a grocer's daughters, she felt sure—in venturing to come and sit on the same bench with *her*—the bench 'for ladies only', under the lee of the funnel! 'Ladies only,' indeed! Did the baggages pretend they considered themselves ladies? Oh, that placid old gentleman in the episcopal gaiters was their father, was he? Well, a bishop should bring up his daughters better, having his children in subjection with all gravity. Instead of which—'Lois, my smelling-salts!' This was a beastly boat; such an odour of machinery; they had no decent boats nowadays; with all our boasted improvements, she could remember well when the cross-Channel service was much better conducted than it was at present. But *that* was before we had compulsory education. The working classes were driving trade out of the country, and the consequence was, we couldn't build a boat which didn't reek like an oil-shop. Even the sailors on board were French—jabbering idiots; not an honest British Jack-tar among the lot of them; though the stewards were English, and very inferior Cockney English at that, with their off-hand ways, and their School Board airs and graces. *She'd* School Board them if they were her servants; *she'd* show them the sort of respect that was due to birth and education. But the children of the lower classes never learnt their catechism nowadays; they were too much occupied with literatoor, jography, and free and drawrin'. Happily for my nerves, a good lurch to leeward put a stop for a while to the course of her thoughts on the present distresses.

At Ostend, the Count made a second gallant attempt to capture the jewel-case, which Lady Georgina automatically repulsed. She had a fixed habit, I believe, of sticking fast to that jewel-case; for she was too overpowered by the Count's urbanity, I feel sure, to suspect for a moment his honesty of purpose. But whenever she travelled, I fancy, she clung to her case as if her life depended upon it: it contained the whole of her valuable diamonds.

We had twenty minutes for refreshments at Ostend, during which interval my old lady declared with warmth that I *must* look after her registered luggage; though, as it was booked through to Cologne, I could not even see it till we crossed the German frontier; for the Belgian *douaniers* seal up the van as soon as the through baggage for Germany is unloaded. To satisfy her, however, I went through the formality of pretending to inspect it, and rendered myself hateful to the head of the *douane* by asking various foolish and inept questions, on which Lady Georgina insisted. When I had finished this silly and uncongenial task—for I am not by nature fussy, and it is hard to assume fussiness as another person's proxy—I returned to our *coupé* which I had arranged for in London. To my great amazement, I found the Cantankerous Old Lady and the egregious Count comfortably seated there. 'Monsieur has been good enough to accept a place in our carriage,' she observed, as I entered.

He bowed and smiled. 'Or, rather, madame has been so kind as to offer me one,' he corrected.

'Would you like some lunch, Lady Georgina?' I asked, in my chilliest voice. 'There are ten minutes to spare, and the *buffet* is excellent.'

'An admirable inspiration,' the Count murmured. 'Permit me to escort you, miladi.'

'You will come, Lois?' Lady Georgina asked.

'No, thank you,' I answered, for I had an idea. 'I am a capital sailor, but the sea takes away my appetite.'

'Then you'll keep our places,' she said, turning to me. 'I hope you won't allow them to stick in any horrid foreigners! They will try to force them on you unless you insist. *I* know their tricky ways. You have the tickets, I trust? And the *bulletin* for the *coupé*? Well, mind you don't lose the paper for the registered luggage. Don't let those dreadful porters touch my cloaks. And if anybody attempts to get in, be sure you stand in front of the door as they mount to prevent them.'

The Count handed her out; he was all high courtly politeness. As Lady Georgina descended, he made yet another dexterous effort to relieve her of the jewel-case. I don't think she noticed it, but automatically once more she waved him aside. Then she turned to me. 'Here, my dear,' she said, handing it to me, 'you'd better take care of it. If I lay it down in the *buffet* while I am eating my soup, some rogue may run away with it. But mind, don't let it out of your hands on any account. Hold it so, on your knee; and, for Heaven's sake, don't part with it.'

By this time my suspicions of the Count were profound. From the first I had doubted him; he was so blandly plausible. But as we landed at Ostend, I had accidentally overheard a low whispered conversation when he passed a shabby-looking man, who had travelled in a second-class carriage from London. 'That succeeds?' the shabby-looking man had muttered under his breath in French, as the haughty nobleman with the waxed moustache brushed by him.

'That succeeds admirably,' the Count had answered, in the same soft undertone. '*Ça réussit à merveille*'.

I understood him to mean that he had prospered in his attempt to impose on Lady Georgina.

They had been gone five minutes at the *buffet*, when the Count came back hurriedly to the door of the *coupé* with a *nonchalant* air. 'Oh, mademoiselle', he said, in an off-hand tone, 'Lady Georgina has sent me to fetch her jewel-case.'

77

I gripped it hard with both hands. '*Pardon*, M. le Comte,' I answered; 'Lady Georgina entrusted it to *my* safe keeping, and, without her leave, I cannot give it up to anyone.'

'You mistrust me?' he cried, looking black. 'You doubt my honour? You doubt my word when I say that miladi has sent me?'

'*Du tout*,' I answered, calmly. 'But I have Lady Georgina's orders to stick to this case; and till Lady Georgina returns, I stick to it.'

He murmured some indignant remark below his breath, and walked off. The shabby-looking passenger was pacing up and down the platform outside in a badly made dust-coat. As they passed, their lips moved. The Count's seemed to mutter, '*C'est un coup manqué*'.

However, he did not desist even so. I saw he meant to go on with his dangerous little game. He returned to the *buffet* and rejoined Lady Georgina. I felt sure it would be useless to warn her, so completely had the Count succeeded in gulling her; but I took my own steps. I examined the jewel-case closely. It had a leather outer covering; within was a strong steel box, with stout bands of metal to bind it. I took my cue at once, and acted for the best on my own responsibility.

When Lady Georgina and the Count returned, they were like old friends together. The quails in aspic and the sparkling hock had evidently opened their hearts to one another. As far as Malines, they laughed and talked without ceasing. Lady Georgina was now in her finest vein of spleen: her acid wit grew sharper and more caustic each moment. Not a reputation in Europe had a rag left to cover it as we steamed in beneath the huge iron roof of the main central junction.

I had observed all the way from Ostend that the Count had been anxious lest we might have to give up our *coupé* at Malines. I assured him more than once that his fears were groundless, for I had arranged at Charing Cross that it should run right through to the German frontier. But he waved me aside, with one lordly hand. I had not told Lady Georgina of his vain attempt to take possession of her jewel-case; and the bare fact of my silence made him increasingly suspicious of me.

'Pardon me, mademoiselle,' he said, coldly; 'you do not understand these lines as well as I do. Nothing is more common than for those rascals of railway clerks to sell one a place in a *coupé* or a *wagon-lit*, and then never reserve it, or turn one out half way. It is very possible miladi may have to descend at Malines.'

Lady Georgina bore him out by a large variety of selected stories concerning the various atrocities of the rival companies which had stolen her luggage on her way to Italy. As for *trains de luxe*, they were dens of robbers.

So when we reached Malines, just to satisfy Lady Georgina, I put out my head and enquired of a porter. As I anticipated, he replied that there was no change; we went through to Verviers.

The Count, however, was still unsatisfied. He descended, and made some remarks a little further down the platform to an official in the gold-banded cap of a *chef-de-gare*, or some such functionary. Then he returned to us, all fuming. 'It is as I said,' he exclaimed, flinging open the door. 'These rogues have deceived us. The *coupé* goes no further. You must dismount at once, miladi, and take the train just opposite.'

I felt sure he was wrong, and I ventured to say so. But Lady Georgina cried, 'Nonsense, child! The *chef-de-gare* must know. Get out at once! Bring my bag and the rugs! Mind that cloak! Don't forget the sandwich-tin! Thanks, Count; will you kindly take charge of my umbrellas? Hurry up, Lois; hurry up; the train is just starting!'

I scrambled after her, with my fourteen bundles, keeping a quiet eye meanwhile on the jewel-case.

We took our seats in the opposite train, which I noticed was marked 'Amsterdam, Bruxelles, Paris'. But I said nothing. The Count jumped in, jumped about, arranged our parcels, jumped out again. He spoke to a porter: then he rushed back excitedly. '*Mille pardons*, miladi,' he cried. 'I find the *chef-de-gare* has cruelly deceived me. You were right, after all, mademoiselle! We must return to the *coupé*!'

With singular magnanimity, I refrained from saying, 'I told you so.'

Lady Georgina, very flustered and hot by this time, tumbled out once more, and bolted back to the *coupé*. Both trains were just starting. In her hurry, at last, she let the Count take possession of her jewel-case. I rather fancy that as he passed one window he handed it in to the shabby-looking passenger; but I am not certain. At any rate, when we were comfortably seated in our own compartment once more, and he stood on the footboard just about to enter, of a sudden, he made an unexpected dash back, and flung himself wildly into a Paris carriage. At the self-same moment, with a piercing shriek, both trains started.

Lady Georgina flung up her hands in a frenzy of horror. 'My diamonds!' she cried aloud. 'Oh, Lois, my diamonds!'

'Don't distress yourself,' I answered, holding her back, or I verily believe she would have leapt from the train. 'He has only taken the outer shell, with the sandwich-case inside it. *Here* is the steel box!' And I produced it, triumphantly.

She seized it, overjoyed. 'How did this happen?' she cried, hugging it, for she loved those diamonds.

'Very simply,' I answered, 'I saw the man was a rogue, and that he had a confederate with him in another carriage. So, while you were gone to the *buffet* at Ostend, I slipped the box out of the case, and put in the sandwich-tin, that he might carry it off, and we might have proofs against him. All you have to do now is to inform the conductor, who will telegraph to stop the train to Paris. I spoke to him about that at Ostend, so that everything is ready.'

She positively hugged me. 'My dear,' she cried, 'you are the cleverest little woman I ever met in my life! Who on earth could have suspected such a polished gentleman? Why, you're worth your weight in gold. What ever shall I do without you at Schlangenbad?'

5

L. T. MEADE AND ROBERT EUSTACE

Mr Bovey's Unexpected Will

AMONGST all my patients there were none who excited my sense of curiosity like Miss Florence Cusack. I never thought of her without a sense of baffled enquiry taking possession of me, and I never visited her without the hope that some day I should get to the bottom of the mystery which surrounded her.

Miss Cusack was a young and handsome woman. She possessed to all appearance superabundant health, her energies were extraordinary, and her life completely out of the common. She lived alone in a large house in Kensington Court Gardens, kept a good staff of servants, and went much into society. Her beauty, her sprightliness, her wealth, and, above all, her extraordinary life, caused her to be much talked about. As one glanced at this handsome girl with her slender figure, her eyes of the darkest blue, her raven black hair and clear complexion, it was almost impossible to believe that she was a power in the police courts, and highly respected by every detective in Scotland Yard.

I shall never forget my first visit to Miss Cusack. I had been asked by a brother doctor to see her in his absence. Strong as she was, she was subject to periodical and very acute nervous attacks. When I entered her house she came up to me eagerly.

'Pray do not ask me too many questions or look too curious, Dr Lonsdale,' she said; 'I know well that my whole condition is abnormal; but, believe me, I am forced to do what I do.'

'What is that?' I enquired.

'You see before you,' she continued, with emphasis, 'the most acute and, I believe, successful lady detective in the whole of London.'

'Why do you lead such an extraordinary life?' I asked.

'To me the life is fraught with the very deepest interest,' she answered. 'In any case,' and now the colour faded from her cheeks, and her eyes grew full of emotion, 'I have no choice: I am under a promise, which I must fulfil. There are times, however, when I need help—such help as you, for instance, can give me. I have never seen you before, but I like your face. If the time should ever come, will you give me your assistance?'

I asked her a few more questions, and finally agreed to do what she wished.

From that hour Miss Cusack and I became the staunchest friends. She constantly invited me to her house, introduced me to her friends, and gave me her confidence to a marvellous extent.

On my first visit I noticed in her study two enormous brazen bull-dogs. They were splendidly cast, and made a striking feature in the arrangements of the room: but I did not pay them any special attention until she happened to mention that there was a story, and a strange one, in connection with them.

'But for these dogs,' she said, 'and the mystery attached to them, I should not be the woman I am, nor would my life be set apart for the performance of duties at once herculean and ghastly.'

When she said these words her face once more turned pale, and her eyes flashed with an ominous fire.

On a certain afternoon in November 1894, I received a telegram from Miss Cusack, asking me to put aside all other work and go to her at once. Handing my patients over to the care of my partner, I started for her house. I found her in her study and alone. She came up to me holding a newspaper in her hand.

'Do you see this?' she asked. As she spoke she pointed to the agony column. The following words met my eyes:

'Send more sand and charcoal dust. Core and mould ready for casting.— Joshua Linklater.'

I read these curious words twice, then glanced at the eager face of the young girl.

'I have been waiting for this,' she said, in a tone of triumph.

'But what can it mean?' I said. 'Core and mould ready for casting?'

She folded up the paper, and laid it deliberately on the table.

'I thought that Joshua Linklater would say something of the kind,' she continued. 'I have been watching for a similar advertisement in all the dailies for the last three weeks. This may be of the utmost importance.'

'Will you explain?' I said.

'I may never have to explain, or, on the other hand, I may,' she answered. 'I have not really sent for you to point out this advertisement, but in connection with another matter. Now, pray, come into the next room with me.'

She led me into a prettily and luxuriously furnished boudoir on the same floor. Standing by the hearth was a slender fairhaired girl, looking very little more than a child.

'May I introduce you to my cousin, Letitia Ransom?' said Miss Cusack, eagerly. 'Pray sit down, Letty,' she continued addressing the girl with a certain asperity, 'Dr Lonsdale is the man of all others we want. Now, doctor, will you give me your very best attention, for I have an extraordinary story to relate.'

At Miss Cusack's words Miss Ransom immediately seated herself. Miss Cusack favoured her with a quick glance, and then once more turned to me.

'You are much interested in queer mental phases, are you not?' she said.

'I certainly am,' I replied.

'Well, I should like to ask your opinion with regard to such a will as this.'

Once again she unfolded a newspaper, and, pointing to a paragraph, handed it to me. I read as follows:

EXTRAORDINARY TERMS OF A MISER'S WILL.

Mr Henry Bovey, who died last week at a small house at Kew, has left one of the most extraordinary wills on record. During his life his eccentricities and miserly habits were well known, but this eclipses them all, by the surprising method in which he has disposed of his property.

Mr Bovey was unmarried, and, as far as can be proved, has no near relations in the world. The small balance at his banker's is to be used for defraying fees, duties, and sundry charges, also any existing debts, but the main bulk of his securities were recently realised, and the money in sovereigns is locked in a safe in his house.

A clause in the will states that there are three claimants to this property, and that the one whose net bodily weight is nearest to the weight of these sovereigns is to become the legatee. The safe containing the property is not to be opened till the three claimants are present; the competition is then to take place, and the winner is at once to remove his fortune.

Considerable excitement has been manifested over the affair, the amount of the fortune being unknown. The date of the competition is also kept a close secret for obvious reasons.

'Well,' I said, laying the paper down, 'whoever this Mr Bovey was, there is little doubt that he must have been out of his mind. I never heard of a more crazy idea.'

'Nevertheless it is to be carried out,' replied Miss Cusack. 'Now listen, please, Dr Lonsdale. This paper is a fortnight old. It is now three weeks since the death of Mr Bovey, his will has been proved, and the time has come for the carrying out of the competition. I happen to know two of the claimants well, and intend to be present at the ceremony.'

I did not make any answer, and after a pause she continued—

'One of the gentlemen who is to be weighed against his own fortune is Edgar Wimburne. He is engaged to my cousin Letitia. If he turns out to be the successful claimant there is nothing to prevent their marrying at once; if otherwise—' here she turned and looked full at Miss Ransom, who stood up, the colour coming and going in her cheeks—'if otherwise Mr Campbell Graham has to be dealt with.'

'Who is he?' I asked.

'Another claimant, a much older man than Edgar. Nay, I must tell you everything. He is a claimant in a double sense, being also a lover, and a very ardent one, of Letitia's.

'Lettie must be saved,' she said, looking at me, 'and I believe I know how to do it.'

'You spoke of three claimants,' I interrupted; 'who is the third?'

'Oh, he scarcely counts, unless indeed he carries off the prize. He is William Tyndall, Mr Bovey's servant and retainer.'

'And when, may I ask, is this momentous competition to take place?' I continued.

'Tomorrow morning at half-past nine, at Mr Bovey's house. Will you come with us tomorrow, Dr Lonsdale, and be present at the weighing?'

'I certainly will,' I answered, 'it will be a novel experience.'

'Very well; can you be at this house a little before half-past eight, and we will drive straight to Kew?'

I promised to do so, and soon after took my leave. The next day I was at Miss Cusack's house in good time. I found waiting for me Miss Cusack herself, Miss Ransom, and Edgar Wimburne.

A moment or two later we all found ourselves seated in a large landau, and in less than an hour had reached our destination. We drew up at a small dilapidated-looking house, standing in a row of prim suburban villas, and found that Mr Graham, the lawyer, and the executors had already arrived.

The room into which we had been ushered was fitted up as a sort of study. The furniture was very poor and scanty, the carpet was old, and the only ornaments on the walls were a few tattered prints yellow with age.

As soon as ever we came in, Mr Southby, the lawyer, came forward and spoke.

'We are met here today,' he said, 'as you are all of course aware, to carry out the clause of Mr Bovey's last will and testament. What reasons prompted him to make these extraordinary conditions we do not know; we only know that we are bound to carry them out. In a safe in his bedroom there is, according to his own statement, a large sum of money in gold, which is to be the property of the one of these three gentlemen whose weight shall nearest approach to the weight of the gold. Messrs. Hutchinson and Co. have been kind enough to supply one of their latest weighing machines, which has been carefully checked, and now if you three gentlemen will kindly come with me into the next room we will begin the business at once. Perhaps you, Dr Lonsdale, as a medical man, will be kind enough to accompany us.'

Leaving Miss Cusack and Miss Ransom we then went into the old man's bedroom, where the three claimants undressed and were carefully weighed. I append their respective weights, which I noted down:

Graham	13 stone	9 lbs.	6 oz.
Tyndall	11 stone	6 lbs.	3 oz.
Wimburne	12 stone	11 lbs.	

Having resumed their attire, Miss Cusack and Miss Ransom were summoned, and the lawyer, drawing out a bunch of keys, went across to a large iron safe which had been built into the wall.

We all pressed round him, everyone anxious to get the first glimpse of the old man's hoard. The lawyer turned the key, shot back the lock, and flung open the heavy doors. We found that the safe was literally packed with small canvas bags—indeed, so full was it that as the doors swung open two of the bags fell to the floor with a heavy crunching noise. Mr Southby lifted them up, and then cutting the strings of one, opened it. It was full of bright sovereigns.

An exclamation burst from us all. If all those bags contained gold there was a fine fortune awaiting the successful candidate! The business was now begun in earnest. The lawyer rapidly extracted bag after bag, untied the string, and shot the contents with a crash into the great copper scale pan, while the attendant kept adding weights to the other side to balance it, calling out the amounts as he did so. No one spoke, but our eyes were fixed as if by some strange fascination on the pile of yellow metal that rose higher and higher each moment.

As the weight reached one hundred and fifty pounds, I heard the old servant behind me utter a smothered oath. I turned and glanced at him; he was staring at the gold with a fierce expression of disappointment and avarice. He at any rate was out of the reckoning, as at eleven stone six, or one hundred and sixty pounds, he could be nowhere near the weight of the sovereigns, there being still eight more bags to untie.

The competition, therefore, now lay between Wimburne and Graham. The latter's face bore strong marks of the agitation which consumed him: the veins stood out like cords on his forehead, and his lips trembled. It would evidently be a near thing, and the suspense was almost intolerable. The lawyer continued to deliberately add to the pile. As the last bag was shot into the scale, the attendant put four ten-pound weights into the other side. It was too much. The gold rose at once. He took one off, and then the two great pans swayed slowly up and down, finally coming to a dead stop.

'Exactly one hundred and eighty pounds, gentlemen,' he cried, and a shout went up from us all. Wimburne at twelve stone eleven, or one hundred and seventy-nine pounds, had won.

I turned and shook him by the hand.

'I congratulate you most heartily.' I cried. 'Now let us calculate the amount of your fortune.'

I took a piece of paper from my pocket and made a rough calculation. Taking £56 to the pound avoirdupois, there were at least ten thousand and eighty sovereigns in the scale before us.

'I can hardly believe it,' cried Miss Ransom.

I saw her gazing down at the gold, then she looked up into her lover's face.

'Is it true?' she said, panting as she spoke.

'Yes, it is true,' he answered. Then he dropped his voice. 'It removes all difficulties.' I heard him whisper to her.

Her eyes filled with tears, and she turned aside to conceal her emotion.

'There is no doubt whatever as to your ownership of this money, Mr Wimburne,' said the lawyer, 'and now the next thing is to ensure its safe transport to the bank.'

As soon as the amount of the gold had been made known, Graham, without bidding goodbye to anyone, abruptly left the room, and I assisted the rest of the men in shovelling the sovereigns into a stout canvas bag, which we then lifted and placed in a four-wheeled cab which had arrived for the purpose of conveying the gold to the city.

'Surely someone is going to accompany Mr Wimburne?' said Miss Cusack at this juncture. 'My dear Edgar,' she continued, 'you are not going to be so mad as to go alone?'

To my surprise, Wimburne coloured, and then gave a laugh of annoyance.

'What could possibly happen to me?' he said. 'Nobody knows that I am carrying practically my own weight in gold into the city.'

'If Mr Wimburne wishes I will go with him,' said Tyndall, now coming forward. The old man had to all appearance got over his disappointment, and spoke eagerly.

'The thing is fair and square,' he added. 'I am sorry I did not win, but I'd rather you had it, sir, than Mr Graham. Yes, that I would, and I congratulate you, sir.'

'Thank you, Tyndall,' replied Wimburne, 'and if you like to come with me I shall be very glad of your company.'

The bag of sovereigns being placed in the cab, Wimburne bade us all a hasty goodbye, told Miss Ransom that he would call to see her at Miss Cusack's house that evening, and, accompanied by Tyndall, started off. As we watched the cab turn the corner I heard Miss Ransom utter a sigh.

'I do hope it will be all right,' she said, looking at me. 'Don't you think it is a risky thing to drive with so much gold through London?'

I laughed in order to reassure her.

'Oh, no, it is perfectly safe,' I answered, 'safer perhaps than if the gold were conveyed in a more pretentious vehicle. There is nothing to announce the fact that it is bearing ten thousand and eighty sovereigns to the bank.'

A moment or two later I left the two ladies and returned to my interrupted duties. The affair of the weighing, the strange clause in the will, Miss Ransom's eager pathetic face, Wimburne's manifest anxiety, had all impressed me considerably, and I could scarcely get the affair off my mind. I hoped that the young couple would now be married quickly, and I could not help being heartily glad that Graham had lost, for I had by no means taken to his appearance.

My work occupied me during the greater part of the afternoon, and I did not get back again to my own house until about six o'clock. When I did so I was told to my utter amazement that Miss Cusack had arrived and was waiting to see me with great impatience. I went at once into my consulting room, where I found her pacing restlessly up and down.

'What is the matter?' I asked.

'Matter!' she cried: 'have you not heard? Why, it has been cried in the streets already—the money is gone, was stolen on the way to London. There was a regular highway robbery in the Richmond Road, in broad daylight too. The facts are simply these: Two men in a dogcart met the cab, shot the driver, and after a desperate struggle, in which Edgar Wimburne was badly hurt, seized the gold and drove off. The thing was planned, of course—planned to a moment.'

'But what about Tyndall?' I asked.

'He was probably in the plot. All we know is that he has escaped and has not been heard of since.'

'But what a daring thing!' I cried. 'They will be caught, of course: they cannot have gone far with the money.'

'You do not understand their tricks, Dr Lonsdale: but I do,' was her quick answer, 'and I venture to guarantee that if we do not get that money back before the morning, Edgar Wimburne has seen the last of his fortune. Now, I mean to follow up this business, all night if necessary.'

I did not reply. Her dark, bright eyes were blazing with excitement, and she began to pace up and down.

'You must come with me,' she continued, 'you promised to help me if the necessity should arise.'

'And I will keep my word,' I answered.

'That is an immense relief.' She gave a deep sigh as she spoke.

'What about Miss Ransom?' I asked.

'Oh, I have left Letty at home. She is too excited to be of the slightest use.'

'One other question,' I interrupted, 'and then I am completely at your service. You mentioned that Wimburne was hurt.'

'Yes, but I believe not seriously. He has been taken to the hospital. He has already given evidence, but it amounts to very little. The robbery took place in a lonely part of the road, and just for the moment there was no one in sight.'

'Well,' I said, as she paused, 'you have some scheme in your head, have you not?'

'I have,' she answered. 'The fact is this: from the very first I feared some such catastrophe as has really taken place. I have known Mr Graham for a long time, and—distrusted him. He has passed for a man of position and means, but I believe him to be a mere adventurer. There is little doubt that all his future depended on his getting this fortune. I saw his face when the scales declared in Edgar Wimburne's favour —but there! I must ask you to accompany me to Hammersmith immediately. On the way I will tell you more.'

'We will go in my carriage,' I said, 'it happens to be at the door.'

We started directly. As we had left the more noisy streets Miss Cusack continued—

'You remember the advertisement I showed you yesterday morning?'

I nodded.

'You naturally could make no sense of it, but to me it was fraught with much meaning. This is by no means the first advertisement which has appeared under the name of Joshua Linklater. I have observed similar advertisements, and all, strange to say, in connection with founder's work, appearing at intervals in the big dailies for the last four or five months, but my attention was never specially directed to them until a circumstance occurred of which I am about to tell you.'

'What is that?' I asked.

'Three weeks ago a certain investigation took me to Hammersmith in order to trace a stolen necklace. It was necessary that I should go to a small pawnbroker's shop—the man's name was Higgins. In my queer work, Dr Lonsdale, I employ many disguises. That night, dressed quietly as a domestic servant on her evening out, I entered the pawnbroker's. I wore a thick veil and a plainly trimmed hat. I entered one of the little boxes where one stands to pawn goods, and waited for the man to appear.

'For the moment he was engaged, and looking through a small window in the door I saw to my astonishment that the pawnbroker was in earnest conversation with no less a person than Mr Campbell Graham. This was the last place I should have expected to see Mr Graham in, and I immediately used both my eyes and ears. I heard the pawnbroker address him as Linklater.

'Immediately the memory of the advertisements under that name flashed through my brain. From the attitude of the two men there was little doubt that they were discussing a matter of the utmost importance, and as Mr Graham, *alias* Linklater, was leaving the shop, I distinctly overheard the following words: "In all probability Bovey will die tonight. I may or may not be successful, but in order to insure against loss we must be prepared. It is not safe for me to come here often—look out for advertisement—it will be in the agony column.'"

'I naturally thought such words very strange, and when I heard of Mr Bovey's death and read an account of the queer will it seemed to me that I began to see daylight. It was also my business to look out for the advertisement, and when I saw it yesterday morning you may well imagine that my keenest suspicions were aroused. I immediately suspected foul play, but could do nothing except watch and await events.

Directly I heard the details of the robbery I wired to the inspector at Hammersmith to have Higgins's house watched. You remember that Mr Wimburne left Kew in the cab at ten o'clock: the robbery must therefore have taken place some time about ten-twenty. The news reached me shortly after eleven, and my wire was sent off about eleven-fifteen. I mention these hours, as much may turn upon them. Just before I came to you I received a wire from the police-station containing startling news. This was sent off about five-thirty. Here, you had better read it.'

As she spoke she took a telegram from her pocket and handed it to me. I glanced over the words it contained.

'Just heard that cart was seen at Higgins's this morning. Man and assistant arrested on suspicion. House searched. No gold there. Please come down at once.'

'So they have bolted with it?' I said.

'That we shall see,' was her reply.

Shortly afterwards we arrived at the police station. The inspector was waiting for us, and took us at once into a private room.

'I am glad you were able to come, Miss Cusack,' he said, bowing with great respect to the handsome girl.

'Pray tell me what you have done,' she answered, 'there is not a moment to spare.'

'When I received your wire,' he said, 'I immediately placed a man on duty to watch Higgins's shop, but evidently before I did this the cart must have arrived and gone—the news with regard to the cart being seen outside Higgins's shop did not reach me till four-thirty. On receiving it I immediately arrested both Higgins and his assistant, and we searched the house from attic to cellar, but have found no gold whatever. There is little doubt that the pawnbroker received the gold, and has already removed it to another quarter.'

'Did you find a furnace in the basement?' suddenly asked Miss Cusack.

'We did,' he replied, in some astonishment; 'but why do you ask?'

To my surprise Miss Cusack took out of her pocket the advertisement which she had shown me that morning and handed it the inspector. The man read the queer words aloud in a slow and wondering voice:

'Send more sand and charcoal dust. Core and mould ready for casting—
JOSHUA LINKLATER.'

'I can make nothing of it, miss,' he said, glancing at Miss Cusack.
'These words seem to me to have something to do with founder's
work.'

'I believe they have,' was her eager reply. 'It is also highly probable
that they have something to do with the furnace in the basement of
Higgins's shop.'

'I do not know what you are talking about, miss, but you have
something at the back of your head which does not appear.'

'I have,' she answered, 'and in order to confirm certain suspicions I
wish to search the house.'

'But the place has just been searched by us,' was the man's almost
testy answer. 'It is impossible that a mass of gold should be there and
be overlooked; every square inch of space has been accounted for.'

'Who is in the house now?'

'No one; the place is locked up, and one of our men is on duty.'

'What size is the furnace?'

'Unusually large,' was the inspector's answer.

Miss Cusack gave a smile which almost immediately vanished.

'We are wasting time,' she said; 'let us go there immediately.'

'I must do so, of course, if nothing else will satisfy you, miss; but I
assure you——'

'Oh, don't let us waste any more time in arguing,' said Miss Cusack,
her impatience now getting the better of her. 'I have a reason for what
I do, and must visit the pawnbroker's immediately.'

The man hesitated no longer, but took a bunch of keys down from
the wall. A blaze of light from a public-house guided us to the pawnbroker's, which bore the well-known sign, the three golden balls.
These were just visible through the fog above us. The inspector nodded to the man on duty, and unlocking the door we entered a narrow
passage into which the swing doors of several smaller compartments
opened. The inspector struck a match, and, lighting the lantern,
looked at Miss Cusack, as much as to say, 'What do you propose to do
now?'

'Take me to the room where the furnace is,' said the lady.

'Come this way,' he replied.

We turned at once in the direction of the stairs which led to the basement, and entered a room on the right. At the further end was an open range which had evidently been enlarged in order to allow the consumption of a great quantity of fuel, and upon it now stood an iron vessel, shaped as a chemist's crucible. Considerable heat still radiated from it. Miss Cusack peered inside, then she slowly commenced raking out the ashes with an iron rod, examining them closely and turning them over and over. Two or three white fragments she examined with peculiar care.

'One thing at least is abundantly clear,' she said at last; 'gold has been melted here, and within a very short time; whether it was the sovereigns or not we have yet to discover.'

'But surely, Miss Cusack,' said the inspector, 'no one would be rash enough to destroy sovereigns.'

'I am thinking of Joshua Linklater's advertisement,' she said. ' "*Send more sand and charcoal dust.*" This,' she continued, once more examining the white fragments, 'is undoubtedly sand.'

She said nothing further, but went back to the ground floor and now commenced a systematic search on her own account.

At last we reached the top floor, where the pawnbroker and his assistant had evidently slept. Here Miss Cusack walked at once to the window and flung it open. She gazed out for a minute, and then turned to face us. Her eyes looked brighter than ever, and a certain smile played about her face.

'Well, miss,' said the police inspector, 'we have now searched the whole house, and I hope you are satisfied.'

'I am,' she replied.

'The gold is not here, miss.'

'We will see,' she said. As she spoke she turned once more and bent slightly out, as if to look down through the murky air at the street below.

The inspector gave an impatient exclamation.

'If you have quite finished, miss, we must return to the station,' he said. 'I am expecting some men from Scotland Yard to go into this affair.'

'I do not think they will have much to do,' she answered, 'except, indeed, to arrest the criminal.' As she spoke she leant a little further out of the window, and then withdrawing her head said quietly, 'Yes, we may as well go back now; I have quite finished. Things are exactly as I expected to find them; we can take the gold away with us.'

Both the inspector and I stared at her in utter amazement.

'What do you mean, Miss Cusack?' I cried.

'What I say,' she answered, and now she gave a light laugh; 'the gold is here, close to us; we have only to take it away. Come,' she added, 'look out, both of you. Why, you are both gazing at it.'

I glanced round in utter astonishment. My expression of face was reproduced in that of the inspector's.

'Look,' she said, 'what do you call that?' As she spoke she pointed to the sign that hung outside—the sign of the three balls.

'Lean out and feel that lower ball,' she said to the inspector.

He stretched out his arm, and as his fingers touched it he started back.

'Why, it is hot,' he said; 'what in the world does it mean?'

'It means the lost gold,' replied Miss Cusack; 'it has been cast as that ball. I said that the advertisement would give me the necessary clue, and it has done so. Yes, the lost fortune is hanging outside the house. The gold was melted in the crucible downstairs, and cast as this ball between twelve o'clock and four-thirty today. Remember it was after four-thirty that you arrested the pawnbroker and his assistant.'

To verify her extraordinary words was the work of a few moments. Owing to its great weight, the inspector and I had some difficulty in detaching the ball from its hook. At the same time we noticed that a very strong stay, in the shape of an iron-wire rope, had been attached to the iron frame from which the three balls hung.

'You will find, I am sure,' said Miss Cusack, 'that this ball is not of solid gold; if it were, it would not be the size of the other two balls. It has probably been cast round a centre of plaster of Paris to give it the same size as the others. This explains the advertisement with regard to the charcoal and sand. A ball of that size in pure gold would weigh nearly three hundred pounds, or twenty stone.'

'Well,' said the inspector, 'of all the curious devices that I have ever seen or heard of, this beats the lot. But what did they do with the real ball? They must have put it somewhere.'

'They burnt it in the furnace, of course,' she answered; 'these balls, as you know, are only wood covered with gold paint. Yes, it was a clever idea, worthy of the brain of Mr Graham; and it might have hung there for weeks and been seen by thousands passing daily, till Mr Higgins was released from imprisonment, as nothing whatever could be proved against him.'

Owing to Miss Cusack's testimony, Graham was arrested that night, and, finding that circumstances were dead against him, he confessed the whole. For long years he was one of a gang of coiners, but managed to pass as a gentleman of position. He knew old Bovey well, and had heard him speak of the curious will he had made. Knowing of this, he determined, at any risk, to secure the fortune, intending, when he had obtained it, to immediately leave the country. He had discovered the exact amount of the money which he would leave behind him, and had gone carefully into the weight which such a number of sovereigns would make. He knew at once that Tyndall would be out of the reckoning, and that the competition would really be between himself and Wimburne. To provide against the contingency of Wimburne's being the lucky man, he had planned the robbery; the gold was to be melted, and made into a real golden ball, which was to hang over the pawnshop until suspicion had died away.

6

BARONESS ORCZY

The Man in the Inverness Cape

I HAVE heard many people say—people, too, mind you, who read their daily paper regularly—that it is quite impossible for anyone to 'disappear' within the confines of the British Isles. At the same time these wise people invariably admit one great exception to their otherwise unimpeachable theory, and that is the case of Mr Leonard Marvell, who, as you know, walked out one afternoon from the Scotia Hotel in Cromwell Road and has never been seen or heard of since.

Information had originally been given to the police by Mr Marvell's sister Olive, a Scotchwoman of the usually accepted type: tall, bony, with sandy-coloured hair, and a somewhat melancholy expression in her blue-grey eyes.

Her brother, she said, had gone out on a rather foggy afternoon. I think it was the 3rd of February, just about a year ago. His intention had been to go and consult a solicitor in the City—whose address had been given him recently by a friend—about some private business of his own.

Mr Marvell had told his sister that he would get a train at South Kensington Station to Moorgate Street, and walk thence to Finsbury Square. She was to expect him home by dinner-time.

As he was, however, very irregular in his habits, being fond of spending his evenings at restaurants and music-halls, the sister did not feel the least anxious when he did not return home at the appointed time. She had her dinner in the table d'hôte room, and went to bed soon after 10.00.

She and her brother occupied two bedrooms and a sitting-room on the second floor of the little private hotel. Miss Marvell, moreover, had a maid always with her, as she was somewhat of an invalid. This girl, Rosie Campbell, a nice-looking Scotch lassie, slept on the top floor.

It was only on the following morning, when Mr Leonard did not put in an appearance at breakfast, that Miss Marvell began to feel anxious. According to her own account, she sent Rosie in to see if anything was the matter, and the girl, wide-eyed and not a little frightened, came back with the news that Mr Marvell was not in his room, and that his bed had not been slept in that night.

With characteristic Scottish reserve, Miss Olive said nothing about the matter at the time to anyone, nor did she give information to the police until two days later, when she herself had exhausted every means in her power to discover her brother's whereabouts.

She had seen the lawyer to whose office Leonard Marvell had intended going that afternoon, but Mr Statham, the solicitor in question, had seen nothing of the missing man.

With great adroitness Rosie, the maid, had made enquiries at South Kensington and Moorgate Street stations. At the former, the booking clerk, who knew Mr Marvell by sight, distinctly remembered selling him a first-class ticket to one of the City stations in the early part of the afternoon; but at Moorgate Street, which is a very busy station, no one recollected seeing a tall, red-haired Scotchman in an Inverness cape—such was the description given of the missing man. By that time the fog had become very thick in the City; traffic was disorganized, and everyone felt fussy, ill-tempered, and self-centred.

These, in substance, were the details which Miss Marvell gave to the police on the subject of her brother's strange disappearance.

At first she did not appear very anxious; she seemed to have great faith in Mr Marvell's power to look after himself; moreover, she declared positively that her brother had neither valuables nor money about his person when he went out that afternoon.

But as day succeeded day and no trace of the missing man had yet been found, matters became more serious, and the search instituted by our fellows at the Yard waxed more keen.

A description of Mr Leonard Marvell was published in the leading London and provincial dailies. Unfortunately, there was no good photograph of him extant, and descriptions are apt to prove vague.

Very little was known about the man beyond his disappearance, which had rendered him famous. He and his sister had arrived at the Scotia Hotel about a month previously, and subsequently they were joined by the maid Campbell.

Scotch people are far too reserved ever to speak of themselves or their affairs to strangers. Brother and sister spoke very little to anyone at the hotel. They had their meals in their sitting-room, waited on by the maid, who messed with the staff. But, in face of the present terrible calamity, Miss Marvell's frigidity relaxed before the police inspector, to whom she gave what information she could about her brother.

'He was like a son to me,' she explained with scarcely restrained tears, 'for we lost our parents early in life, and as we were left very, very badly off, our relations took but little notice of us. My brother was years younger than I am—and though he was a little wild and fond of pleasure, he was as good as gold to me, and has supported us both for years by journalistic work. We came to London from Glasgow about a month ago, because Leonard got a very good appointment on the staff of the *Daily Post*.'

All this, of course, was soon proved to be true; and although, on minute enquiries being instituted in Glasgow, but little seemed to be known about Mr Leonard Marvell in that city, there seemed no doubt that he had done some reporting for the *Courier*, and that latterly, in response to an advertisement, he had applied for and obtained regular employment on the *Daily Post*.

The latter enterprising halfpenny journal, with characteristic magnanimity, made an offer of £50 reward to any of its subscribers who gave information which would lead to the discovery of the whereabouts of Mr Leonard Marvell.

But time went by, and that £50 remained unclaimed.

2

Lady Molly had not seemed as interested as she usually was in cases of this sort. With strange flippancy—wholly unlike herself—she remarked that one Scotch journalist more or less in London did not vastly matter.

I was much amused, therefore, one morning about three weeks

after the mysterious disappearance of Mr Leonard Marvell, when Jane, our little parlour-maid, brought in a card accompanied by a letter.

The card bore the name 'Miss Olive Marvell'. The letter was the usual formula from the chief, asking Lady Molly to have a talk with the lady in question, and to come and see him on the subject after the interview.

With a smothered yawn my dear lady told Jane to show in Miss Marvell.

'There are two of them, my lady,' said Jane, as she prepared to obey.

'Two what?' asked Lady Molly with a laugh.

'Two ladies, I mean,' explained Jane.

'Well! Show them both into the drawing-room,' said Lady Molly, impatiently.

Then, as Jane went off on this errand, a very funny thing happened; funny, because during the entire course of my intimate association with my dear lady, I had never known her act with such marked indifference in the face of an obviously interesting case. She turned to me and said:

'Mary, you had better see these two women, whoever they may be; I feel that they would bore me to distraction. Take note of what they say, and let me know. Now, don't argue,' she added with a laugh, which peremptorily put a stop to my rising protest, 'but go and interview Miss Marvell and Co.'.

Needless to say, I promptly did as I was told, and the next few seconds saw me installed in our little drawing-room, saying polite preliminaries to the two ladies who sat opposite to me.

I had no need to ask which of them was Miss Marvell. Tall, ill-dressed in deep black, with a heavy crape veil over her face, and black cotton gloves, she looked the uncompromising Scotchwoman to the life. In strange contrast to her depressing appearance, there sat beside her an overdressed, much behatted, peroxided young woman, who bore the stamp of *the* profession all over her pretty, painted face.

Miss Marvell, I was glad to note, was not long in plunging into the subject which had brought her here.

'I saw a gentleman at Scotland Yard,' she explained, after a short preamble, 'because Miss—er—Lulu Fay came to me at the hotel this very morning with a story which, in my opinion, should have been told to the police directly my brother's disappearance became known, and not three weeks later.'

The emphasis which she laid on the last few words, and the stern look with which she regarded the golden-haired young woman beside her, showed the disapproval with which the rigid Scotchwoman viewed any connection which her brother might have had with the lady, whose very name seemed unpleasant to her lips.

Miss—er—Luly Fay blushed even through her rouge, and turned a pair of large, liquid eyes imploringly upon me.

'I—I didn't know. I was frightened,' she stammered.

'There's no occasion to be frightened now,' retorted Miss Marvell, 'and the sooner you try and be truthful about the whole matter, the better it will be for all of us.'

And the stern woman's lips closed with a snap, as she deliberately turned her back on Miss Fay and began turning over the leaves of a magazine which happened to be on a table close to her hand.

I muttered a few words of encouragement, for the little actress looked ready to cry. I spoke as kindly as I could, telling her that if indeed she could throw some light on Mr Marvell's present whereabouts it was her duty to be quite frank on the subject.

She 'hem'-ed and 'ha'-ed for awhile, and her simpering ways were just beginning to tell on my nerves, when she suddenly started talking very fast.

'I am principal boy at the Grand,' she explained with great volubility; 'and I knew Mr Leonard Marvell well—in fact—er—he paid me a good deal of attention and—— '

'Yes—and—— ?' I queried, for the girl was obviously nervous.

There was a pause. Miss Fay began to cry.

'And it seems that my brother took this young—er—lady to supper on the night of February 3rd, after which no one has ever seen or heard of him again,' here interposed Miss Marvell, quietly.

'Is that so?' I asked.

Lulu Fay nodded, whilst heavy tears fell upon her clasped hands.

'But why did you not tell this to the police three weeks ago?' I ejaculated, with all the sternness at my command.

'I—I was frightened,' she stammered.

'Frightened? Of what?'

'I am engaged to Lord Mountnewte and——'

'And you did not wish him to know that you were accepting the attentions of Mr Leonard Marvell—was that it? Well,' I added, with involuntary impatience, 'what happened after you had supper with Mr Marvell?'

'Oh! I hope—I hope that nothing happened,' she said through more tears; 'we had supper at the Trocadero, and he saw me into my brougham. Suddenly, just as I was driving away, I saw Lord Mountnewte standing quite close to us in the crowd.'

'Did the two men know one another?' I asked.

'No,' replied Miss Fay; 'at least, I didn't think so, but when I looked back through the window of my carriage I saw them standing on the kerb talking to each other for a moment, and then walk off together towards Piccadilly Circus. That is the last I have seen of either of them,' continued the little actress with a fresh flood of tears. 'Lord Mountnewte hasn't spoken to me since, and Mr Marvell has disappeared with my money and my diamonds.'

'Your money and your diamonds?' I gasped in amazement.

'Yes; he told me he was a jeweller, and that my diamonds wanted resetting. He took them with him that evening, for he said that London jewellers were clumsy thieves, and that he would love to do the work for me himself. I also gave him two hundred pounds, which he said he would want for buying the gold and platinum required for the settings. And now he has disappeared—and my diamonds—and my money! Oh! I have been very—very foolish—and——'

Her voice broke down completely. Of course, one often hears of the idiocy of girls giving money and jewels unquestioningly to clever adventurers who know how to trade upon their inordinate vanity. There was, therefore, nothing very out of the way in the story just told me by Miss—er—Lulu Fay, until the moment when Miss Marvell's quiet voice, with its marked Scotch burr, broke in upon the short silence which had followed the actress's narrative.

'As I explained to the chief detective-inspector at Scotland Yard,' she said calmly, 'the story which this young—er—lady tells is only partly true. She may have had supper with Mr Leonard Marvell on the night of February 3rd, and he may have paid her certain attentions; but he never deceived her by telling her that he was a jeweller, nor did he obtain possession of her diamonds and her money through false statements. My brother was the soul of honour and loyalty. If, for some reason which Miss—er—Lulu Fay chooses to keep secret, he had her jewels and money in his possession on the fatal February 3rd, then I think his disappearance is accounted for. He has been robbed and perhaps murdered.'

Like a true Scotchwoman she did not give way to tears, but even her harsh voice trembled slightly when she thus bore witness to her brother's honesty, and expressed the fears which assailed her as to his fate.

Imagine my plight! I could ill forgive my dear lady for leaving me in this unpleasant position—a sort of peacemaker between two women who evidently hated one another, and each of whom was trying her best to give the other 'the lie direct'.

I ventured to ring for our faithful Jane and to send her with an imploring message to Lady Molly, begging her to come and disentangle the threads of this muddled skein with her clever fingers; but Jane returned with a curt note from my dear lady, telling me not to worry about such a silly case, and to bow the two women out of the flat as soon as possible and then come for a nice walk.

I wore my official manner as well as I could, trying not to betray the 'prentice hand. Of course, the interview lasted a great deal longer, and there was considerably more talk than I can tell you of in a brief narrative. But the gist of it all was just as I have said. Miss Lulu Fay stuck to every point of the story which she had originally told Miss Marvell. It was the latter uncompromising lady who had immediately marched the younger woman off to Scotland Yard in order that she might repeat her tale to the police. I did not wonder that the chief promptly referred them both to Lady Molly.

Anyway, I made excellent shorthand notes of the conflicting stories which I heard; and I finally saw, with real relief, the two women walk out of our little front door.

3

Miss—er—Lulu Fay, mind you, never contradicted in any one particular the original story which she had told me, about going out to supper with Leonard Marvell, entrusting him with £200 and the diamonds, which he said he would have reset for her, and seeing him finally in close conversation with her recognized *fiancé*, Lord Mountnewte. Miss Marvell, on the other hand, very commendably refused to admit that her brother acted dishonestly towards the girl. If he had her jewels and money in his possession at the time of his disappearance, then he had undoubtedly been robbed, or perhaps murdered, on his way back to the hotel, and if Lord Mountnewte had been the last to speak to him on that fatal night, then Lord Mountnewte must be able to throw some light on the mysterious occurrence.

Our fellows at the Yard were abnormally active. It seemed, on the face of it, impossible that a man, healthy, vigorous, and admittedly sober, should vanish in London between Piccadilly Circus and Cromwell Road without leaving the slightest trace of himself or of the valuables said to have been in his possession.

Of course, Lord Mountnewte was closely questioned. He was a young Guardsman of the usual pattern, and, after a great deal of vapid talk which irritated Detective-Inspector Saunders not a little, he made the following statement—

'I certainly am acquainted with Miss Lulu Fay. On the night in question I was standing outside the Troc, when I saw this young lady at her own carriage window talking to a tall man in an Inverness cape. She had, earlier in the day, refused my invitation to supper, saying that she was not feeling very well, and would go home directly after the theatre; therefore I felt, naturally, a little vexed. I was just about to hail a taxi, meaning to go on to the club, when, to my intense astonishment, the man in the Inverness cape came up to me and asked me if I could tell him the best way to get back to Cromwell Road.'

'And what did you do?' asked Saunders.

'I walked a few steps with him and put him on his way,' replied Lord Mountnewte, blandly.

In Saunders's own expressive words, he thought that story 'fishy'. He could not imagine the arm of coincidence being quite so long as to cause these two men—who presumably were both in love with the same girl, and who had just met at a moment when one of them was obviously suffering pangs of jealousy—to hold merely a topographical conversation with one another. But it was equally difficult to suppose that the eldest son and heir of the Marquis of Loam should murder a successful rival and then rob him in the streets of London.

Moreover, here came the eternal and unanswerable questions: If Lord Mountnewte had murdered Leonard Marvell, where and how had he done it, and what had he done with the body?

I dare say you are wondering by this time why I have said nothing about the maid, Rosie Campbell.

Well, plenty of very clever people (I mean those who write letters to the papers and give suggestions to every official department in the kingdom) thought that the police ought to keep a very strict eye upon that pretty Scotch lassie. For she was very pretty, and had quaint, demure ways which rendered her singularly attractive, in spite of the fact that, for most masculine tastes, she would have been considered too tall. Of course, Saunders and Danvers kept an eye on her—you may be sure of that—and got a good deal of information about her from the people at the hotel. Most of it, unfortunately, was irrelevant to the case. She was maid-attendant to Miss Marvell, who was feeble in health, and who went out but little. Rosie waited on her master and mistress upstairs, carrying their meals to their private room, and doing their bedrooms. The rest of the day she was fairly free, and was quite sociable downstairs with the hotel staff.

With regard to her movements and actions on that memorable 3rd of February, Saunders—though he worked very hard—could glean but little useful information. You see, in a hotel of that kind, with an average of thirty to forty guests at one time, it is extremely difficult to state positively what any one person did or did not do on that particular day.

Most people at the Scotia remembered that Miss Marvell dined in the *table d'hôte* room on that 3rd of February; this she did about once a fortnight, when her maid had an evening 'out'.

The hotel staff also recollected fairly distinctly that Miss Rosie Campbell was not in the steward's room at supper-time that evening, but no one could remember definitely when she came in.

One of the chambermaids who occupied the bedroom adjoining hers, said that she heard her moving about soon after midnight; the hall porter declared that he saw her come in just before half-past twelve when he closed the doors for the night.

But one of the ground-floor valets said that, on the morning of the 4th, he saw Miss Marvell's maid, in hat and coat, slip into the house and upstairs, very quickly and quietly, soon after the front doors were opened, namely, about 7.00 a.m.

Here, of course, was a direct contradiction between the chamber-maid and hall porter on the one side, and the valet on the other, whilst Miss Marvell said that Campbell came into her room and made her some tea long before seven o'clock every morning, including that of the 4th.

I assure you our fellows at the Yard were ready to tear their hair out by the roots, from sheer aggravation at this maze of contradictions which met them at every turn.

The whole thing seemed so simple. There was nothing 'to it' as it were, and but very little real suggestion of foul play, and yet Mr Leonard Marvell had disappeared, and no trace of him could be found.

Everyone now talked freely of murder. London is a big town, and this would not have been the first instance of a stranger—for Mr Leonard Marvell was practically a stranger in London—being enticed to a lonely part of the city on a foggy night, and there done away with and robbed, and the body hidden in an out-of-the-way cellar, where it might not be discovered for months to come.

But the newspaper-reading public is notably fickle, and Mr Leonard Marvell was soon forgotten by everyone save the chief and the batch of our fellows who had charge of the case.

Thus I heard through Danvers one day that Rosie Campbell had left Miss Marvell's employ, and was living in rooms in Findlater Terrace, near Walham Green.

I was alone in our Maida Vale flat at the time, my dear lady having gone to spend the weekend with the Dowager Lady Loam, who was an old friend of hers; nor, when she returned, did she seem any more interested in Rosie Campbell's movements than she had been hitherto.

Yet another month went by, and I for one had absolutely ceased to think of the man in the Inverness cape, who had so mysteriously and so completely vanished in the very midst of busy London, when, one morning early in January, Lady Molly made her appearance in my room, looking more like the landlady of a disreputable gambling-house than anything else I could imagine.

'What in the world——?' I began.

'Yes! I think I look the part,' she replied, surveying with obvious complacency the extraordinary figure which confronted her in the glass.

My dear lady had on a purple cloth coat and skirt of a peculiarly vivid hue, and of a singular cut, which made her matchless figure look like a sack of potatoes. Her soft brown hair was quite hidden beneath a 'transformation', of that yellow-reddish tint only to be met with in very cheap dyes.

As for her hat! I won't attempt to describe it. It towered above and around her face, which was plentifully covered with brick-red and with that kind of powder which causes the cheeks to look a deep mauve.

My dear lady looked, indeed, a perfect picture of appalling vulgarity.

'Where are you going in this elegant attire?' I asked in amazement.

'I have taken rooms in Findlater Terrace,' she replied lightly. 'I feel that the air of Walham Green will do us both good. Our amiable, if somewhat slatternly, landlady expects us in time for luncheon. You will have to keep rigidly in the background, Mary, all the while we are there. I said that I was bringing an invalid niece with me, and, as a pre-liminary, you may as well tie two or three thick veils over your face. I think I may safely promise that you won't be dull.'

And we certainly were not dull during our brief stay at 34, Findlater Terrace, Walham Green. Fully equipped, and arrayed in our extra-ordinary garments, we duly arrived there, in a rickety four-wheeler, on the top of which were perched two seedy-looking boxes.

The landlady was a toothless old creature, who apparently thought washing a quite unnecessary proceeding. In this she was evidently at one with every one of her neighbours. Findlater Terrace looked unspeakably squalid; groups of dirty children congregated in the gutters and gave forth discordant shrieks as our cab drove up.

Through my thick veils I thought that, some distance down the road, I spied a horsy-looking man in ill-fitting riding-breeches and gaiters, who vaguely reminded me of Danvers.

Within half an hour of our installation, and whilst we were eating a tough steak over a doubtful tablecloth, my dear lady told me that she had been waiting a full month, until rooms in this particular house happened to be vacant. Fortunately the population in Findlater Terrace is always a shifting one, and Lady Molly had kept a sharp eye on No. 34, where, on the floor above, lived Miss Rosie Campbell. Directly the last set of lodgers walked out of the ground-floor rooms, we were ready to walk in.

My dear lady's manners and customs, whilst living at the above aristocratic address, were fully in keeping with her appearance. The shrill, rasping voice which she assumed echoed from attic to cellar.

One day I heard her giving vague hints to the landlady that her husband, Mr Marcus Stein, had had a little trouble with the police about a small hotel which he had kept somewhere near Fitzroy Square, and where 'young gentlemen used to come and play cards of a night'. The landlady was also made to understand that the worthy Mr Stein was now living temporarily at His Majesty's expense, whilst Mrs Stein had to live a somewhat secluded life, away from her fashionable friends.

The misfortunes of the pseudo Mrs Stein in no way marred the amiability of Mrs Tredwen, our landlady. The inhabitants of Findlater Terrace care very little about the antecedents of their lodgers, so long as they pay their week's rent in advance, and settle their 'extras' without much murmur.

This Lady Molly did, with a generosity characteristic of an ex-lady of means. She never grumbled at the quantity of jam and marmalade which we were supposed to have consumed every week, and which anon reached titanic proportions. She tolerated Mrs Tredwen's cat, tipped Ermyntrude—the tousled lodging-house slavey—lavishly, and lent the upstairs lodger her spirit-lamp and curling-tongs when Miss Rosie Campbell's got out of order.

A certain degree of intimacy followed the loan of those curling-tongs. Miss Campbell, reserved and demure, greatly sympathized with the lady who was not on the best of terms with the police. I kept steadily in the background. The two ladies did not visit each other's rooms, but they held long and confidential conversations on the landings, and I gathered, presently, that the pseudo Mrs Stein had succeeded in persuading Rosie Campbell that, if the police were watching No. 34, Findlater Terrace, at all, it was undoubtedly on account of the unfortunate Mr Stein's faithful wife.

I found it a little difficult to fathom Lady Molly's intentions. We had been in the house over three weeks, and nothing whatever had happened. Once I ventured on a discreet query as to whether we were to expect the sudden reappearance of Mr Leonard Marvell.

'For if that's all about it,' I argued, 'then surely the men from the Yard could have kept the house in view, without all this inconvenience and masquerading on our part.'

But to this tirade my dear lady vouchsafed no reply.

She and her newly acquired friend were, about this time, deeply interested in the case known as the 'West End Shop Robberies', which no doubt you recollect, since they occurred such a very little while ago. Ladies who were shopping in the large drapers' emporiums during the crowded and busy sale time, lost reticules, purses, and valuable parcels, without any trace of the clever thief being found.

The drapers, during sale-time, invariably employ detectives in plain clothes to look after their goods, but in this case it was the customers who were robbed, and the detectives, attentive to every attempt at 'shoplifting', had had no eyes for the more subtle thief.

I had already noticed Miss Rosie Campbell's keen look of excitement whenever the pseudo Mrs Stein discussed these cases with her. I was not a bit surprised, therefore, when, one afternoon at about teatime, my dear lady came home from her habitual walk, and, at the top of her shrill voice, called out to me from the hall:

'Mary! Mary! they've got the man of the shop robberies. He's given the silly police the slip this time, but they know who he is now, and I suppose they'll get him presently. 'Tisn't anybody I know,' she added, with that harsh, common laugh which she had adopted for her part.

I had come out of the room in response to her call, and was standing just outside our own sitting-room door. Mrs Tredwen, too, bedraggled and unkempt, as usual, had sneaked up the area steps, closely followed by Ermyntrude.

But on the half-landing just above us the trembling figure of Rosie Campbell, with scared white face and dilated eyes, looked on the verge of a sudden fall.

Still talking shrilly and volubly, Lady Molly ran up to her, but

Campbell met her half-way, and the pseudo Mrs Stein, taking vigorous hold of her wrist, dragged her into our own sitting-room.

'Pull yourself together, now,' she said with rough kindness; 'that owl Tredwen is listening, and you needn't let her know too much. Shut the door, Mary. Lor' bless you, m'dear, I've gone through worse scares than these. There! you just lie down on this sofa a bit. My niece'll make you a cup o' tea; and I'll go and get an evening paper, and see what's going on. I suppose you are very interested in the shop robbery man, or you wouldn't have took on so.'

Without waiting for Campbell's contradiction to this statement, Lady Molly flounced out of the house.

Miss Campbell hardly spoke during the next ten minutes that she and I were left alone together. She lay on the sofa with eyes wide open, staring up at the ceiling, evidently still in a great state of fear.

I had just got tea ready when Lady Molly came back. She had an evening paper in her hand, but threw this down on the table directly she came in.

'I could only get an early edition,' she said breathlessly, 'and the silly thing hasn't got anything in it about the matter.'

She drew near to the sofa, and, subduing the shrillness of her voice, she whispered rapidly, bending down towards Campbell:

'There's a man hanging about at the corner down there. No, no; it's not the police,' she added quickly, in response to the girl's sudden start of alarm. 'Trust me, my dear, for knowing a 'tec when I see one! Why, I'd smell one half a mile off. No; my opinion is that it's your man, my dear, and that he's in a devil of a hole.'

'Oh! he oughtn't to come here,' ejaculated Campbell in great alarm. 'He'll get me into trouble and do himself no good. He's been a fool!' she added, with a fierceness wholly unlike her usual demure placidity, 'getting himself caught like that. Now I suppose we shall have to hook it—if there's time.'

'Can I do anything to help you?' asked the pseudo Mrs Stein. "You know I've been through all this myself, when they was after Mr Stein. Or perhaps Mary could do something.'

'Well, yes,' said the girl, after a slight pause, during which she seemed to be gathering her wits together; 'I'll write a note, and you shall take it, if you will, to a friend of mine—a lady who lives in the

Cromwell Road. But if you still see a man lurking about at the corner of the street, then, just as you pass him, say the word "Campbell", and if he replies "Rosie", then give *him* the note. Will you do that?'

'Of course I will, my dear, Just you leave it all to me.'

And the pseudo Mrs Stein brought ink and paper and placed them on the table. Rosie Campbell wrote a brief note, and then fastened it down with a bit of sealing-wax before she handed it over to Lady Molly. The note was addressed to Miss Marvell, Scotia Hotel, Cromwell Road.

'You understand?' she said eagerly. 'Don't give the note to the man unless he says "Rosie" in reply to the word "Campbell".'

'All right—all right!' said Lady Molly, slipping the note into her reticule. 'And you go up to your room, Miss Campbell; it's no good giving that old fool Tredwen too much to gossip about.'

Rosie Campbell went upstairs, and presently my dear lady and I were walking rapidly down the badly lighted street.

'Where is the man?' I whispered eagerly as soon as we were out of earshot of No. 34.

'There is no man,' replied Lady Molly, quickly.

'But the West End shop thief?' I asked.

'He hasn't been caught yet, and won't be either, for he is far too clever a scoundrel to fall into an ordinary trap.'

She did not give me time to ask further questions, for presently, when we had reached Reporton Square, my dear lady handed me the note written by Campbell, and said:

'Go straight on to the Scotia Hotel, and ask for Miss Marvell; send up the note to her, but don't let her see you, as she knows you by sight. I must see the chief first, and will be with you as soon as possible. Having delivered the note, you must hang about outside as long as you can. Use your wits; she must not leave the hotel before I see her.'

There was no hansom to be got in this elegant quarter of the town, so, having parted from my dear lady, I made for the nearest Underground station, and took a train for South Kensington.

Thus it was nearly seven o'clock before I reached the Scotia. In answer to my enquiries for Miss Marvell, I was told that she was ill in bed and could see no one. I replied that I had only brought a note for her, and would wait for a reply.

Acting on my dear lady's instructions, I was as slow in my movements as ever I could be, and was some time in finding the note and handing it to a waiter, who then took it upstairs.

Presently he returned with the message: 'Miss Marvell says there is no answer.'

Whereupon I asked for pen and paper at the office, and wrote the following brief note on my own responsibility, using my wits as my dear lady had bidden me to do.

'Please, madam,' I wrote, 'will you send just a line to Miss Rosie Campbell? She seems very upset and frightened at some news she has had.'

Once more the waiter ran upstairs, and returned with a sealed envelope, which I slipped into my reticule.

Time was slipping by very slowly. I did not know how long I should have to wait about outside in the cold, when, to my horror, I heard a hard voice, with a marked Scotch accent, saying:

'I am going out, waiter, and shan't be back to dinner. Tell them to lay a little cold supper upstairs in my room.'

The next moment Miss Marvell, with coat, hat, and veil, was descending the stairs.

My plight was awkward. I certainly did not think it safe to present myself before the lady; she would undoubtedly recollect my face. Yet I had orders to detain her until the appearance of Lady Molly.

Miss Marvell seemed in no hurry. She was putting on her gloves as she came downstairs. In the hall she gave a few more instructions to the porter, whilst I, in a dark corner in the background, was vaguely planning an assault or an alarm of fire.

Suddenly, at the hotel entrance, where the porter was obsequiously holding open the door for Miss Marvell to pass through, I saw the latter's figure stiffen; she took one step back as if involuntarily, then, equally quickly, attempted to dart across the threshold, on which a group—composed of my dear lady, of Saunders, and of two or three people scarcely distinguishable in the gloom beyond—had suddenly made its appearance.

Miss Marvell was forced to retreat into the hall; already I had heard Saunders's hurriedly whispered words:

'Try and not make a fuss in this place, now. Everything can go off quietly, you know.'

Danvers and Cotton, whom I knew well, were already standing one each side of Miss Marvell, whilst suddenly amongst this group I recognized Fanny, the wife of Danvers, who is one of our female searchers at the Yard.

'Shall we go up to your own room?' suggested Saunders.

'I think that is quite unnecessary,' interposed Lady Molly. 'I feel convinced that Mr Leonard Marvell will yield to the inevitable quietly, and follow you without giving any trouble.'

Marvell, however, did make a bold dash for liberty. As Lady Molly had said previously, he was far too clever to allow himself to be captured easily. But my dear lady had been cleverer. As she told me subsequently, she had from the first suspected that the trio who lodged at the Scotia Hotel were really only a duo—namely, Leonard Marvell and his wife. The latter impersonated a maid most of the time; but among these two clever people the three characters were interchangeable. Of course, there was no Miss Marvell at all. Leonard was alternately dressed up as man or woman, according to the requirements of his villainies.

'As soon as I heard that Miss Marvell was very tall and bony,' said Lady Molly, 'I thought that there might be a possibility of her being merely a man in disguise. Then there was the fact—but little dwelt on by either the police or public—that no one seems ever to have seen brother and sister together, nor was the entire trio ever seen at one and the same time.

'On that 3rd of February Leonard Marvell went out. No doubt he changed his attire in a lady's waiting-room at one of the railway stations; subsequently he came home, now dressed as Miss Marvell, and had dinner in the table d'hôte room so as to set up a fairly plausible alibi. But ultimately it was his wife, the pseudo Rosie Campbell, who stayed indoors that night, whilst he, Leonard Marvell, when going out after dinner, impersonated the maid until he was clear of the hotel; then he reassumed his male clothes once more, no doubt in the deserted waiting-room of some railway station, and met Miss Lulu Fay at supper, subsequently returning to the hotel in the guise of the maid.

'You see the game of criss-cross, don't you? This interchanging of characters was bound to baffle everyone. Many clever scoundrels have assumed disguises, sometimes personating members of the opposite sex to their own, but never before have I known two people play the part of three. Thus, endless contradictions followed as to the hour when Campbell the maid went out and when she came in, for at one time it was she herself who was seen by the valet, and at another it was Leonard Marvell dressed in her clothes.'

He was also clever enough to accost Lord Mountnewte in the open street, thus bringing further complications into this strange case.

After the successful robbery of Miss Fay's diamonds, Leonard Marvell and his wife parted for awhile. They were waiting for an opportunity to get across the Channel and there turn their booty into solid cash. Whilst Mrs Marvell, *alias* Rosie Campbell, led a retired life in Findlater Terrace, Leonard kept his hand in with West End shop robberies.

Then Lady Molly entered the lists. As usual, her scheme was bold and daring; she trusted her own intuition and acted accordingly.

When she brought home the false news that the author of the shop robberies had been spotted by the police, Rosie Campbell's obvious terror confirmed her suspicions. The note written by the latter to the so-called Miss Marvell, though it contained nothing in any way incriminating, was the crowning certitude that my dear lady was right, as usual, in all her surmises.

And now Mr Leonard Marvell will be living for a couple of years at the tax-payers' expense; he has 'disappeared' temporarily from the public eye.

Rosie Campbell—i.e. Mrs Marvell—has gone to Glasgow. I feel convinced that two years hence we shall hear of the worthy couple again.

7

HUGH C. WEIR

The Man With Nine Lives

Now that I seek a point of beginning in the curious comradeship between Madelyn Mack and myself, the weird problems of men's knavery that we have confronted together come back to me with almost a shock.

Perhaps the events which crowd into my memory followed each other too swiftly for thoughtful digest at the time of their occurrence. Perhaps only a sober retrospect can supply a properly appreciative angle of view.

Madelyn Mack! What newspaper reader does not know the name? Who, even among the most casual followers of public events, does not recall the young woman who found the missing heiress, Virginia Denton, after a three months' disappearance; who convicted 'Archie' Irwin, chief of the 'fire bug trust'; who located the absconder, Wolcott, after a pursuit from Chicago to Khartoom; who solved the riddle of the double Peterson murder; who—

But why continue the enumeration of Miss Mack's achievements? They are of almost household knowledge, at least that portion which, from one cause or another, have found their way into the newspaper columns. Doubtless those admirers of Miss Mack, whose opinions have been formed through the press-chronicles of her exploits, would be startled to know that not one in ten of her cases has ever been recorded outside of her own file cases. And many of them—the most sensational from a newspaper viewpoint—will never be!

It is the woman, herself, however, who has seemed to me always a greater mystery than any of the problems to whose unraveling she has brought her wonderful genius. In spite of the deluge of printer's ink that she has inspired, I question if it has been given to more than a dozen persons to know the true Madelyn Mack.

I do not refer, of course, to her professional career. The salient points of that portion of her life, I presume, are more or less generally known—the college girl confronted suddenly with the necessity of earning her own living; the epidemic of mysterious 'shoplifting' cases chronicled in the newspaper she was studying for employment advertisements; her application to the New York department stores, that had been victimized, for a place on their detective staffs, and their curt refusal; her sudden determination to undertake the case as a free-lance, and her remarkable success, which resulted in the conviction of the notorious Madame Bousard, and which secured for Miss Mack her first position as assistant house-detective with the famous Niegel dry-goods firm. I sometimes think that this first case, and the realization which it brought her of her peculiar talent, is Madelyn's favorite—that its place in her memory is not even shared by the recovery of Mrs Niegel's fifty-thousand-dollar pearl necklace, stolen a few months after the employment of the college girl detective at the store, and the reward for which, incidentally, enabled the ambitious Miss Mack to open her own office.

Next followed the Bergner kidnapping case, which gave Madelyn her first big advertising broadside, and which brought the beginning of the steady stream of business that resulted, after three years, in her Fifth Avenue suite in the Maddox Building, where I found her on that—to me—memorable afternoon when a sapient Sunday editor dispatched me for an interview with the woman who had made so conspicuous a success in a man's profession.

I can see Madelyn now, as I saw her then—my first close-range view of her. She had just returned from Omaha that morning, and was planning to leave for Boston on the midnight express. A suitcase and a fat portfolio of papers lay on a chair in a corner. A young woman stenographer was taking a number of letters at an almost incredible rate of dictation. Miss Mack finished the last paragraph as she rose from a flat-top desk to greet me.

I had vaguely imagined a masculine-appearing woman, curt of voice, sharp of feature, perhaps dressed in a severe, tailor-made gown.

I saw a young woman of maybe twenty-five, with red and white cheeks, crowned by a softly waved mass of dull gold hair, and a pair of vivacious, grey-blue eyes that at once made one forget every other detail of her appearance. There was a quality in the eyes which for a long time I could not define. Gradually I came to know that it was the spirit of optimism, of joy in herself, and in her life, and in her work, the exhilaration of doing things. And there was something contagious in it. Almost unconsciously you found yourself *believing* in her and in her sincerity.

Nor was there a suggestion foreign to her sex in my appraisal. She was dressed in a simply embroidered white shirt-waist and white broadcloth skirt. One of Madelyn's few peculiarities is that she always dresses either in complete white or complete black. On her desk was a jar of white chrysanthemums.

'How do I do it?' she repeated, in answer to my question, in a tone that was almost a laugh. 'Why—just by hard work, I suppose. Oh, there isn't anything wonderful about it! You can do almost anything, you know, if you make yourself really *think* you can! I am not at all unusual or abnormal. I work out my problems just as I would work out a problem in mathematics, only instead of figures I deal with human motives. A detective is always given certain known factors, and I keep building them up, or subtracting them, as the case may be, until I know that the answer *must* be correct.

'There are only two real rules for a successful detective, hard work and common sense—not uncommon sense such as we associate with our old friend, Sherlock Holmes, but common, *business* sense. And, of course, imagination! That may be one reason why I have made what you call a success. A woman, I think, always has a more acute imagination than a man!'

'Do you then prefer women operatives on your staff?' I asked.

She glanced up with something like a twinkle from the jade paper-knife in her hands.

'Shall I let you into a secret? All of my staff, with the exception of my stenographer, are men. But I do most of my work in person. The factor of imagination can't very well be used second, or third, or fourth handed. And then, if I fail, I can only blame Madelyn Mack! Some day,'—the gleam in her grey-blue eyes deepened,—'some day I hope to reach a point where I can afford to do only consulting work or personal investigation. The business details of an office staff, I am afraid, are a bit too much of routine for me!'

The telephone jingled. She spoke a few crisp sentences into the receiver, and turned. The interview was over.

When I next saw her, three months later, we met across the body of Morris Anthony, the murdered bibliophic. It was a chance discovery of mine which Madelyn was good enough to say suggested to her the solution of the affair, and which brought us together in the final melodramatic climax in the grim mansion on Washington Square, when I presume my hysterical warning saved her from the fangs of Dr Lester Randolph's hidden cobra. In any event, our acquaintanceship crystallized gradually into a comradeship, which revolutionized two angles of my life.

Not only did it bring to me the stimulus of Madelyn Mack's personality, but it gave me exclusive access to a fund of newspaper 'copy' that took me from scant-paid Sunday 'features' to a 'space' arrangement in the city room, with an income double that which I had been earning. I have always maintained that in our relationship Madelyn gave all, and I contributed nothing. Although she invariably made instant disclaimer, and generally ended by carrying me up to the 'Rosary', her chalet on the Hudson, as a cure for what she termed my attack of the 'blues', she was never able to convince me that my protest was not justified!

It was at the 'Rosary' where Miss Mack found haven from the stress of business. She had copied its design from an ivy-tangled Swiss chalet that had attracted her fancy during a summer vacation ramble through the Alps, and had built it on a jagged bluff of the river at a point near enough to the city to permit of fairly convenient motoring, although, during the first years of our friendship, when she was held close to the commercial grindstone, weeks often passed without her being able to snatch a day there. In the end, it was the gratitude of Chalmers Walker for her remarkable work which cleared his chorus-girl wife from the seemingly unbreakable coil of circumstantial evidence in the murder of Dempster, the theatrical broker, that enabled Madelyn to realize her long-cherished dream of setting up as a consulting expert. Although she still maintained an office in town, it was confined to one room and a small reception hall, and she limited her attendance there to two days of the week. During the remainder of the time, when not engaged directly on a case, she seldom appeared in the city at all. Her flowers and her music—she was passionately devoted to both—appeared to content her effectually.

I charged her with growing old, to which she replied with a shrug. I upbraided her as a cynic, and she smiled inscrutably. But the manner of her life was not changed. In a way I envied her. It was almost like looking down on the world and watching tolerantly its mad scramble for the rainbow's end. The days I snatched at the 'Rosary', particularly in the summer, when Madelyn's garden looked like nothing so much as a Turner picture, left me with almost a repulsion for the grind of Park Row. But a workaday newspaper woman cannot indulge the dreams of a genius whom fortune has blessed. Perhaps this was why Madelyn's invitations came with a frequency and a subtleness that could not be resisted. Somehow they always reached me when I was in just the right receptive mood.

It was late on a Thursday afternoon of June, the climax of a racking five days for me under the blistering Broadway sun, that Madelyn's motor caught me at the *Bugle* office, and Madelyn insisted on bundling me into the tonneau without even a suitcase.

'We'll reach the Rosary in time for a fried chicken supper,' she promised. 'What you need is four or five days' rest where you can't smell the asphalt.'

'You fairy godmother!' I breathed as I snuggled down on the cushions.

Neither of us knew that already the crimson trail of crime was twisting toward us—that within twelve hours we were to be pitch-forked from a quiet weekend's rest into the vortex of tragedy.

2

We had breakfasted late and leisurely. When at length we had finished, Madelyn had insisted on having her phonograph brought to the rose-garden, and we were listening to Sturveysant's matchless rendering of 'The Jewel Song'—one of the three records for which Miss Mack had sent the harpist her check for two hundred dollars the day before. I had taken the occasion to read her a lazy lesson on extravagance. The beggar had probably done the work in less than two hours!

As the plaintive notes quivered to a pause, Susan, Madelyn's housekeeper, crossed the garden, and laid a little stack of letters and the morning papers on a rustic table by our bench. Madelyn turned to her correspondence with a shrug.

'From the divine to the prosaic!'

Susan sniffed with the freedom of seven years of service.

'I heard one of them Dago fiddling chaps at Hammerstein's last week who could beat that music with his eyes closed!'

Madelyn stared at her sorrowfully.

'At your age—Hammerstein's!'

Susan tossed her prim rows of curls, glanced contemptuously at the phonograph by way of retaliation, and made a dignified retreat. In the doorway she turned.

'Oh, Miss Madelyn, I am baking one of your old-fashioned strawberry shortcakes for lunch!'

'Really?' Madelyn raised a pair of sparkling eyes. 'Susan, you're a dear!'

A contented smile wreathed Susan's face even to the tips of her precise curls. Madelyn's gaze crossed to me.

'What are you chuckling over, Nora?'

'From a psychological standpoint, the pair of you have given me two interesting studies,' I laughed. 'A single sentence compensates Susan for a week of your glumness!'

Madelyn extended a hand toward her mail.

'And what is the other feature that appeals to your dissecting mind?'

'Fancy a world-known detective rising to the point of enthusiasm at the mention of strawberry shortcake!'

'Why not? Even a detective has to be human once in a while!' Her eyes twinkled. 'Another point for my memoirs, Miss Noraker!'

As her gaze fell to the half-opened letter in her hand, my eyes traveled across the garden to the outlines of the chalet, and I breathed a sigh of utter content. Broadway and Park Row seemed very, very far away. In a momentary swerving of my gaze, I saw that a line as clear cut as a pencil-stroke had traced itself across Miss Mack's forehead.

The suggestion of lounging indifference in her attitude had

vanished like a wind-blown veil. Her glance met mine suddenly. The twinkle I had last glimpsed in her eyes had disappeared. Silently she pushed a square sheet of close, cramped writing across the table to me.

'MY DEAR MADAM:

'When you read this, it is quite possible that it will be a letter from a dead man.

'I have been told by no less an authority than my friend, Cosmo Hamilton, that you are a remarkable woman. While I will say at the outset that I have little faith in the analytical powers of the feminine brain, I am prepared to accept Hamilton's judgement.

'I cannot, of course, discuss the details of my problem in correspondence.

'As a spur to quick action, I may say, however, that, during the past five months, my life has been attempted no fewer than eight different times, and I am convinced that the ninth attempt, if made, will be successful. The curious part of it lies in the fact that I am absolutely unable to guess the reason for the persistent vendetta. So far as I know, there is no person in the world who should desire my removal. And yet I have been shot at from ambush on four occasions, thugs have rushed me once, a speeding automobile has grazed me twice, and this evening I found a cunning little dose of cyanide of potassium in my favorite cherry pie!

'All of this, too, in the shadow of a New Jersey skunk farm! It is high time, I fancy, that I secure expert advice. Should the progress of the mysterious vendetta, by any chance, render me unable to receive you personally, my niece, Miss Muriel Jansen, I am sure, will endeavor to act as a substitute.

'Respectfully Yours,

'WENDELL MARSH.'

'THREE FORKS JUNCTION, N.J.,
June 16.'

At the bottom of the page a lead pencil had scrawled the single line in the same cramped writing:

'For God's sake, hurry!'

Madelyn retained her curled-up position on the bench, staring across at a bush of deep crimson roses.

'Wendell Marsh?' She shifted her glance to me musingly. 'Haven't I seen that name somewhere lately?' (Madelyn pays me the compliment of saying that I have a card-index brain for newspaper history!)

'If you have read the Sunday supplements,' I returned drily, with a vivid remembrance of Wendell Marsh as I had last seen him, six months before, when he crossed the gangplank of his steamer, fresh from England, his face browned from the Atlantic winds. It was a face to draw a second glance—almost gaunt, self-willed, with more than a hint of cynicism. (Particularly when his eyes met the waiting press group!) Someone had once likened him to the pictures of Oliver Cromwell.

'Wendell Marsh is one of the greatest newspaper copy-makers that ever dodged an interviewer,' I explained. 'He hates reporters like an upstate farmer hates an automobile, and yet has a flock of them on his trail constantly. His latest exploit to catch the spotlight was the purchase of the Bainford relics in London. Just before that he published a three-volume history on "The World's Great Cynics". Paid for the publication himself.'

Then came a silence between us, prolonging itself. I was trying, rather unsuccessfully, to associate Wendell Marsh's half-hysterical letter with my mental picture of the austere millionaire. . . .

'For God's sake, hurry!'

What wrenching terror had reduced the ultra-reserved Mr Marsh to an appeal like this? As I look back now I know that my wildest fancy could not have pictured the ghastliness of the truth!

Madelyn straightened abruptly.

'Susan, will you kindly tell Andrew to bring around the car at once? If you will find the New Jersey automobile map, Nora, we'll locate Three Forks Junction.'

'You are going down?' I asked mechanically.

She slipped from the bench.

'I am beginning to fear,' she said irrelevantly, 'that we'll have to defer our strawberry shortcake!'

3

The sound eye of Daniel Peddicord, liveryman by avocation, and sheriff of Merino County by election, drooped over his florid left cheek. Mr Peddicord took himself and his duties to the tax-payers of Merino County seriously.

Having lowered his sound eye with befitting official dubiousness, while his glass eye stared guilelessly ahead, as though it took absolutely no notice of the procedure, Mr Peddicord jerked a fat, red thumb toward the winding stairway at the rear of the Marsh hall.

'I reckon as how Mr Marsh is still up there, Miss Mack. You see, I told 'em not to disturb the body until—'

Our stares brought the sentence to an abrupt end. Mr Peddicord's sound eye underwent a violent agitation.

'You don't mean that you haven't—heard?'

The silence of the great house seemed suddenly oppressive. For the first time I realized the oddity of our having been received by an ill-at-ease policeman instead of by a member of the family. I was abruptly conscious of the incongruity between Mr Peddicord's awkward figure and the dim, luxurious background.

Madelyn gripped the chief's arm, bringing his sound eye circling around to her face.

'Tell me what has happened!'

Mr Peddicord drew a huge red handkerchief over his forehead.

'Wendell Marsh was found dead in his library at eight o'clock this morning! He had been dead for hours.'

Tick-tock! Tick-tock! Through my daze beat the rhythm of a tall, gaunt clock in the corner. I stared at it dully. Madelyn's hands had caught themselves behind her back, her veins swollen into sharp blue ridges. Mr Peddicord still gripped his red handkerchief.

'It sure is queer you hadn't heard! I reckoned as how that was what had brought you down. It—it looks like murder!'

In Madelyn's eyes had appeared a greyish glint like cold steel.

'Where is the body?'

'Upstairs in the library. Mr Marsh had worked—'

'Will you kindly show me the room?'

I do not think we noted at the time the crispness in her tones, certainly not with any resentment. Madelyn had taken command of the situation quite as a matter of course.

'Also, will you have my card sent to the family?'

Mr Peddicord stuffed his handkerchief back into a rear trousers' pocket. A red corner protruded in jaunty abandon from under his blue coat.

'Why, there ain't no family—at least none but Muriel Jansen.' His head cocked itself cautiously up the stairs. 'She's his niece, and I reckon now everything here is hers. Her maid says as how she is clear bowled over. Only left her room once since—since it happened. And that was to tell me as how nothing was to be disturbed.' Mr Peddicord drew himself up with the suspicion of a frown. 'Just as though an experienced officer wouldn't know *that* much!'

Madelyn glanced over her shoulder to the end of the hall. A hatchet-faced man in russet livery stood staring at us with wooden eyes.

Mr Peddicord shrugged.

'That's Peters, the butler. He's the chap what found Mr Marsh.'

I could feel the wooden eyes following us until a turn in the stairs blocked their range.

A red-glowing room—oppressively red. Scarlet-frescoed walls, deep red draperies, cherry-upholstered furniture, Turkish-red rugs, rows on rows of red-bound books. Above, a great, flat glass roof, open to the sky from corner to corner, through which the splash of the sun on the rich colors gave the weird semblance of a crimson pool almost in the room's exact center. Such was Wendell Marsh's library—as eccentrically designed as its master.

It was the wreck of a room that we found. Shattered vases littered the floor—books were ripped savagely apart—curtains were hanging in ribbons—a heavy leather rocker was splintered.

The wreckage might have marked the death-struggle of giants. In the midst of the destruction, Wendell Marsh was twisted on his back. His face was shriveled, his eyes were staring. There was no hint of a wound or even a bruise. In his right hand was gripped an object partially turned from me.

I found myself stepping nearer, as though drawn by a magnet. There is something hypnotic in such horrible scenes! And then I barely checked a cry.

Wendell Marsh's dead fingers held a pipe—a strangely carved, red sandstone bowl, and a long, glistening stem.

Sheriff Peddicord noted the direction of my glance.

'Mr Marsh got that there pipe in London, along with those other relics he brought home. They do say as how it was the first pipe ever smoked by a white man. The Indians of Virginia gave it to a chap named Sir Walter Raleigh. Mr Marsh had a new stem put to it, and his butler says he smoked it every day. Queer, ain't it, how some folks' tastes do run?'

The sheriff moistened his lips under his scraggly yellow moustache.

'Must have been some fight what done this!' His head included the wrecked room in a vague sweep.

Madelyn strolled over to a pair of the ribboned curtains, and fingered them musingly.

'But that isn't the queerest part.' The chief glanced at Madelyn expectantly. 'There was no way for anyone else to get out—or in!'

Madelyn stooped lower over the curtains. They seemed to fascinate her. 'The door?' she hazarded absently. 'It was locked?'

'From the inside. Peters and the footman saw the key when they broke in this morning. . . . Peters swears he heard Mr Marsh turn it when he left him writing at ten o'clock last night.'

'The windows?'

'Fastened as tight as a drum—and, if they wasn't, it's a matter of a good thirty foot to the ground.'

'The roof, perhaps?'

'A cat *might* get through it—it every part wasn't clamped as tight as the windows.'

Mr Peddicord spoke with a distinct inflection of triumph. Madelyn was still staring at the curtains.

'Isn't it rather odd,' I ventured, 'that the sounds of the struggle, or whatever it was, didn't alarm the house?'

Sheriff Peddicord plainly regarded me as an outsider. He answered my question with obvious shortness.

'You could fire a blunderbuss up here and no one would be the wiser. They say as how Mr Marsh had the room made sound-proof. And, besides, the servants have a building to themselves, all except Miss Jansen's maid, who sleeps in a room next to her at the other end of the house.'

My eyes circled back to Wendell Marsh's knotted figure—his

shriveled face—horror-frozen eyes—the hand gripped about the fantastic pipe. I think it was the pipe that held my glance. Of all incongruities, a pipe in the hand of a dead man!

Maybe it was something of the same thought that brought Madelyn of a sudden across the room. She stooped, straightened the cold fingers, and rose with the pipe in her hand.

A new stem had obviously been added to it, of a substance which I judged to be jessamine. At its end, teeth-marks had bitten nearly through. The stone bowl was filled with the cold ashes of half-consumed tobacco. Madelyn balanced it musingly.

'Curious, isn't it, Sheriff, that a man engaged in a life-or-death struggle should cling to a heavy pipe?'

'Why—I suppose so. But the question, Miss Mack, is what became of that there other man? It isn't natural as how Mr Marsh could have fought with himself.'

'The other man?' Madelyn repeated mechanically. She was stirring the rim of the dead ashes.

'And how in tarnation was Mr Marsh killed?'

Madelyn contemplated a dust-covered finger.

'Will you do me a favor, Sheriff?'

'Why, er—of course.'

'Kindly find out from the butler if Mr Marsh had cherry pie for dinner last night!'

The sheriff gulped.

'Che-cherry pie?'

Madelyn glanced up impatiently.

'I believe he was very fond of it.'

The sheriff shuffled across to the door uncertainly. Madelyn's eyes flashed to me.

'You might go, too, Nora.'

For a moment I was tempted to flat rebellion. But Madelyn affected not to notice the fact. She is always so aggravatingly sure of her own way!—With what I tried to make a mood of aggrieved silence, I followed the sheriff's blue-coated figure. As the door closed, I saw that Madelyn was still balancing Raleigh's pipe.

From the top of the stairs, Sheriff Peddicord glanced across at me suspiciously.

'I say, what I would like to know is what became of that there other man!'

4

A wisp of a black-gowned figure, peering through a dormer window at the end of the second-floor hall, turned suddenly as we reached the landing. A white, drawn face, suggesting a tired child, stared at us from under a frame of dull-gold hair, drawn low from a careless part. I knew at once it was Muriel Jansen, for the time, at least, mistress of the house of death.

'Has the coroner come yet, Sheriff?'

She spoke with one of the most liquid voices I have ever heard. Had it not been for her bronze hair, I would have fancied her at once of Latin descent. The fact of my presence she seemed scarcely to notice, not with any suggestion of aloofness, but rather as though she had been drained even of the emotion of curiosity.

'Not yet, Miss Jansen. He should be here now.'

She stepped closer to the window, and then turned slightly.

'I told Peters to telegraph to New York for Dr Dench when he summoned you. He was one of Uncle's oldest friends. I—I would like him to be here when—when the coroner makes his examination.'

The sheriff bowed awkwardly.

'Miss Mack is upstairs now.'

The pale face was staring at us again with raised eyebrows.

'Miss Mack? I don't understand.' Her eyes shifted to me.

'She had a letter from Mr Marsh by this morning's early post,' I explained. 'I am Miss Noraker. Mr Marsh wanted her to come down at once. She didn't know, of course—couldn't know—that—that he was—dead!'

'A letter from—Uncle?' A puzzled line gathered in her face.

I nodded.

'A distinctly curious letter. But—Miss Mack would perhaps prefer to give you the details.'

The puzzled line deepened. I could feel her eyes searching mine intently.

'I presume Miss Mack will be down soon,' I volunteered. 'If you wish, however, I will tell her—'

'That will hardly be necessary. But—you are quite sure—a letter?'

'Quite sure,' I returned, somewhat impatiently.

And then, without warning, her hands darted to her head, and she swayed forward. I caught her in my arms with a side-view of Sheriff Peddicord staring, open-mouthed.

'Get her maid!' I gasped.

The sheriff roused into belated action. As he took a cumbersome step toward the nearest door, it opened suddenly. A gaunt, middle-aged woman, in a crisp white apron, digested the situation with cold, grey eyes. Without a word, she caught Muriel Jansen in her arms.

'She has fainted,' I said rather vaguely. 'Can I help you?'

The other paused with her burden.

'When I need you, I'll ask you!' she snapped, and banged the door in our faces.

In the wake of Sheriff Peddicord, I descended the stairs. A dozen question-marks were spinning through my brain. Why had Muriel Jansen fainted? Why had the mention of Wendell Marsh's letter left such an atmosphere of bewildered doubt? Why had the dragon-like maid—for such I divined her to be—faced us with such hostility? The undercurrent of hidden secrets in the dim, silent house seemed suddenly intensified.

With a vague wish for fresh air and the sun on the grass, I sought the front veranda, leaving the sheriff in the hall, mopping his face with his red handkerchief.

A carefully tended yard of generous distances stretched an inviting expanse of graded lawn before me. Evidently Wendell Marsh had provided a discreet distance between himself and his neighbors. The advance guard of a morbid crowd was already shuffling about the gate. I knew that it would not be long, too, before the press-siege would begin.

I could picture frantic city editors pitchforking their star men New Jerseyward. I smiled at the thought. The *Bugle*, the slave-driver that presided over my own financial destinies,—was assured of a generous 'beat' in advance. The next train from New York was not due until late afternoon.

From the staring line about the gate, the figure of a well-set-up young man in blue serge detached itself with swinging step.

'A reporter?' I breathed, incredulous.

With a glance at me, he ascended the steps, and paused at the door, awaiting an answer to his bell. My stealthy glances failed to place him among the 'stars' of New York newspaperdom. Perhaps he was a local correspondent. With smug expectancy, I awaited his discomfiture when Peters received his card. And then I rubbed my eyes. Peters was stepping back from the door, and the other was following him with every suggestion of assurance.

I was still gasping when a maid, broom in hand, zigzagged toward my end of the veranda. She smiled at me with a pair of friendly black eyes.

'Are you a detective?'

'Why?' I parried.

She drew her broom idly across the floor.

'I—I always thought detectives different from other people.'

She sent a rivulet of dust through the railing, with a side glance still in my direction.

'Oh, you will find them human enough,' I laughed, 'outside of detective stories!'

She pondered my reply doubtfully.

'I thought it about time Mr Truxton was appearing!' she ventured suddenly.

'Mr Truxton?'

'He's the man that just came—Mr Homer Truxton. Miss Jansen is going to marry him!'

A light broke through my fog.

'Then he is not a reporter?'

'Mr Truxton? He's a lawyer.' The broom continued its dilatory course. 'Mr Marsh didn't like him—so they *say*!'

I stepped back, smoothing my skirts. I have learned the cardinal rule of Madelyn never to pretend too great an interest in the gossip of a servant.

The maid was mechanically shaking out a rug.

'For my part, I always thought Mr Truxton far and away the pick of Miss Jansen's two steadies. I never could understand what she could see in Dr Dench! Why, he's old enough to be her—'

In the doorway, Sheriff Peddicord's bulky figure beckoned.

'Don't you reckon as how it's about time we were going back to Miss Mack?' he whispered.

'Perhaps,' I assented rather reluctantly.

From the shadows of the hall, the sheriff's sound eye fixed itself on me belligerently.

'I say, what I would like to know is what became of that there other man!'

As we paused on the second landing the well-set-up figure of Mr Homer Truxton was bending toward a partially opened door. Beyond his shoulder, I caught a fleeting glimpse of a pale face under a border of rumpled dull-gold hair. Evidently Muriel Jansen had recovered from her faint.

The door closed abruptly, but not before I had seen that her eyes were red with weeping.

Madelyn was sunk into a red-backed chair before a huge, flat-top desk in the corner of the library, a stack of Wendell Marsh's red-bound books, from a wheel-cabinet at her side, bulked before her. She finished the page she was reading—a page marked with a broad blue pencil—without a hint that she had heard us enter.

Sheriff Peddicord stared across at her with a disappointment that was almost ludicrous. Evidently Madelyn was falling short of his conception of the approved attitudes for a celebrated detective!

'Are you a student of Elizabethan literature, Sheriff?' she asked suddenly.

The sheriff gurgled weakly.

'If you are, I am quite sure you will be interested in Mr Marsh's collection. It is the most thorough on the subject that I have ever seen. For instance, here is a volume on the inner court life of Elizabeth—perhaps you would like me to read you this random passage?'

The sheriff drew himself up with more dignity than I thought he possessed.

'We are investigating a crime, Miss Mack!'

Madelyn closed the book with a sigh.

'So we are! May I ask what is your report from the butler?'

'Mr Marsh did *not* have cherry pie for dinner last night!' the sheriff snapped.

'You are quite confident?'

And then abruptly the purport of the question flashed to me.

'Why, Mr Marsh, himself, mentioned the fact in his letter!' I burst out.

Madelyn's eyes turned to me reprovingly.

'You must be mistaken, Nora.'

With a lingering glance at the books on the desk, she rose, Sheriff Peddicord moved toward the door, opened it, and faced about with an abrupt clearing of his throat.

'Begging your pardon, Miss Mack, have—have you found any *clues* in the case?'

Madelyn had paused again at the ribboned curtains.

'Clues? The man who made Mr Marsh's death possible, Sheriff, was an expert chemist, of Italian origin, living for some time in London— and he died three hundred years ago!'

From the hall we had a fleeting view of Sheriff Peddicord's face, flushed as red as his handkerchief, and then it and the handkerchief disappeared.

I whirled on Madelyn sternly.

'You are carrying your absurd joke, Miss Mack, altogether too—'

I paused, gulping in my turn. It was as though I had stumbled from the shadows into an electric glare.

Madelyn had crossed to the desk, and was gently shifting the dead ashes of Raleigh's pipe into an envelope. A moment she sniffed at its bowl, peering down at the crumpled body at her feet.

'The pipe!' I gasped. 'Wendell Marsh was poisoned with the pipe!'

Madelyn sealed the envelope slowly.

'Is that fact just dawning on you, Nora?'

'But the rest of it—what you told the—'

Madelyn thrummed on the bulky volume of Elizabethan history.

'Some day, Nora, if you will remind me, I will give you the material for what you call a Sunday "feature" on the historic side of murder as a fine art!'

In a curtain-shadowed nook of the side veranda Muriel Jansen was awaiting us, pillowed back against a bronze-draped chair, whose colors almost startlingly matched the gold of her hair. Her resemblance to a tired child was even more pronounced than when I had last seen her.

I found myself glancing furtively for signs of Homer Truxton, but he had disappeared.

Miss Jansen took the initiative in our interview with a nervous abruptness, contrasting oddly with her hesitancy at our last meeting.

'I understand, Miss Mack, that you received a letter from my uncle asking your presence here. May I see it?'

The eagerness of her tones could not be mistaken.

From her wrist-bag Madelyn extended the square envelope of the morning post, with its remarkable message. Twice Muriel Jansen's eyes swept slowly through its contents. Madelyn watched her with a little frown. A sudden tenseness had crept into the air, as though we were all keying ourselves for an unexpected climax. And then, like a thunder-clap, it came.

'A curious communication,' Madelyn suggested. 'I had hoped you might be able to add to it?'

The tired face in the bronze-draped chair stared across the lawn.

'I can. The most curious fact of your communication, Miss Mack, is that *Wendell Marsh did not write it!*'

Never have I admired more keenly Madelyn's remarkable poise. Save for an almost imperceptible indrawing of her breath, she gave no hint of the shock which must have stunned her as it did me. I was staring with mouth agape. But, then, I presume you have discovered by this time that I was not designed for a detective!

Strangely enough, Muriel Jansen gave no trace of wonder in her announcement. Her attitude suggested a sense of detachment from the subject as though suddenly it had lost its interest. And yet, less than an hour ago, it had prostrated her in a swoon.

'You mean the letter is a forgery?' asked Madelyn quietly.

'Quite obviously.'

'And the attempts on Mr Marsh's life to which it refers?'

'There have been none. I have been with my uncle continuously for six months. I can speak definitely.'

Miss Jansen fumbled in a white-crocheted bag.

'Here are several specimens of Mr Marsh's writing. I think they should be sufficient to convince you of what I say. If you desire others—'

I was gulping like a truant schoolgirl as Madelyn spread on her lap the three notes extended to her. Casual business and personal references they were, none of more than half a dozen lines. Quite enough, however, to complete the sudden chasm at our feet—quite enough to emphasize a bold, aggressive penmanship, almost perpendicular, without the slightest resemblance to the cramped, shadowy writing of the morning's astonishing communication.

Madelyn rose from her chair, smoothing her skirts thoughtfully. For a moment she stood at the railing, gazing down upon a trellis of yellow roses, her face turned from us. For the first time in our curious friendship, I was actually conscious of a feeling of pity for her! The blank wall which she faced seemed so abrupt—so final!

Muriel Jansen shifted her position slightly.

'Are you satisfied, Miss Mack?'

'Quite.' Madelyn turned, and handed back the three notes. 'I presume this means that you do not care for me to continue the case?'

I whirled in dismay. I had never thought of this possibility.

'On the contrary, Miss Mack, it seems to me an additional reason why you should continue!'

I breathed freely again. At least we were not to be dismissed with the abruptness that Miss Jansen's maid had shown! Madelyn bowed rather absently.

'Then if you will give me another interview, perhaps this afternoon—'

Miss Jansen fumbled with the lock of her bag. For the first time her voice lost something of its directness.

'Have—have you any explanation of this astonishing—forgery?'

Madelyn was staring out toward the increasing crowd at the gate. A sudden ripple had swept through it.

'Have you ever heard of a man by the name of Orlando Julio, Miss Jansen?'

My own eyes, following the direction of Madelyn's gaze, were brought back sharply to the veranda. For the second time, Muriel Jansen had crumpled back in a faint.

As I darted toward the servants' bell Madelyn checked me. Striding up the walk were two men with the unmistakable air of physicians. At Madelyn's motioning hand they turned toward us.

The foremost of the two quickened his pace as he caught sight of the figure in the chair. Instinctively I knew that he was Dr Dench—and it needed no profound analysis to place his companion as the local coroner.

With a deft hand on Miss Jansen's heartbeats, Dr Dench raised a ruddy, brown-whiskered face enquiringly toward us.

'Shock!' Madelyn explained. 'Is it serious?'

The hand on the wavering breast darted toward a medicine case, and selected a vial of brownish liquid. The gaze above it continued its scrutiny of Madelyn's slender figure.

Dr Dench was of the rugged, German type, steel-eyed, confidently sure of movement, with the physique of a splendidly muscled animal. If the servant's tattle was to be credited, Muriel Jansen could not have attracted more opposite extremes in her suitors.

The coroner—a rusty-suited man of middle age, in quite obvious professional awe of his companion—extended a glass of water. Miss Jansen wearily opened her eyes before it reached her lips.

Dr Dench restrained her sudden effort to rise.

'Drink this, please!' There was nothing but professional command in his voice. If he loved the grey-pallored girl in the chair, his emotions were under superb control.

Madelyn stepped to the background, motioning me quietly.

'I fancy I can leave now safely. I am going back to town.'

'Town?' I echoed.

'I should be back the latter part of the afternoon. Would it inconvenience you to wait here?'

'But, why on earth—' I began.

'Will you tell the butler to send around the car? Thanks!'

When Madelyn doesn't choose to answer questions she ignores

them. I subsided as gracefully as possible. As her machine whirled under the porte-cochere, however, my curiosity again overflowed my restraint.

'At least, who is Orlando Julio?' I demanded.

Madelyn carefully adjusted her veil.

'The man who provided the means for the death of Wendell Marsh!' And she was gone.

I swept another glance at the trio on the side veranda, and with what I tried to convince myself was a philosophical shrug, although I knew perfectly well it was merely a pettish fling, sought a retired corner of the rear drawing-room, with my pad and pencil.

After all, I was a newspaper woman, and it needed no elastic imagination to picture the scene in the city room of the *Bugle*, if I failed to send a proper accounting of myself.

A few minutes later a tread of feet, advancing to the stairs, told me that the coroner and Dr Dench were ascending for the belated examination of Wendell Marsh's body. Miss Jansen had evidently recovered, or been assigned to the ministrations of her maid. Once Peters, the wooden-faced butler, entered ghostly to inform me that luncheon would be served at one, but effaced himself almost before my glance returned to my writing.

I partook of the meal in the distinguished company of Sheriff Peddicord. Apparently Dr Dench was still busied in his grewsome task upstairs, and it was not surprising that Miss Jansen preferred her own apartments.

However much the sheriff's professional poise might have been jarred by the events of the morning, his appetite had not been affected. His attention was too absorbed in the effort to do justice to the Marsh hospitality to waste time in table talk.

He finished his last spoonful of strawberry ice-cream with a heavy sigh of contentment, removed the napkin, which he had tucked under his collar, and, as though mindful of the family's laundry bills, folded it carefully and wiped his lips with his red handkerchief. It was not until then that our silence was interrupted.

Glancing cautiously about the room, and observing that the butler had been called kitchenward, to my amazement he essayed a confidential wink.

'I say,' he ventured enticingly, leaning his elbow on the table, 'what I would like to know is what became of that there other man!'

'Are you familiar with the Fourth Dimension, Sheriff?' I returned solemnly. I rose from my chair, and stepped toward him confidentially in my turn. 'I believe that a thorough study of that subject would answer your question.'

It was three o'clock when I stretched myself in my corner of the drawing-room, and stuffed the last sheets of my copy paper into a special-delivery-stamped envelope.

My story was done. And Madelyn was not there to blue-pencil the Park Row adjectives! I smiled rather gleefully as I patted my hair, and leisurely addressed the envelope. The city editor would be satisfied, if Madelyn wasn't!

As I stepped into the hall, Dr Dench, the coroner, and Sheriff Peddicord were descending the stairs. Evidently the medical examination had been completed. Under other circumstances the three expressions before me would have afforded an interesting study in contrasts—Dr Dench trimming his nails with professional stoicism, the coroner endeavoring desperately to copy the other's *sang froid*, and the sheriff buried in an owl-like solemnity.

Dr Dench restored his knife to his pocket.

'You are Miss Mack's assistant, I understand?' I bowed.

'Miss Mack has been called away. She should be back, however, shortly.'

I could feel the doctor's appraising glance dissecting me with much the deliberateness of a surgical operation. I raised my eyes suddenly, and returned his stare. It was a virile, masterful face—and, I had to admit, coldly handsome!

Dr Dench snapped open his watch.

'Very well then, Miss, Miss—'

'Noraker!' I supplied crisply.

The blond beard inclined the fraction of an inch.

'We will wait.'

'The autopsy?' I ventured. 'Has it—'

'The result of the autopsy I will explain to—Miss Mack!'

I bit my lip, felt my face flush as I saw that Sheriff Peddicord was trying to smother a grin, and turned with a rather unsuccessful shrug.

Now, if I had been of a vindictive nature, I would have opened my envelope and inserted a retaliating paragraph that would have returned the snub of Dr Dench with interest. I flatter myself that I consigned the envelope to the Three Forks post-office, in the rear of the Elite Dry Goods Emporium, with its contents unchanged.

As a part recompense, I paused at a corner drug store, and permitted a young man with a gorgeous pink shirt to make me a chocolate ice-cream soda. I was bent over an asthmatic straw when, through the window, I saw Madelyn's car skirt the curb.

I rushed out to the sidewalk, while the young man stared dazedly after me. The chauffeur swerved the machine as I tossed a dime to the Adonis of the fountain.

Madelyn shifted to the end of the seat as I clambered to her side. One glance was quite enough to show that her town-mission, whatever it was, had ended in failure. Perhaps it was the consciousness of this fact that brought my eyes next to her blue turquoise locket. It was open. I glared accusingly.

'So you have fallen back on the cola stimulant again, Miss Mack?'

She nodded glumly, and perversely slipped into her mouth another of the dark, brown berries, on which I have known her to keep up for forty-eight hours without sleep, and almost without food.

For a moment I forgot even my curiosity as to her errand.

'I wish the duty would be raised so high you couldn't get those things into the country!'

She closed her locket, without deigning a response. The more volcanic my outburst, the more glacial Madelyn's coldness—particularly on the cola topic. I shrugged in resignation. I might as well have done so in the first place!

I straightened my hat, drew my handkerchief over my flushed face, and coughed questioningly. Continued silence. I turned in desperation.

'Well?' I surrendered.

'Don't you know enough, Nora Noraker, to hold your tongue?'

My pent-up emotions snapped.

'Look here, Miss Mack, I have been snubbed by Dr Dench and the coroner, grinned at by Sheriff Peddicord, and I am not going to be crushed by you! What is your report,—good, bad, or indifferent?'

Madelyn turned from her stare into the dust-yellow road.

'I have been a fool, Nora—a blind, bigoted, self-important fool!'

I drew a deep breath.

'Which means—'

From her bag Madelyn drew the envelope of dead tobacco ashes from the Marsh library, and tossed it over the side of the car. I sank back against the cushions.

'Then the tobacco after all—'

'Is nothing but tobacco—harmless tobacco!'

'But the pipe—I thought the pipe—'

'That's just it! The pipe, my dear girl, killed Wendell Marsh! But I don't know how! *I don't know how*!'

'Madelyn,' I said severely, 'you are a woman, even if you are making your living at a man's profession! What you need is a good cry!'

6

Dr Dench, pacing back and forth across the veranda, knocked the ashes from an amber-stemmed meerschaum, and advanced to meet us as we alighted. The coroner and Sheriff Peddicord were craning their necks from wicker chairs in the background. It was easy enough to surmise that Dr Dench had parted from them abruptly in the desire for a quiet smoke to marshall his thoughts.

'Fill your pipe again if you wish,' said Madelyn. 'I don't mind.'

Dr Dench inclined his head, and dug the mouth of his meerschaum into a fat leather pouch. A spiral of blue smoke soon curled around his face. He was one of that type of men to whom a pipe lends a distinction of studious thoughtfulness.

With a slight gesture he beckoned in the direction of the coroner.

'It is proper, perhaps, that Dr Williams in his official capacity should be heard first.'

Through the smoke of his meerschaum, his eyes were searching Madelyn's face. It struck me that he was rather puzzled as to just how seriously to take her.

The coroner shuffled nervously. At his elbow, Sheriff Peddicord fumbled for his red handkerchief.

'We have made a thorough examination of Mr Marsh's body, Miss Mack, a most thorough examination—'

'Of course he was not shot, nor stabbed, nor strangled, nor sand-bagged?' interrupted Madelyn crisply.

The coroner glanced at Dr Dench uncertainly. The latter was smoking with inscrutable face.

'Nor poisoned!' finished the coroner with a quick breath.

A blue smoke curl from Dr Dench's meerschaum vanished against the sun. The coroner jingled a handful of coins in his pocket. The sound jarred on my nerves oddly. Not poisoned! Then Madelyn's theory of the pipe—

My glance swerved in her direction. Another blank wall—the blankest in this riddle of blank walls!

But the bewilderment I had expected in her face I did not find. The black dejection I had noticed in the car had dropped like a whisked-off cloak. The tired lines had been erased as by a sponge. Her eyes shone with that tense glint which I knew came only when she saw a befogged way swept clear before her.

'You mean that you *found* no trace of poison?' she corrected.

The coroner drew himself up.

'Under the supervision of Dr Dench, we have made a most complete probe of the various organs,—lungs, stomach, heart—'

'And brain, I presume?'

'Brain? Certainly not!'

'And you?' Madelyn turned toward Dr Dench. 'You subscribe to Dr Williams' opinion?'

Dr Dench removed his meerschaum.

'From our examination of Mr Marsh's body, I am prepared to state emphatically that there is no trace of toxic condition of any kind!'

'Am I to infer then that you will return a verdict of—natural death?'

Dr Dench stirred his pipe-ashes.

'I was always under the impression, Miss Mack, that the verdict in a case of this kind must come from the coroner's jury.'

Madelyn pinned back her veil, and removed her gloves.

'There is no objection to my seeing the body again?'

The coroner stared.

'Why, er—the undertaker has it now. I don't see why he should object, if you wish—'

Madelyn stepped to the door. Behind her, Sheriff Peddicord stirred suddenly.

'I say, what I would like to know, gents, is what became of that there other man!'

It was not until six o'clock that I saw Madelyn again, and then I found her in Wendell Marsh's red library. She was seated at its late tenant's huge desk. Before her were a vial of whitish-grey powder, a small, rubber, inked roller, a half a dozen sheets of paper, covered with what looked like smudges of black ink, and Raleigh's pipe. I stopped short, staring.

She rose with a shrug.

'Fingerprints,' she explained laconically. 'This sheet belongs to Miss Jansen; the next to her maid; the third to the butler, Peters; the fourth to Dr Dench; the fifth to Wendell Marsh, himself. It was my first experiment in taking the "prints" of a dead man. It was— interesting.'

'But what has that to do with a case of this kind?' I demanded.

Madelyn picked up the sixth sheet of smudged paper.

'We have here the fingerprints of Wendell Marsh's murderer!'

I did not even cry my amazement. I suppose the kaleidoscope of the day had dulled my normal emotions. I remember that I readjusted a loose pin in my waist before I spoke.

'The murderer of Wendell Marsh!' I repeated mechanically. 'Then he *was* poisoned?'

Madelyn's eyes opened and closed without answer.

I reached over to the desk, and picked up Mr Marsh's letter of the morning post at Madelyn's elbow.

'You have found the man who forged this?'

'It was *not* forged!'

In my daze I dropped the letter to the floor.

'You have discovered then the other man in the death-struggle that wrecked the library?'

'There was no other man!'

Madelyn gathered up her possessions from the desk. From the edge of the row of books she lifted a small, red-bound volume, perhaps four inches in width, and then with a second thought laid it back.

'By the way, Nora, I wish you would come back here at eight o'clock. If this book is still where I am leaving it, please bring it to me! I think that will be all for the present.'

'All?' I gasped. 'Do you realize that—'

Madelyn moved toward the door.

'I think eight o'clock will be late enough for your errand,' she said without turning.

The late June twilight had deepened into a somber darkness when, my watch showing ten minutes past the hour of my instructions, I entered the room on the second floor that had been assigned to Miss Mack and myself. Madelyn at the window was staring into the shadow-blanketed yard.

'Well?' she demanded.

'Your book is no longer in the library!' I said crossly.

Madelyn whirled with a smile.

'Good! And now if you will be so obliging as to tell Peters to ask Miss Jansen to meet me in the rear drawing-room, with any of the friends of the family she desires to be present, I think we can clear up our little puzzle.'

7

It was a curious group that the graceful Swiss clock in the bronze drawing-room of the Marsh house stared down upon as it ticked its way past the half hour after eight. With a grave, rather insistent bow, Miss Mack had seated the other occupants of the room as they answered her summons. She was the only one of us that remained standing.

Before her were Sheriff Peddicord, Homer Truxton, Dr Dench, and Muriel Jansen. Madelyn's eyes swept our faces for a moment in silence, and then she crossed the room and closed the door.

'I have called you here,' she began, 'to explain the mystery of Mr Marsh's death.' Again her glance swept our faces. 'In many respects it has provided us with a peculiar, almost an unique problem.

'We find a man, in apparently normal health, dead. The observer argues at once foul play; and yet on his body is no hint of wound or bruise. The medical examination discovers no trace of poison. The autopsy shows no evidence of crime. Apparently we have eliminated all forms of unnatural death.

'I have called you here because the finding of the autopsy is incorrect, or rather incomplete. We are not confronted by natural death—but by a crime. And I may say at the outset that I am not the only person to know this fact. My knowledge is shared by one other in this room.'

Sheriff Peddicord rose to his feet and rather ostentatiously stepped to the door and stood with his back against it. Madelyn smiled faintly at the movement.

'I scarcely think there will be an effort at escape, Sheriff,' she said quietly.

Muriel Jansen was crumpled back into her chair, staring. Dr Dench was studying Miss Mack with the professional frown he might have directed at an abnormality on the operating table. It was Truxton who spoke first in the fashion of the impulsive boy.

'If we are not dealing with natural death, how on earth then was Mr Marsh killed?'

Madelyn whisked aside a light covering from a stand at her side, and raised to view Raleigh's red sand-stone pipe. For a moment she balanced it musingly.

'The three-hundred-year-old death tool of Orlando Julio,' she explained. 'It was this that killed Wendell Marsh!'

She pressed the bowl of the pipe into the palm of her hand. 'As an instrument of death, it is *almost* beyond detection. We examined the ashes, and found nothing but harmless tobacco. The organs of the victim showed no trace of foul play.'

She tapped the long stem gravely.

'But the examination of the organs did *not* include the brain. And it is through the brain that the pipe strikes, killing first the mind in a nightmare of insanity, and then the body. That accounts for the wreckage that we found—the evidences apparently of *two* men engaged in a desperate struggle. The wreckage was the work of only one man—a maniac in the moment before death. The drug with which we are dealing drives its victim into an insane fury before his body succumbs. I believe such cases are fairly common in India.'

'Then Mr Marsh was poisoned after all?' cried Truxton. He was the only one of Miss Mack's auditors to speak.

'No, not poisoned! You will understand as I proceed. The pipe, you will find, contains apparently but one bowl and one channel, and at a superficial glance is filled only with tobacco. In reality, there is a lower chamber concealed beneath the upper bowl, to which extends a second channel. This secret chamber is charged with a certain compound of Indian hemp and dhatura leaves, one of the most powerful brain stimulants known to science—and one of the most dangerous if used above a certain strength. From the lower chamber it would leave no trace, of course, in the ashes above.

'Between the two compartments of the pipe is a slight connecting opening, sufficient to allow the hemp beneath to be ignited gradually by the burning tobacco. When a small quantity of the compound is used, the smoker is stimulated as by no other drug, not even opium. Increase the quantity above the danger point, and mark the result. The victim is not poisoned in the strict sense of the word, but literally *smothered to death by the fumes!*'

In Miss Mack's voice was the throb of the student before the creation of the master.

'I should like this pipe, Miss Jansen, if you ever care to dispose of it!'

The girl was still staring woodenly.

'It was Orlando Julio, the medieval poisoner,' she gasped, 'that Uncle described—'

'In his seventeenth chapter of "The World's Great Cynics",' finished Madelyn. 'I have taken the liberty of reading the chapter in manuscript form. Julio, however, was not the discoverer of the drug. He merely introduced it to the English public. As a matter of fact, it is one of the oldest stimulants of the East. It is easy to assume that it was not as a stimulant that Julio used it, but as a baffling instrument of murder. The mechanism of the pipe was his own invention, of course. The smoker, if not in the secret, would be completely oblivious to his danger. He might even use the pipe in perfect safety—until its lower chamber was loaded!'

Sheriff Peddicord, against the door, mopped his face with his red handkerchief, like a man in a daze. Dr Dench was still studying Miss Mack with his intent frown. Madelyn swerved her angle abruptly.

'Last night was not the first time the hemp-chamber of Wendell Marsh's pipe had been charged. We can trace the effect of the drug on his brain for several months—hallucinations, imaginative enemies seeking his life, incipient insanity. That explains his astonishing letter to me. Wendell Marsh was not a man of nine lives, but only one. The perils which he described were merely fantastic figments of the drug. For instance, the episode of the poisoned cherry pie. There was no pie at all served at the table yesterday.

'The letter to me was not a forgery, Miss Jansen, although you were sincere enough when you pronounced it such. The complete change in your uncle's handwriting was only another effect of the drug. It was this fact, in the end, which led me to the truth. You did not perceive that the dates of your notes and mine were *six months apart*! I knew that some terrific mental shock *must* have occurred in the meantime.

'And then, too, the ravages of a drug-crazed victim were at once suggested by the curtains of the library. They were not simply torn, but fairly *chewed* to pieces!'

A sudden tension fell over the room. We shifted nervously, rather avoiding one another's eyes. Madelyn laid the pipe back on the stand. She was quite evidently in no hurry to continue. It was Truxton again who put the leading question of the moment.

'If Mr Marsh was killed as you describe, Miss Mack, *who* killed him?'

Madelyn glanced across at Dr Dench.

'Will you kindly let me have the red leather book that you took from Mr Marsh's desk this evening, Doctor?'

The physician met her glance steadily.

'You think it—necessary?'

'I am afraid I must insist.'

For an instant Dr Dench hesitated. Then, with a shrug, he reached into a coat-pocket and extended the red-bound volume, for which Miss Mack had dispatched me on the fruitless errand to the library. As Madelyn opened it we saw that it was not a printed volume, but filled with several hundred pages of close, cramped writing. Dr Dench's gaze swerved to Muriel Jansen as Miss Mack spoke.

'I have here the diary of Wendell Marsh, which shows us that he had been in the habit of seeking the stimulant of Indian hemp, or "hasheesh" for some time, possibly as a result of his retired, sedentary life and his close application to his books. Until his purchase of the Bainford relics, however, he had taken the stimulant in the comparatively harmless form of powdered leaves or "bhang", as it is termed in the Orient. His acquisition of Julio's drug-pipe, and an accidental discovery of its mechanism, led him to adopt the compound of hemp and dhatura, prepared for smoking—in India called "charas". No less an authority than Captain E. N. Windsor, bacteriologist of the Burmese government, states that it is directly responsible for a large percentage of the lunacy of the Orient. Wendell Marsh, however, did not realize his danger, nor how much stronger the latter compound is than the form of the drug to which he had been accustomed.

'Dr Dench endeavored desperately to warn him of his peril, and free him from the bondage of the habit as the diary records, but the victim was too thoroughly enslaved. In fact, the situation had reached a point just before the final climax when it could no longer be concealed. The truth was already being suspected by the older servants. I assume this was why you feared my investigations in the case, Miss Jansen.'

Muriel Jansen was staring at Madelyn in a sort of dumb appeal.

'I can understand and admire Dr Dench's efforts to conceal the fact from the public—first, in his supervision of the inquest, which might have stumbled on the truth, and then in his removal of the betraying diary, which I left purposely exposed in the hope that it might inspire such an action. Had it *not* been removed, I might have suspected another explanation of the case—in spite of certain evidence to the contrary!'

Dr Dench's face had gone white.

'God! Miss Mack, do you mean that after all it was not suicide?'

'It was not suicide,' said Madelyn quietly. She stepped across toward the opposite door.

'When I stated that my knowledge that we are not dealing with natural death was shared by another person in this room, I might have added that it was shared by still a third person—*not in the room!*'

With a sudden movement she threw open the door before her. From the adjoining ante-room lurched the figure of Peters, the butler. He stared at us with a face grey with terror, and then crumpled to his knees. Madelyn drew away sharply as he tried to catch her skirts.

'You may arrest the murderer of Wendell Marsh, Sheriff!' she said gravely. 'And I think perhaps you had better take him outside.'

She faced our bewildered stares as the drawing-room door closed behind Mr Peddicord and his prisoner. From her stand she again took Raleigh's sand-stone pipe, and with it two sheets of paper, smudged with the prints of a human thumb and fingers.

'It was the pipe in the end which led me to the truth, not only as to the method but the identity of the assassin,' she explained. 'The hand, which placed the fatal charge in the concealed chamber, left its imprint on the surface of the bowl. The fingers, grimed with the dust of the drug, made an impression which I would have at once detected had I not been so occupied with what I might find *inside* that I forgot what I might find *outside*! I am very much afraid that I permitted myself the great blunder of the modern detective—lack of thoroughness.

'Comparison with the fingerprints of the various agents in the case, of course, made the next step a mere detail of mathematical comparison. To make my identity sure, I found that my suspect possessed not only the opportunity and the knowledge for the crime, but the motive.

'In his younger days Peters was a chemist's apprentice; a fact which he utilized in his master's behalf in obtaining the drugs which had become so necessary a part of Mr Marsh's life. Had Wendell Marsh appeared in person for so continuous a supply, his identity would soon have made the fact a matter of common gossip. He relied on his servant for his agent, a detail which he mentions several times in his diary, promising Peters a generous bequest in his will as a reward. I fancy that it was the dream of this bequest, which would have meant a small fortune to a man in his position, that set the butler's brain to work on his treacherous plan of murder.'

Miss Mack's dull gold hair covered the shoulders of her white *peignoir* in a great, thick braid. She was propped in a nest of pillows, with her favourite romance, 'The Three Musketeers', open at the   historic siege of Porthos in the wine cellar. We had elected to spend the night at the Marsh house.

Madelyn glanced up as I appeared in the doorway of our room.

'Allow me to present a problem to your analytical skill, Miss Mack,'

I said humbly. 'Which man does your knowledge of feminine psychology say Muriel Jansen will reward—the gravely protecting physician, or the boyishly admiring Truxton?'

'If she were thirty,' retorted Madelyn, yawning, 'she would be wise enough to choose Dr Dench. But, as she is only twenty-two, it will be Truxton.'

With a sigh, she turned again to the swashbuckling exploits of the gallant Porthos.

8

ANNA KATHARINE GREEN

An Intangible Clue

'HAVE you studied the case?'

'Not I.'

'Not studied the case which for the last few days has provided the papers with such conspicuous headlines?'

'I do not read the papers. I have not looked at one in a whole week.'

'Miss Strange, your social engagements must be of a very pressing nature just now?'

'They are.'

'And your business sense in abeyance?'

'How so?'

'You would not ask if you had read the papers.'

To this she made no reply save by a slight toss of her pretty head. If her employer felt nettled by this show of indifference, he did not betray it save by the rapidity of his tones as, without further preamble and possibly without real excuse, he proceeded to lay before her the case in question.

'Last Tuesday night a woman was murdered in this city; an old woman, in a lonely house where she has lived for years. Perhaps you remember this house? It occupies a not inconspicuous site in Seventeenth Street—a house of the olden time?'

'No, I do not remember.'

The extreme carelessness of Miss Strange's tone would have been fatal to her socially; but then, she would never have used it socially. This they both knew, yet he smiled with his customary indulgence.

'Then I will describe it.'

She looked around for a chair and sank into it. He did the same.

'It has a fanlight over the front door.'

She remained impassive.

'And two old-fashioned strips of parti-coloured glass on either side.'

'And a knocker between its panels which may bring money some day.'

'Oh, you do remember! I thought you would, Miss Strange.'

'Yes. Fanlights over doors are becoming very rare in New York.'

'Very well, then. That house was the scene of Tuesday's tragedy. The woman who has lived there in solitude for years was foully murdered. I have since heard that the people who knew her best have always anticipated some such violent end for her. She never allowed maid or friend to remain with her after five in the afternoon; yet she had money—some think a great deal—always in the house.'

'I am interested in the house, not in her.'

'Yet, she was a character—as full of whims and crotchets as a nut is of meat. Her death was horrible. She fought—her dress was torn from her body in rags. This happened, you see, before her hour for retiring; some think as early as six in the afternoon. And'—here he made a rapid gesture to catch Violet's wandering attention—'in spite of this struggle; in spite of the fact that she was dragged from room to room—that her person was searched—and everything in the house searched—that drawers were pulled out of bureaus—doors wrenched off of cupboards—china smashed upon the floor—whole shelves denuded and not a spot from cellar to garret left unransacked, no direct clue to the perpetrator has been found—nothing that gives any idea of his personality save his display of strength and great cupidity. The police have even deigned to consult me,—an unusual procedure—but I could find nothing, either. Evidences of fiendish purpose abound—of relentless search—but no clue to the man himself. It's uncommon, isn't it, not to have *any* clue?'

'I suppose so.' Miss Strange hated murders and it was with difficulty she could be brought to discuss them. But she was not going to be let off; not this time.

'You see,' he proceeded insistently, 'it's not only mortifying to the police but disappointing to the press, especially as few reporters believe in the No-thoroughfare business. They say, and we cannot but agree with them, that no such struggle could take place and no such repeated goings to and fro through the house without some vestige being left by which to connect this crime with its daring perpetrator.'

Still she stared down at her hands—those little hands so white and fluttering, so seemingly helpless under the weight of their many rings, and yet so slyly capable.

'She must have queer neighbours,' came at last, from Miss Strange's reluctant lips. 'Didn't they hear or see anything of all this?'

'She has no neighbours—that is, after half-past five o'clock. There's a printing establishment on one side of her, a deserted mansion on the other side, and nothing but warehouses back and front. There was no one to notice what took place in her small dwelling after the printing house was closed. She was the most courageous or the most foolish of women to remain there as she did. But nothing except death could budge her. She was born in the room where she died; was married in the one where she worked; saw husband, father, mother, and five sisters carried out in turn to their graves through the door with the fanlight over the top—and these memories held her.'

'You are trying to interest me in the woman. Don't.'

'No, I'm not trying to interest you in her, only trying to explain her. There was another reason for her remaining where she did so long after all residents had left the block. She had a business.'

'Oh!'

'She embroidered monograms for fine ladies.'

'She did? But you needn't look at me like that. She never embroidered any for me.'

'No? She did first-class work. I saw some of it. Miss Strange, *if* I could get you into that house for ten minutes—not to see her but to pick up the loose intangible thread which I am sure is floating around in it somewhere—wouldn't you go?'

Violet slowly rose—a movement which he followed to the letter.

'Must I express in words the limit I have set for myself in our affair?' she asked. 'When, for reasons I have never thought myself called upon to explain, I consented to help you a little now and then with some matter where a woman's tact and knowledge of the social world might tell without offence to herself or others, I never thought it would be necessary for me to state that temptation must stop with

149

such cases, or that I should not be asked to touch the sordid or the bloody. But it seems I was mistaken, and that I must stoop to be explicit. The woman who was killed on Tuesday might have interested me greatly as an embroiderer, but as a victim, not at all. What do you see in me, or miss in me, that you should drag me into an atmosphere of low-down crime?'

'Nothing, Miss Strange. You are by nature, as well as by breeding, very far removed from everything of the kind. But you will allow me to suggest that no crime is low-down which makes imperative demand upon the intellect and intuitive sense of its investigator. Only the most delicate touch can feel and hold the thread I've just spoken of, and *you* have the most delicate touch I know.'

'Do not attempt to flatter me. I have no fancy for handling befouled spider webs. Besides, if I had—if such elusive filaments fascinated me—how could I, well-known in person and name, enter upon such a scene without prejudice to our mutual compact?'

'Miss Strange'—she had reseated herself, but so far he had failed to follow her example (an ignoring of the subtle hint that her interest might yet be caught, which seemed to annoy her a trifle), 'I should not even have suggested such a possibility had I not seen a way of introducing you there without risk to your position or mine. Among the boxes piled upon Mrs Doolittle's table—boxes of finished work, most of them addressed and ready for delivery—was one on which could be seen the name of—shall I mention it?'

'Not mine? You don't mean mine? That would be too odd—too ridiculously odd. I should not understand a coincidence of that kind; no, I should not, notwithstanding the fact that I have lately sent out such work to be done.'

'Yet it was your name, very clearly and precisely written—your whole name, Miss Strange. I saw and read it myself.'

'But I gave the order to Madame Pirot on Fifth Avenue. How came my things to be found in the house of this woman of whose horrible death we have been talking?'

'Did you suppose that Madame Pirot did such work with her own hands?—or even had it done in her own establishment? Mrs Doolittle was universally employed. She worked for a dozen firms. You will find the biggest names on most of her packages. But on this one—I allude to the one addressed to you—there was more to be seen than the name. These words were written on it in another hand. *Send without opening.* This struck the police as suspicious; sufficiently so, at least, for them to desire your presence at the house as soon as you can make it convenient.'

'To open the box?'

'Exactly.'

The curl of Miss Strange's disdainful lip was a sight to see. ·

'You wrote those words yourself,' she coolly observed. 'While someone's back was turned, you whipped out your pencil and——.'

'Resorted to a very pardonable subterfuge highly conducive to the public's good. But never mind that. Will you go?'

Miss Strange became suddenly demure.

'I suppose I must,' she grudgingly conceded. 'However obtained, a summons from the police cannot be ignored even by Peter Strange's daughter.'

Another man might have displayed his triumph by smile or gesture; but this one had learned his role too well. He simply said:

'Very good. Shall it be at once? I have a taxi at the door.'

But she failed to see the necessity of any such hurry. With sudden dignity she replied:

'That won't do. If I go to this house it must be under suitable conditions. I shall have to ask my brother to accompany me.'

'Your brother!'

'Oh, he's safe. He—he knows.'

'Your *brother knows*?' Her visitor, with less control than usual, betrayed very openly his uneasiness.

'He does and—*approves*. But that's not what interests us now, only so far as it makes it possible for me to go with propriety to that dreadful house.'

A formal bow from the other and the words:

'They may expect you, then. Can you say when?'

'Within the next hour. But it will be a useless concession on my part,' she pettishly complained. 'A place that has been gone over by a dozen detectives is apt to be brushed clean of its cobwebs, even if such ever existed.'

'That's the difficulty,' he acknowledged; and did not dare to add another word; she was at that particular moment so very much the great lady, and so little his confidential agent.

He might have been less impressed, however, by this sudden assumption of manner, had he been so fortunate as to have seen how she employed the three-quarters of an hour's delay for which she had asked.

She read those neglected newspapers, especially the one containing the following highly coloured narration of this ghastly crime:

'A door ajar—an empty hall—a line of sinister looking blotches marking a guilty step diagonally across the flagging—silence—and an unmistakable odour repugnant to all humanity—such were the indications which met the eyes of Officer O'Leary on his first round last night, and led to the discovery of a murder which will long thrill the city by its mystery and horror.

'Both the house and the victim are well known.' Here followed a description of the same and of Mrs Doolittle's manner of life in her ancient home, which Violet hurriedly passed over to come to the following:

'As far as one can judge from appearances, the crime happened in this wise: Mrs Doolittle had been in her kitchen, as the tea-kettle found singing on the stove goes to prove, and was coming back through her bedroom, when the wretch, who had stolen in by the front door which, to save steps, she was unfortunately in the habit of leaving on the latch till all possibility of customers for the day was over, sprang upon her from behind and dealt her a swinging blow with the poker he had caught up from the hearthstone.

'Whether the struggle which ensued followed immediately upon this first attack or came later, it will take medical experts to determine. But, whenever it did occur, the fierceness of its character is shown by the grip taken upon her throat and the traces of blood which are to be seen all over the house. If the wretch had lugged her into her workroom and thence to the kitchen, and thence back to the spot of first assault, the evidences could not have been more ghastly. Bits of her clothing torn off by a ruthless hand, lay scattered over all these floors. In her bedroom, where she finally breathed her last, there could be seen mingled with these a number of large but worthless glass beads; and close against one of the base-boards, the string which had held them, as shown by the few remaining beads still clinging to it. If in pulling the string from her neck he had hoped to light upon some valuable booty, his fury at his disappointment is evident. You can almost see the frenzy with which he flung the would-be necklace at the wall, and kicked about and stamped upon its rapidly rolling beads.

'Booty! That was what he was after; to find and carry away the poor needlewoman's supposed hoardings. If the scene baffles description—if, as some believe, he dragged her yet living from spot to spot, demanding information as to her places of concealment under threat of repeated blows, and, finally baffled, dealt the finishing stroke and proceeded on the search alone, no greater devastation could have taken place in this poor woman's house or effects. Yet such was his precaution and care for himself that he left no fingerprint behind him nor any other token which could lead to personal identification. Even though his footsteps could be traced in much the order I have mentioned, they were of so indeterminate and shapeless a character as to convey little to the intelligence of the investigator.

'That these smears (they could not be called footprints) not only crossed the hall but appeared in more than one place on the staircase proves that he did not confine his search to the lower storey; and perhaps one of the most interesting features of the case lies in the indications given by these marks of the raging course he took through these upper rooms. As the accompanying diagram will show [we omit the diagram] he went first into the large front chamber, thence to the rear where we find two rooms, one unfinished and filled with accumulated stuff most of which he left lying loose upon the floor, and the other plastered, and containing a window opening upon an alley-way at the side, but empty of all furniture and without even a carpet on the bare boards.

'Why he should have entered the latter place, and why, having entered he should have crossed to the window, will be plain to those who have studied the conditions. The front chamber windows were tightly shuttered, the attic ones cumbered with boxes and shielded from approach by old bureaus and discarded chairs. This one only was free and, although darkened by the proximity of the house neighbouring it across the alley, was the only spot on the storey where sufficient light could be had at this late hour for the examination of any object of whose value he was doubtful. That he had come across such an object and had brought it to this window for some such purpose is very satisfactorily demonstrated by the discovery of a worn-out wallet of ancient make lying on the floor directly in front of this window—a proof of his cupidity but also proof of his ill-luck. For this wallet, when lifted and opened, was found to contain two hundred or more dollars in old bills, which, if not the full hoard of their industrious owner, was certainly worth the taking by one who had risked his neck for the sole purpose of theft.

'This wallet, and the flight of the murderer without it, give to this affair, otherwise simply brutal, a dramatic interest which will be appreciated not only by the very able detectives already hot upon the chase, but by all other enquiring minds anxious to solve a mystery of which so estimable a woman has been the unfortunate victim. A problem is presented to the police——'

There Violet stopped.

When, not long after, the superb limousine of Peter Strange stopped before the little house in Seventeenth Street, it caused a veritable sensation, not only in the curiosity-mongers lingering on the sidewalk, but to the two persons within—the officer on guard and a belated reporter.

Though dressed in her plainest suit, Violet Strange looked much too fashionable and far too young and thoughtless to be observed, without emotion, entering a scene of hideous and brutal crime. Even the young man who accompanied her promised to bring a most incongruous element into this atmosphere of guilt and horror, and, as the detective on guard whispered to the man beside him, might much better have been left behind in the car.

But Violet was great for the proprieties and young Arthur followed her in.

Her entrance was a *coup du théâtre*. She had lifted her veil in crossing the sidewalk and her interesting features and general air of timidity were very fetching. As the man holding open the door noted the impression made upon his companion, he muttered with sly facetiousness:

'You think you'll show her nothing; but I'm ready to bet a fiver that she'll want to see it all and that you'll show it to her.'

The detective's grin was expressive, notwithstanding the shrug with which he tried to carry it off.

And Violet? The hall into which she now stepped from the most vivid sunlight had never been considered even in its palmiest days as possessing cheer even of the stately kind. The ghastly green light infused through it by the coloured glass on either side of the doorway seemed to promise yet more dismal things beyond.

'Must I go in there?' she asked, pointing, with an admirable simulation of nervous excitement, to a half-shut door at her left. 'Is there where it happened? Arthur, do you suppose that there is where it happened?'

'No, no, Miss,' the officer made haste to assure her. 'If you are Miss Strange' (Violet bowed), 'I need hardly say that the woman was struck in her bedroom. The door beside you leads into the parlour, or as she would have called it, her workroom. You needn't be afraid of going in there. You will see nothing but the disorder of her boxes. They were pretty well pulled about. Not all of them though, he added, watching her as closely as the dim light permitted. There is one which gives no sign of having been tampered with. It was done up in wrapping paper and is addressed to you, which in itself would not have seemed worthy of our attention had not these lines been scribbled on it in a man's handwriting: '*Send without opening.*'

'How odd!' exclaimed the little minx with widely opened eyes and an air of guileless innocence. 'Whatever can it mean? Nothing serious I am sure, for the woman did not even know me. She was employed to do this work by Madame Pirot.'

'Didn't you know that it was to be done here?'

'No. I thought Madame Pirot's own girls did her embroidery for her.'

'So that you were surprised——'

'Wasn't I!'

'To get our message.'

'I didn't know what to make of it.'

The earnest, half-injured look with which she uttered this disclaimer, did its appointed work. The detective accepted her for what she seemed and, oblivious to the reporter's satirical gesture, crossed to the work-room door, which he threw wide open with the remark:

'I should be glad to have you open that box in our presence. It is undoubtedly all right, but we wish to be sure. You know what the box should contain?'

'Oh, yes, indeed; pillowcases and sheets, with a big S embroidered on them.

'Very well. Shall I undo the string for you?'

'I shall be much obliged,' said she, her eye flashing quickly about the room before settling down upon the knot he was deftly loosening.

Her brother, gazing indifferently in from the doorway, hardly noticed this look; but the reporter at his back did, though he failed to detect its penetrating quality.

'Your name is on the other side,' observed the detective as he drew away the string and turned the package over.

The smile which just lifted the corner of her lips was not in answer to this remark, but to her recognition of her employer's handwriting in the words under her name: *Send without opening.* She had not misjudged him.

'The cover you may like to take off yourself,' suggested the officer, as he lifted the box out of its wrapper.

'Oh, I don't mind. There's nothing to be ashamed of in embroidered linen. Or perhaps that is not what you are looking for?'

No one answered. All were busy watching her whip off the lid and lift out the pile of sheets and pillowcases with which the box was closely packed.

'Shall I unfold them?' she asked.

The detective nodded.

Taking out the topmost sheet, she shook it open. Then the next and the next till she reached the bottom of the box. Nothing of a criminating nature came to light. The box as well as its contents was without mystery of any kind. This was not an unexpected result of course, but the smile with which she began to refold the pieces and throw them back into the box, revealed one of her dimples which was almost as dangerous to the casual observer as when it revealed both.

'There,' she exclaimed, 'you see! Household linen exactly as I said. Now may I go home?'

'Certainly, Miss Strange.'

The detective stole a sly glance at the reporter. She was not going in for the horrors then after all.

But the reporter abated nothing of his knowing air, for while she spoke of going, she made no move towards doing so, but continued to look about the room till her glances finally settled on a long dark curtain shutting off an adjoining room.

'There's where she lies, I suppose,' she feelingly exclaimed. 'And not one of you knows who killed her. Somehow, I cannot understand that. Why don't you know when that's what you're hired for?' The innocence with which she uttered this was astonishing. The detective began to look sheepish and the reporter turned aside to hide his smile. Whether in another moment either would have spoken no one can say, for, with a mock consciousness of having said something foolish, she caught up her parasol from the table and made a start for the door.

But of course she looked back.

'I was wondering,' she recommenced, with a half wistful, half speculative air, 'whether I should ask to have a peep at the place where it all happened.'

The reporter chuckled behind the pencil-end he was chewing, but the officer maintained his solemn air, for which act of self-restraint he was undoubtedly grateful when in another minute she gave a quick impulsive shudder not altogether assumed, and vehemently added: 'But I couldn't stand the sight; no, I couldn't! I'm an awful coward when it comes to things like that. Nothing in all the world would induce me to look at the woman or her room. But I should like—' here both her dimples came into play though she could not be said exactly to smile—'just one little look upstairs, where he went poking about so long without any fear it seems of being interrupted. Ever since I've read about it I have seen, in my mind, a picture of his wicked figure sneaking from room to room, tearing open drawers and flinging out the contents of closets just to find a little money—a little, little money! I shall not sleep tonight just for wondering how those high up attic rooms really look.'

Who could dream that back of this display of mingled childishness and audacity there lay hidden purpose, intellect, and a keen knowledge of human nature. Not the two men who listened to this seemingly irresponsible chatter. To them she was a child to be humoured and humour her they did. The dainty feet which had already found their way to that gloomy staircase were allowed to ascend, followed it is true by those of the officer who did not dare to smile back at the reporter because of the brother's watchful and none too conciliatory eye.

At the stair head she paused to look back.

'I don't see those horrible marks which the papers describe as running all along the lower hall and up these stairs.'

'No, Miss Strange; they have gradually been rubbed out, but you will find some still showing on these upper floors.'

'Oh! oh! where? You frighten me—frighten me horribly! But—but—if you don't mind, I should like to see.'

Why should not a man on a tedious job amuse himself? Piloting her over to the small room in the rear, he pointed down at the boards. She gave one look and then stepped gingerly in.

'Just look!' she cried; 'a whole string of marks going straight from door to window. They have no shape, have they,—just blotches? I wonder why one of them is so much larger than the rest?'

This was no new question. It was one which everybody who went into the room was sure to ask, there was such a difference in the size and appearance of the mark nearest the window. The reason—well, minds were divided about that, and no one had a satisfactory theory. The detective therefore kept discreetly silent.

This did not seem to offend Miss Strange. On the contrary it gave her an opportunity to babble away to her heart's content.

'One, two, three, four, five, six,' she counted, with a shudder at every count. 'And one of them bigger than the others.' She might have added, 'It is the trail of one foot, and strangely intermingled at that,' but she did not, though we may be quite sure that she noted the fact. 'And where, just where did the old wallet fall? Here? or *here*?'

She had moved as she spoke, so that in uttering the last 'here', she stood directly before the window. The surprise she received there nearly made her forget the part she was playing. From the character of the light in the room, she had expected, on looking out, to confront a nearby wall, but not a window in that wall. Yet that was what she saw directly facing her from across the old-fashioned alley separating this house from its neighbour; twelve unshuttered and uncurtained panes through which she caught a darkened view of a room almost as forlorn and devoid of furniture as the one in which she then stood.

When quite sure of herself, she let a certain portion of her surprise appear.

'Why, look!' she cried, 'if you can't see right in next door! What a lonesome-looking place! From its desolate appearance I should think the house quite empty.'

'And it is. That's the old Shaffer homestead. It's been empty for a year.'

'Oh, empty!' And she turned away, with the most inconsequent air in the world, crying out as her name rang up the stair, 'There's Arthur calling. I suppose he thinks I've been here long enough. I'm sure I'm very much obliged to you, officer. I really shouldn't have slept a wink tonight, if I hadn't been given a peep at these rooms, which I had imagined so different.' And with one additional glance over her shoulder, that seemed to penetrate both windows and the desolate space beyond, she ran quickly out and down in response to her brother's reiterated call.

'Drive quickly!—as quickly as the law allows, to Hiram Brown's office in Duane Street.'

Arrived at the address named, she went in alone to see Mr Brown. He was her father's lawyer and a family friend.

Hardly waiting for his affectionate greeting, she cried out quickly. 'Tell me how I can learn anything about the old Shaffer house in Seventeenth Street. Now, don't look so surprised. I have very good reasons for my request and—and—I'm in an awful hurry.'

'But——'

'I know, I know; there's been a dreadful tragedy next door to it; but it's about the Shaffer house itself I want some information. Has it an agent, a——'

'Of course it has an agent, and here is his name.'

Mr Brown presented her with a card on which he had hastily written both name and address.

She thanked him, dropped him a mocking curtsey full of charm, whispered 'Don't tell father', and was gone.

Her manner to the man she next interviewed was very different. As soon as she saw him she subsided into her usual society manner. With just a touch of the conceit of the successful débutante, she announced herself as Miss Strange of Seventy-second Street. Her business with him was in regard to the possible renting of the Shaffer house. She had an old lady friend who was desirous of living downtown.

In passing through Seventeenth Street, she had noticed that the old Shaffer house was standing empty and had been immediately struck with the advantages it possessed for her elderly friend's occupancy. Could it be that the house was for rent? There was no sign on it to that effect, but—etc.

His answer left her nothing to hope for.

'It is going to be torn down,' he said.

'Oh, what a pity!' she exclaimed. 'Real colonial, isn't it! I wish I could see the rooms inside before it is disturbed. Such doors and such dear old-fashioned mantelpieces as it must have! I just dote on the Colonial. It brings up such pictures of the old days; weddings, you know, and parties;—all so different from ours and so much more interesting.'

Is it the chance shot that tells? Sometimes. Violet had no especial intention in what she said save as a prelude to a pending request, but nothing could have served her purpose better than that one word, *wedding*. The agent laughed and giving her his first indulgent look, remarked genially:

'Romance is not confined to those ancient times. If you were to enter that house today you would come across evidences of a wedding as romantic as any which ever took place in all the seventy odd years of its existence. A man and a woman were married there day before yesterday who did their first courting under its roof forty years ago. He has been married twice and she once in the interval; but the old love held firm and now at the age of sixty and over they have come together to finish their days in peace and happiness. Or so we will hope.'

'Married! married in that house and on the day that——'

She caught herself up in time. He did not notice the break.

'Yes, in memory of those old days of courtship, I suppose. They came here about five, got the keys, drove off, went through the ceremony in that empty house, returned the keys to me in my own apartment, took the steamer for Naples, and were on the sea before midnight. Do you not call that quick work as well as highly romantic?'

'Very.' Miss Strange's cheek had paled. It was apt to when she was greatly excited. 'But I don't understand,' she added, the moment after. 'How could they do this and nobody know about it? I should have thought it would have got into the papers.'

'They are quiet people. I don't think they told their best friends. A simple announcement in the next day's journals testified to the fact of their marriage, but that was all. I would not have felt at liberty to mention the circumstances myself, if the parties were not well on their way to Europe.'

'Oh, how glad I am that you did tell me! Such a story of constancy and the hold which old associations have upon sensitive minds! But——'

'Why, Miss? What's the matter? You look very much disturbed.'

'Don't you remember? Haven't you thought? Something else happened that very day and almost at the same time on that block. Something very dreadful——'

'Mrs Doolittle's murder?'

'Yes. It was as near as next door, wasn't it? Oh, if this happy couple had known——'

'But fortunately they didn't. Nor are they likely to, till they reach the other side. You needn't fear that their honeymoon will be spoiled that way.'

'But they may have heard something or seen something before leaving the street. Did you notice how the gentleman looked when he returned you the keys?'

'I did, and there was no cloud on his satisfaction.'

'Oh, how you relieve me!' One—two dimples made their appearance in Miss Strange's fresh, young cheeks. 'Well! I wish them joy. Do you mind telling me their names? I cannot think of them as actual persons without knowing their names.'

'The gentleman was Constantin Amidon; the lady, Marian Shaffer. You will have to think of them now as Mr and Mrs Amidon.'

'And I will. Thank you, Mr Hutton, thank you very much. Next to the pleasure of getting the house for my friend, is that of hearing this charming bit of news in its connection.'

She held out her hand and, as he took it, remarked:

'They must have had a clergyman and witnesses.'

'Undoubtedly.'

'I wish I had been one of the witnesses,' she sighed sentimentally.

'They were two old men.'

'Oh, no! Don't tell me that.'

'Fogies; nothing less.'

'But the clergyman? He must have been young. Surely there was someone there capable of appreciating the situation?'

'I can't say about that; I did not see the clergyman.'

'Oh, well! it doesn't matter.' Miss Strange's manner was as nonchalant as it was charming. 'We will think of him as being *very* young.'

And with a merry toss of her head she flitted away.

But she sobered very rapidly upon entering her limousine.

'Hello!'

'Ah, is that you?'

'Yes, I want a Marconi sent.'

'A Marconi?'

'Yes, to the *Cretic*, which left dock the very night in which we are so deeply interested.'

'Good. Whom to? The Captain?'

'No, to a Mrs Constantin Amidon. But first be sure there is such a passenger.'

'*Mrs*! What idea have you there?'

'Excuse my not stating over the telephone. The message is to be to this effect. Did she at any time immediately before or after her marriage to Mr Amidon get a glimpse of anyone in the adjoining house? No remarks, please. I use the telephone because I am not ready to explain myself. If she did, let her send a written description to you of that person as soon as she reaches the Azores.'

'You surprise me. May I not call or hope for a line from you early tomorrow?'

'I shall be busy till you get your answer.'

He hung up the receiver. He recognized the resolute tone.

But the time came when the pending explanation was fully given to him. An answer had been returned from the steamer, favourable to Violet's hopes. Mrs Amidon had seen such a person and would send a

162

full description of the same at the first opportunity. It was news to fill Violet's heart with pride; the filament of a clue which had led to this great result had been so nearly invisible and had felt so like nothing in her grasp.

To her employer she described it as follows:

'When I hear or read of a case which contains any baffling features, I am apt to feel some hidden chord in my nature thrill to one fact in it and not to any of the others. In this case the single fact which appealed to my imagination was the dropping of the stolen wallet in that upstairs room. Why did the guilty man drop it? and why, having dropped it, did he not pick it up again? But one answer seemed possible. He had heard or seen something at the spot where it fell which not only alarmed him but sent him in flight from the house.'

'Very good; and did you settle to your own mind the nature of that sound or that sight?'

'I did.' Her manner was strangely businesslike. No show of dimples now. 'Satisfied that if any possibility remained of my ever doing this, it would have to be on the exact place of this occurrence or not at all, I embraced your suggestion and visited the house.'

'And that room no doubt.'

'And that room. Women, somehow, seem to manage such things.'

'So I've noticed, Miss Strange. And what was the result of your visit? What did you discover there?'

'This: that one of the blood spots marking the criminal's steps through the room was decidedly more pronounced than the rest; and, what was even more important, that the window out of which I was looking had its counterpart in the house on the opposite side of the alley. In gazing through the one I was gazing through the other; and not only that, but into the darkened area of the room beyond. Instantly I saw how the latter fact might be made to explain the former one. But before I say how, let me ask if it is quite settled among you that the smears on the floor and stairs mark the passage of the criminal's footsteps!'

'Certainly; and very bloody feet they must have been too. His shoes—or rather his one shoe—for the proof is plain that only the right one left its mark—must have become thoroughly saturated to carry its traces so far.'

'Do you think that any amount of saturation would have done this? Or, if you are not ready to agree to that, that a shoe so covered with blood could have failed to leave behind it some hint of its shape, some imprint, however faint, of heel or toe? But nowhere did it do this. We see a smear—and that is all.'

'You are right, Miss Strange; you are always right. And what do you gather from this?'

She looked to see how much he expected from her, and, meeting an eye not quite as free from all ironic suggestion as his words had led her to expect, faltered a little as she proceeded to say:

'My opinion is a girl's opinion, but such as it is you have the right to have it. From the indications mentioned I could draw but this conclusion: that the blood which accompanied the criminal's footsteps was not carried through the house by his shoes;—he wore no shoes; he did not even wear stockings; probably he had none. For reasons which appealed to his judgement, he went about his wicked work barefoot; and it was the blood from his own veins and not from those of his victim which made the trail we have followed with so much interest. Do you forget those broken beads;—how he kicked them about and stamped upon them in his fury? One of them pierced the ball of his foot, and that so sharply that it not only spurted blood but kept on bleeding with every step he took. Otherwise, the trail would have been lost after his passage up the stairs.'

'Fine!' There was no irony in the bureau-chief's eye now. 'You are progressing, Miss Strange. Allow me, I pray, to kiss your hand. It is a liberty I have never taken, but one which would greatly relieve my present stress of feeling.'

She lifted her hand toward him, but it was in gesture, not in recognition of his homage.

'Thank you,' said she, 'but I claim no monopoly on deductions so simple as these. I have not the least doubt that not only yourself but every member of the force has made the same. But there is a little matter which may have escaped the police, may even have escaped you. To that I would now call your attention since through it I have been enabled, after a little necessary groping, to reach the open. You remember the one large blotch on the upper floor where the man dropped the wallet? That blotch, more or less commingled with a fainter one, possessed great significance for me from the first moment I saw it. How came his foot to bleed so much more profusely at that one spot than at any other? There could be but one answer: because here a surprise met him—a surprise so startling to him in his present state of mind, that he gave a quick spring backward, with the result that his wounded foot came down suddenly and forcibly instead of easily as in his previous wary tread. And what was the surprise? I made it my business to find out, and now I can tell you that it was the sight of a woman's face staring upon him from the neighbouring house which he had probably been told was empty. The shock disturbed his judgement. He saw his crime discovered—his guilty secret read, and fled in unreasoning panic. He might better have held on to his wits. It was this display of fear which led me to search after its cause, and consequently to discover that at this especial hour more than one person had been in the Shaffer house; that, in fact, a marriage had been celebrated there under circumstances as romantic as any we read of in books, and that this marriage, privately carried out, had been followed by an immediate voyage of the happy couple on one of the White Star steamers. With the rest you are conversant. I do not need to say anything about what has followed the sending of that Marconi.'

'But I am going to say something about your work in this matter, Miss Strange. The big detectives about here will have to look sharp if——'

'Don't, please! Not yet.' A smile softened the asperity of this interruption. 'The man has yet to be caught and identified. Till that is done I cannot enjoy anyone's congratulations. And you will see that all this may not be so easy. If no one happened to meet the desperate wretch before he had an opportunity to retie his shoelaces, there will be little for you or even for the police to go upon but his wounded foot, his undoubtedly carefully prepared alibi, and later, a woman's confused description of a face seen but for a moment only and that under a personal excitement precluding minute attention. I should not be surprised if the whole thing came to nothing.'

But it did not. As soon as the description was received from Mrs Amidon (a description, by the way, which was unusually clear and precise, owing to the peculiar and contradictory features of the man), the police were able to recognize him among the many suspects always under their eye. Arrested, he pleaded, just as Miss Strange had foretold, an alibi of a seemingly unimpeachable character; but neither it, nor the plausible explanation with which he endeavoured to account for a freshly healed scar amid the callouses of his right foot, could stand before Mrs Amidon's unequivocal testimony that he was the same man she had seen in Mrs Doolittle's upper room on the afternoon of her own happiness and of that poor woman's murder.

The moment when, at his trial, the two faces again confronted each other across a space no wider than that which had separated them on the dread occasion in Seventeenth Street, is said to have been one of the most dramatic in the annals of that ancient courtroom.

9

ARTHUR B. REEVE

The Clairvoyants

'Do you believe in dreams?' Constance Dunlap looked searchingly at her interrogator, as if her face or manner betrayed some new side of her character.

Mrs de Forest Caswell was an attractive woman verging on forty, a chance acquaintance at a shoppers' tea-room downtown who had proved to be an uptown neighbour.

'I have had some rather strange experiences, Mildred,' confessed Constance tentatively. 'Why?'

'Because—' the other woman hesitated, then added, 'why should I not tell you? Last night, Constance, I had the strangest dream. It has left such an impression on me that I can't shake it off, although I have tried all day.'

'Yes? Tell me about it.'

Mildred Caswell paused a moment, then began slowly, as if not to omit anything from her story.

'I dreamt that Forest was dying. I could see him, could see the doctor and the nurse, everything. And yet somehow I could not get to him. I was afraid, with such an oppressive fear. I tried—oh, how I tried! I struggled, and how badly I felt!' and she shuddered at the very recollection.

'There seemed to be a wall,' she resumed, 'a narrow wall in the way, and I couldn't get over it. As often as I tried, I fell. And then I seemed to be pursued by some kind of animal, half bull, half snake. I ran. It followed closely. I seemed to see a crowd of people and I felt that if I could only get to that crowd, somehow I would be safe, perhaps might even get over the wall and—I woke up—almost screaming.'

The woman's face was quite blanched.

'My dear,' remonstrated Constance, 'you must not take it so. Remember—it was only a dream.'

'I know it was only a dream,' she said, 'but you don't know what is behind it.'

Mildred Caswell had from time to time hinted to Constance of the growing incompatibility of her married life, but as Constance was getting used to confidences, she had kept silent, knowing that her friend would tell her in time.

'You must have guessed,' faltered Mrs Caswell, 'that Forest and I are not—not on the best of terms, that we are getting further and further apart.'

It rather startled Constance to hear frankly stated what she already had observed. She wondered how far the estrangement had gone. The fact was that she had rather liked deForest Caswell, although she had only met her friend's husband a few times. In fact she was surprised that momentarily there flashed through her mind the query as to whether Mildred herself might be altogether blameless in the growing uncongeniality.

Mildred Caswell had drawn out of her chatelaine a bit of newspaper and handed it to Constance, not as if it was of any importance to herself but as if it would explain better than she could tell what she meant.

Constance read:

MME. CASSANDRA,
THE VEILED PROPHETESS

Born with a double caul educated in occult mysteries in Egypt and India. Without asking a question, tells your name and reads your secret troubles and the remedy. Reads your dreams. Great questions of life quickly solved. Failure turned to success, the separated brought together, advice on all affairs of life, love, marriage, divorce, business, speculation, and investments. Overcomes all evil influences. Ever ready to help and advise those with capital to find a safe and paying investment. No fee until it succeeds. Could anything be fairer?

THE RETREAT,
——*W. 47th Street.*

'Won't you come with me to Madame Cassandra?' asked Mrs Caswell, as Constance finished reading. 'She always seems to do me so much good.'

'Who is Madame Cassandra?' asked Constance, re-reading the last part of the advertisement.

'I suppose you would call her a dream doctor,' said Mildred.

It was a new idea to Constance, this of a dream doctor to settle the affairs of life. Only a moment she hesitated, then she answered simply, 'Yes, I'll go.'

'The Retreat' was just off Longacre Square among quite a nest of swindlers. A queue of motor cars before the place testified, however, to the prosperity of Madame Cassandra, as they entered the bronze-grilled, plate-glass door and turned on the first floor toward the home of the Adept. As they entered Constance had an uncomfortable feeling of being watched from behind the shades of the apartment. Still, they had no trouble in being admitted, and a soft-voiced coloured attendant welcomed them.

The esoteric flat of Madame Cassandra was darkened, except for the electric lights glowing in amber and rose-coloured shades. There were several women there already. As they entered Constance had noticed a peculiar, dreamy odour. There did not seem to be any hurry, any such thing as time here, so skilfully was the place run. There was no noise; the feet sank in half-inch piles of rugs, and easy-chairs and divans were scattered about.

Puffs of light smoke arose here and there, and Constance awoke to the fact that some were smoking little delicately gold-banded cigarettes. Indeed it was all quite recherché.

Mrs Caswell took one from a maid. So did Constance, but, after a puff or two, managed to put it out, and, later, to secure another, which she kept.

Madame Cassandra herself proved to be a tall, slender, pale woman with dark hair and magnetic eyes—eyes that probably accounted more than anything else for her success. She was clad in a house gown of purplish silk, which clung tightly to her. At her throat a diamond pendant sparkled, while other brilliants adorned her long, slender fingers.

She met Mildred and Constance with outstretched hands.

'So glad to see you, my dears,' purred Madame, leading the way into an inner sanctum.

Mrs Caswell had seated herself with the air of one who worshipped at the shrine, while Constance gazed about curiously.

'Madame,' began Mrs Caswell a little tremulously, 'I have had another of those dreadful dreams.'

'You poor, dear soul,' soothed Madame, stroking her hand. 'Tell me of it—all.'

Quickly Mrs Caswell poured forth her story as she had already told it to Constance.

'My dear Mrs Caswell,' remarked the high priestess slowly, when the story was complete, 'it is all very simple. His love is dead. That is what you fear, and it is the truth. The wall is the wall that he has erected against you. Try to forget it—to forget him. You would be better off. There are other things in the world—'

'Ah, but I cannot live as I am used to, without money,' murmured Mrs Caswell.

'I know,' replied Madame. 'It is that that keeps many a woman with a brute. When financial and economic independence comes, then woman will be free, and only then. Now, listen. Would you like to be free—financially? You remember that delightful Mr Davies who has been here? Yes? Well, he is a regular client of mine now. He is a broker, and never embarks in any enterprise without first consulting me. Just the other day I read his fortune in United Traction. It has gone up five points already and will go fifteen more. If you like, I will give you a card to him. Let me see—yes, I can do that. You too will be lucky in speculation.'

Constance, with one ear open, had been busy looking about the room. In a bookcase she saw a number of books and paused to examine their titles. She was surprised to see among the old style dream books several works on modern psychology, particularly on the interpretation of dreams.

'Of course, Mrs Caswell, I don't want to urge you,' Madame was saying. 'I have only pointed out a way in which you can be independent. And, you know, Mr Davies is a perfect gentleman; so courteous and reliable. I know you will be successful if you take my advice and go to him.'

Mildred said nothing for a few moments, but as she rose to go she remarked, 'Thank you very much. I'll think about it. Anyhow, you've made me feel better.'

'So kind of you to say that,' murmured the Adept. 'I'm sorry you must go, but really I have other appointments. Please come again—with your friend. Goodbye.'

'What do you think of her?' asked Mrs Caswell as they gained the street.

'Very clever,' answered Constance dubiously.

Mrs Caswell looked up quickly. 'You don't like her?'

'To tell the truth,' confessed Constance quietly, 'I have had too much experience in Wall Street myself to trust to a clairvoyant.'

They had scarcely reached the corner before Constance again had that peculiar feeling, which some psychologists have noted, of being stared at. She turned, but saw no one. Still the feeling persisted. She could stand it no longer.

'Don't think me crazy, Mildred,' she said, 'but I just have a desire to walk back a block.'

Constance had turned suddenly. As she glanced keenly about she was aware of a familiar figure gazing into the window of an art store across the street. He had stopped so that, although his back was turned, he could, by a slight change of position, still see, by means of a mirror in the window, what was going on across the street behind him.

One look was enough. It was Drummond, the detective. What did it mean?

Restless, Constance determined that night to go down to the Public Library and see whether any of the books at the clairvoyant's were on the shelves. Fortunately she found some—found, indeed, that they were not all, as she had half suspected, the works of frauds, but that quite a literature had been built up around the new psychology of dreams.

Deeply she delved into the fascinating subjects that had been opened by the studies of the famous Dr Sigmund Freud of Vienna, and, as she read, she began to understand much about Mrs Caswell—and, with a start, about her own self.

At first she revolted against the unpleasant feature of the new dream philosophy—the irresistible conclusion that all humanity, underneath the shell, is sensuous or sensual in nature; that practically all dreams portray some delight of the senses and that sensuous dreams are a large proportion of all visions. But, the more she thought of it, the more clearly was she able to analyse Mrs Caswell's dream and to get at the causes of it: in the estrangement from her husband and perhaps the brutality arising from his ignorance of woman.

She did not see Mildred Caswell again until the following afternoon. But then she seemed unusually bright in contrast with the depression of the day before. Constance was not surprised. Her intuition told her that something had happened, and she hardly needed to guess that Mrs Caswell had followed the advice of the clairvoyant and had been to see the wonderful Mr Davies, to whom the mysteries of the stock market were an open book.

'Have you had any other dreams?' asked Constance casually.

'Yes,' replied Mildred, 'but not like the one that depressed me. Last night I had a very pleasant dream. It seemed that I was breakfasting with Mr Davies. I remember that there was a hot coal fire in the grate. Then suddenly a messenger came in with news that United Traction had advanced twenty points. Wasn't it strange?'

Constance said nothing. In fact it did not seem strange to her at all. The strange thing to her, now that she was a sort of amateur dream reader herself, was that Mrs Caswell did not seem to see the real import of her own dream.

'You have seen Mr Davies today?' Constance ventured.

Mrs Caswell laughed. 'I wasn't going to tell you. You seemed so set against speculating in Wall Street. But since you ask me, I may as well admit it.'

'When did you see him before?' went on Constance. 'Did you have much invested with him already?'

Mrs Caswell glanced up, startled. 'My—you are positively uncanny, Constance. How did you know I had seen him before?'

'One seldom dreams,' said Constance, 'about anything unless it has been suggested by an event of the day before. You saw him today. That would not have inspired the dream of last night. Therefore I concluded that you must have seen him and invested before. Madame Cassandra's mention of him yesterday caused the dream of last night. The dream of last night probably influenced you to see him again today, and you invested in United Traction. That is the way dreams work. Probably more of conduct than we know is influenced by dream life. Now, if you should get fifteen or twenty points you would be in a fair way to join the ranks of those who believe that dreams do come true.'

Mrs Caswell looked at her almost alarmed, then attempted to turn it off with a laugh, 'And perhaps breakfast with him?'

'When I do set up as interpreter of dreams,' answered Constance simply, 'I'll tell you more.'

On one point she had made up her mind. That was to visit Mr Davies herself the next day.

She found his office a typical bucket shop, even down to having a section partitioned off for women clients of the firm. She had not intended to risk anything, and so was prepared when Mr Davies himself approached her courteously. Instinctively Constance distrusted him. He was too cordial, too polite. She could feel the claws hidden in his velvety paw, as it were. There was a debonair assurance about him, the air of a man who thought he understood women, and indeed did understand a certain type. But to Constance, who was essentially a man's woman, Davies was only revolting.

She managed to talk without committing herself, and he in his complacency was glad to hope that he was making a new customer. She had to be careful not to betray any of the real and extensive knowledge about Wall Street which she actually possessed. But the glib misrepresentations about United Traction quite amazed her.

When she rose to go, Davies accompanied her to the door, then out into the hall to the elevator. As he bent over to shake hands, she noted that he held her hand just a little longer than was necessary.

'He's a swindler of the first water,' she concluded as she was whisked down in the elevator. 'I'm sure Mildred is in badly with this crowd, one urging her on in her trouble, the other making it worse and fleecing her into the bargain.'

At the entrance she paused, undecided which was the quickest route home. As by chance she turned just for a moment she thought she caught a fleeting glimpse of Drummond dodging behind a pillar. It was only for an instant but even that apparition was enough.

'I *will* get her out of this safely,' resolved Constance. 'I *will* keep one more fly from his web.'

Constance felt as if even now, she must see Mildred and, although she knew nothing, at least put her on her guard. She did not have long to wait for her chance. It was late in the afternoon when her doorbell sounded.

'Constance, I've been looking for you all day?' sighed Mildred, dropping sobbing into a chair. 'I am—distracted.'

'Why, my dear, what's the matter?' asked Constance. 'Let me make you a cup of coffee?'

Over the steaming little cups Mildred grew more calm.

'Forest has found out in some way that I am speculating in Wall Street,' she confided at length. 'I suppose some of his friends—he has lots down there—told him.'

Momentarily the picture of Drummond back of the post in Davies' building flashed over Constance.

'And he is awfully angry. Oh, I never new him to be so angry—and sarcastic, too.'

'Was it wholly over your money?' asked Constance. 'Was there nothing else?'

Mrs Caswell started. 'You grow more weird, every day, Constance. Yes—there was something else.'

'Mr Davies?'

Mildred had risen. 'Don't—don't—' she cried.

'Then you do really—care for him?' asked Constance mercilessly.

'No—no, a thousand times—no. How can I? I have put all such thoughts out of my mind—long ago.' She paused, then went on more calmly, 'Constance, believe me or not—I am just as good a woman today as I was the day I married Forest. No—I would not even let the thought enter my head—never!'

For perhaps an hour after her friend had gone, Constance sat thinking. What should she do? Something must be done and soon. As she thought, suddenly the truth flashed over her.

Caswell had employed Drummond to shadow his wife in the hope that he might unearth something that might lead to a divorce. Drummond, like so many divorce detectives, was not averse to guiding events, to put it mildly. He had ingratiated himself, perhaps, with the clairvoyant and Davies. Constance had often heard before of clairvoyants and brokers who worked in conjunction to fleece the credulous. Now another and more serious element than the loss of money was involved. Added to them was a divorce detective—and honour itself was at stake. She remembered the drugged cigarettes. She had heard of them before at clairvoyants'. She saw it all—Madame Cassandra playing on Mildred's wounded affections, the broker on both that and her desire to be independent—and Drummond pulling the wires that all might take advantage of her woman's frailty.

That moment Constance determined on action.

First, she telephoned to deForest Caswell at his office. It was an unconventional thing to do to ask him to call, but she made some plausible pretext. She was surprised to find that he accepted it without hesitating. It set her thinking. Drummond must have told him something of her and he had thought this as good a time as any to face her. In that case Drummond would probably come too. She was prepared.

She had intended to have one last talk with Mildred, but had no need to call her. Utterly wretched, the poor little woman came in again to see her as she had done scores of times before, to pour out her heart. Forest had not come home to dinner, had not even taken the trouble to telephone. Constance did not say that she herself was responsible.

'Do you really want to know the truth about your dreams?' asked Constance, after she had prevailed upon Mildred to eat a little.

'I do know,' she returned.

'No, you don't,' went on Constance, now determined to tell her the truth whether she liked it or not. 'That clairvoyant and Mr Davies are in league, playing you for a "sucker", as they say.'

Mrs Caswell did not reply for a moment. Then she drew a long breath and shut her eyes. 'Oh, you don't know how true what she says is to me. She——'

'Listen,' interrupted Constance. 'Mildred, I'm going to be frank,

175

brutally frank. Madame Cassandra has read your character, not the character as you think it is, but your unconscious, subconscious self. She knows that there is no better way to enter into the intimate life of a client, according to the new psychology, than by getting at and analyzing the dreams. And she knows that you can't go far in dream analysis without finding sex. It is one of the strongest natural impulses—though subject to the strongest repression—and hence one of the weakest points of our culture.

'She is actually helping along your alienation for that broker. You yourself have given me the clue in your dreams. Only I am telling you the truth about them. She holds it back and tells you plausible false-hoods to help her own ends. She is trying to arouse in you those passions which you have suppressed, and she has not scrupled to use drugged cigarettes with you and others to do it. You remember the breakfast dream, when I said that much could be traced back to dreams? A thing happens. It causes a dream. That in turn sometimes causes action. No, don't interrupt. Let me finish.

'Take that first dream,' continued Constance, rapidly thrusting home her interpretation so that it would have its full effect. 'You dreamed that your husband was dying and you were afraid. She said it meant love was dead. It did not. The fact is that neurotic fear in a woman has its origin in repressed, unsatisfied love, love which for one reason or another is turned away from its object and has not suc-ceeded in being applied. Then his death. That simply means that you have a feeling that you might be happier if he were away and didn't devil you. It is a survival of childhood, when death is synonymous with absence. I know you don't believe it. But if you had studied the subject as I have in the last few days you'd understand. Madame Cassandra understands.

'And the wall. That was Wall Street, probably, which does divide you two. You tried to get over it and you fell. That means your fear of actually falling, morally, of being a fallen woman.'

Mildred was staring wildly. She might deny but in her heart she must admit.

'The thing that pursued you, half bull, half snake, was Davies and his blandishments. I have seen him. I know what he is. The crowd in a dream always denotes a secret. He is pursuing you, as in the dream.

But he hasn't caught you. He thinks there is in you the same wild demimondaine instinct that with many an ardent woman slumbers unknown in the back of her mind.

'Whatever you may say, you do think of him. When a woman dreams of breakfasting cozily with someone other than her husband it has an obvious meaning. As for the messenger and the message about the United Traction, there, too, was a plain wish, and, as you must see, wishes in one form or another, disguised or distorted, lie at the basis of dreams. Take the coal fire. That, too, is susceptible of interpretation. I think you must have heard the couplet:

> ' "No coal, no fire so hotly glows
> As the sceret love that no one knows." '

Mildred Caswell had risen, an indignant flush on her face.

Constance put her hand on her arm gently to restrain her, knowing that such indignation was the first sign that she had struck at the core of truth in her interpretation.

'My dear,' she urged, 'I'm only telling you the truth, for your own sake, and not to take advantage of you as Madame Cassandra is doing. Please—remember that the best evidence of your normal condition is just what I find, that absence of love would be abnormal. My dear, you are what the psychologists call a consciously frigid, unconsciously passionate woman. Consciously you reject this Davies; unconsciously you accept him. And it is the more dangerous, although you do not know it, because someone else is watching. It was not one of his friends who told your husband——'

Mrs Caswell had paled. 'Is—is there a—detective?' she faltered.

Constance nodded.

Mildred had collapsed completely. She was sobbing in a chair, her head bowed in her hands, her little lace handkerchief soaked. 'What shall I do? What shall I do?'

There was a sudden tap at the door.

'Quick—in there,' whispered Constance, shoving her through the portières into the drawing room.

It was Forest Caswell.

For a moment Constance stood irresolute, wondering just how to meet him, then she said, 'Good evening, Mr Caswell. I hope you will pardon me for asking you to call on me, but, as you know, I've come to know your wife—perhaps better than you do.'

'Not better,' he corrected, seeming to see that it was directness that she was aiming at. 'It is bad enough to get mixed up badly in Wall Street, but what would you yourself say—you are a business woman—what would you say about getting into the clutches of a—a dream doctor—and worse?'

He had put Constance on the defensive in a sentence.

'Don't you ever dream?' she asked quietly.

He looked at her a moment as if doubting even her mentality.

'Lord,' he exclaimed in disgust, 'you, too, defend it?'

'But, don't you dream?' she persisted.

'Why, of course I dream,' he answered somewhat petulantly. 'What of it? I don't guide my actions by it.'

'Do you ever dream of Mildred?' she asked.

'Sometimes,' he admitted reluctantly.

'Ever of other—er—people?' she pursued.

'Yes,' he replied, 'sometimes of other people. But what has that to do with it? I cannot help my dreams. My conduct I can help, and I do help.'

Constance had not expected him to be frank to the extent of taking her into his confidence. Still, she felt that he had told her just enough. She discerned a vague sense of jealousy in his tone which told her more than words that whatever he might have said or done to Mildred he resented, unconsciously, the manner in which she had striven to gain sympathy outside.

'Fortunately he knows nothing of the new theories,' she said to herself.

'Mrs Dunlap,' he resumed, 'since you have been frank with me, I must be equally frank with you. I think you are far too sensible a woman not to understand in just what a peculiar position my wife has placed me.'

He had taken out of his pocket a few sheets of closely typewritten tissue paper. He did not look at them. Evidently he knew the contents by heart. Constance did not need to be told that this was a sheaf of the daily reports of the agency for which Drummond worked.

He paused. She had been watching him searchingly. She was determined not to let him justify himself first.

'Mr Caswell,' she persisted in a low, earnest tone, 'don't be so sure that there is nothing in this dream business. Before you read me those reports from Mr Drummond, let me finish.'

Forest Caswell almost dropped them in surprise.

'Dreams,' she continued, seeing her advantage, 'are wishes, either suppressed or expressed. Sometimes the dream is frank and shows an expressed wish. Other times it shows a suppressed wish, or a wish which in its fulfilment in the dream is disguised or distorted.

'You are the cause of your wife's dreams. She feels in them anxiety. And, according to the modern psychologists who have studied dreams carefully and scientifically, fear and anxiety represent love repressed or suppressed.'

She paused to emphasize the point, glad to note that he was following her.

'That clairvoyant,' she went on, 'has found out the truth. True, it may not have been the part of wisdom for Mildred to have gone to her in the first place. I pass over that. I do not know whether you or she was most to blame at the start. But that woman, in the guise of being her friend, has played on every string of your wife's lonely heart, which you have wrung until it vibrates.

'Then,' she hastened on, 'came your precious friend Drummond—Drummond who has, no doubt, told you a pack of lies about me. You see that?'

She had flung down on the table a cigarette which she had managed to get at Madame Cassandra's.

'Smoke it.'

He lighted it gingerly, took a puff or two, puckered his face, frowned, and rubbed the lighted end on the fireplace to extinguish it.

'What is it?' he asked suspiciously.

'Hashish,' she answered tersely. 'Things were not going fast enough to suit either Madame Cassandra or Drummond. Madame Cassandra helped along the dreams by a drug noted for its effect on the passions. More than that,' added Constance, leaning over toward him and catching his eye, 'Madame Cassandra was working in league with a broker, as so many of these swindlers do. Drummond knew it, whether he told you the truth about it or not. That broker was named Davies.'

She was watching the effect on him. She saw that he had been reserving this for a last shot at her, that he realized she had stolen his own ammunition and appropriated it to herself.

'They were only too glad when Drummond approached them. There you are, three against that poor little woman—no, four, including yourself. Perhaps she was foolish. But it was not so much to her discredit as to that of those who cast her adrift when she had a natural right to protection. Here was a woman with passions which she herself did not understand, and a little money—alone. Her case appealed to me. I knew her dreams. I studied them.'

Caswell was listening in amazement. 'It is dangerous to be with a person who pays attention to such little things,' he said.

Evidently Drummond himself must have been listening. The door buzzer sounded and he stepped in, perhaps to bolster up his client in case he should be weakening.

As he met Constance's eye he smiled superciliously and was about to speak. But she did not give him time even to say good evening.

'Ask him,' she cried, her eyes flashing, for she realized that it had been part of the plan to confront her, perhaps worm out of her just enough to confirm Drummond's own story to Caswell, 'ask him to tell the truth—if he is capable of it—not the truth that will make a good daily report of a hired shadow who colours his report the way he thinks his client desires it, but the real truth.'

'Mr Caswell,' interrupted Drummond, 'this woman——'

'Mr Drummond,' cried Constance, rising and shaking the burnt stub of the little gold-banded cigarette at him to impress it on his mind, 'Mr Drummond, I don't care whether I am a—a she-devil'—she almost hissed the words at him—'but I have evidence enough to go before the district attorney of this city and the grand jury and get indictments for conspiracy against a certain clairvoyant and a bucket-shop operator. To save themselves, they will probably tell all they know about a certain crook who has been using them.'

Caswell looked at her, amazed at her denunciation of the detective. As for Drummond, he turned his back on her as if to ignore her utterly.

'Mr Caswell,' he said bitterly, 'in those reports——'

'Forest Caswell,' insisted Constance, rising and facing him, 'if you have in that heart of yours one shred of manhood it should move you. You—this man—the others—have placed in the path of a woman every provocation, every temptation for financial, physical, and moral ruin. She has consulted a clairvoyant—yes. She has speculated—yes. Yet she was proof against something greater than that. And I know— because I know her unconscious self which her dreams reveal, her inmost soul—I know her better than you do, better than she does herself. I know that even now she is as good and true and would be as loving as—'

Constance had paused and taken a step toward the drawing room. Before she knew it, the portières flew apart and an eager little woman had rushed past her and flung her arms about the neck of the man.

Caswell's features were working, as he gently disengaged her arms, still keeping one hand. Half shoving her aside, ignoring Constance, he had faced Drummond. For a moment the brazen detective flinched.

As he did so, deForest Caswell crumpled up the mass of tissue paper reports and flung them into the fireplace.

'Get out!' he said, suppressing his voice with difficulty. 'Send me— your bill. I'll pay it—but, mind, if it is one penny more than it should be, I'll—I'll fight if it takes me from the district attorney and the grand jury to the highest court of the State. Now—go!'

Caswell turned slowly again toward his wife.

'I've been a brute,' he said simply.

Something almost akin to jealousy rose in Constance's heart as she saw Mildred, safe at last.

Then Caswell turned slowly to her. 'You,' he said, stroking his wife's hand gently, but looking at Constance, 'you are a *real* clairvoyant.'

10

F. TENNYSON JESSE

Lot's Wife

THE hotel was full of just the sort of people you expect to find at hotels. There were the knitting women—grimmer than those harridans who knitted by the guillotine; there were Bright Young Things—to some minds grimmer still. There were family parties with small children who whooped up and down the corridors all day, and screamed when they had to go to bed. There were young men twirling Gallic moustaches and eyeing the smart ladies who sat about in bathing dresses, their slim brown legs unafraid of the eye of man or of the sun.

Solange decided that though within the hotel all was horrible, yet out of doors, in spite of endless motor cars along the highway, all was beautiful. After a winter in England most things would have been beautiful to Solange, but indeed the loveliness of this unspoiled Mediterranean Gulf would have pleased a far more exacting taste than was hers at the moment.

And then, as though to complete the charm, and reward Solange for sordid experiences of the immediate past, beauty was added even to life in the hotel. A young Scottish girl, Flora MacTavish, arrived with her mother, and Flora was one of those rare beings upon whom the eye can rest with endless enchantment. She was young and very fair without being insipid, high of cheek-bone, but with exquisitely tender and full lips. Her clear water-grey eyes were almond-shaped, with a fine line of fair brows set high above them. She was almost too thin for her height, and she more nearly resembled Botticelli's Venus than any human being Solange had ever known.

Foreheads were 'in' again, and Flora's was high, so high that it would have been thought incredibly dowdy, and would have been covered only a few years earlier. That high forehead, the almond-shaped eyes and long delicious nose, that tender mouth, pointed chin, and long thick neck were, so Solange told herself delightedly, not only complete Botticelli, but entirely the fashion of the moment as well. Flora MacTavish was one of those fortunate people who happen to be just right for the period in which they live.

Solange gazed, envied, and admired, for Flora, besides possessing that subtle disproportion which means beauty, had charm. She was not intellectual, but she had that fundamental mixture of sweetness and iron-hard determination possessed by all truly womanly women. Had her bones not been so small, she might have looked thin to angularity, and had her nature not been sweet and unselfish, her mind would have been thin to angularity also. Her ideas were very much at the mercy of anyone whom she met; she was both fluid and obstinate. Compact of honey and rose and pearl, her fundamental sturdiness was only betrayed by her high cheek-bones and a certain way she had of setting her soft, full lips.

She was one of those girls who are perhaps ill-advised to travel with their mothers, for it was possible to see, almost lost in Mrs MacTavish's pink and white cushiony plumpness, in her large bosom and fat, dimpled hands, something of Flora's beauty. Flora, in fact, travelled about with her own future, but she was so enchanting that it took someone with an eye as well trained as was that of Solange to discover it.

Solange made friends with the MacTavishes, not because she thought they would interest her, but simply so that she could have an excuse for looking at Flora, and the more she grew to know her, the more delicious the girl appeared. Her high, clear, fluting voice, her swift rippling movements, the sudden stillnesses into which her long limbs fell, were in keeping with the sophisticated simplicity of her appearance. There was nothing of the ingénue, nothing of the pretty milkmaid, about Flora.

As the days went by, and Professor Fontaine's house, where he and Solange were hoping to spend the summer months, still remained impossible, owing to alterations in the bathroom and the dilatory habits of workpeople in the south, Solange grew more and more to depend for her daily interest on her intercourse with the MacTavishes.

Flora MacTavish might not be a stimulating companion for the mind, but she was a delight for the eye. And then, almost before she realized it, Solange began to be aware that there was some strange undercurrent of feeling upsetting the minds of both mother and daughter, and at once her interest was alert. For several days Flora only appeared at dinner in the evening, and on those occasions Mrs MacTavish would ask Solange to lunch at her table. Flora was out with a friend, she would say, the pursing of her lips not unlike Flora's own little unconscious action. Almost without realizing the fact, Solange knew that Mrs MacTavish disapproved of this friend. Flora herself would flicker through the hotel like a lovely eager flame just in time for dinner, her long, grey eyes shining, her pointed chin tilted up on that long, thick neck of a Botticelli nymph, and during dinner and afterwards she would be aloof and secret, yet alight.

One day Mrs MacTavish broke down, though with evident diffi-culty, her Scottish habit of reticence and confided her anxieties to Solange over the luncheon table where Flora had left them to a tête-à-tête meal.

'She is my only one, Miss Fontaine, and I am so worried I don't know what to do. It is a man, of course. All the trouble in the world is made by men. If I had my way, I really believe I'd shut them all up in monasteries, or something.'

Solange, refraining from pointing out that had this excellent method of settling the sex problem obtained some twenty years ago, there would have been no Flora to worry a devoted mother, nodded sympathy, and Mrs MacTavish, her plump face creased with worry, poured out all her trouble. Flora was in love, and the man she loved was, for all he knew to the contrary, a married man.

'How do you mean, "for all he knows to the contrary"? asked Solange interested.

'His wife ran away,' said Mrs MacTavish. 'It's over a year ago now, and although I believe he spent money like water trying to find her, he hasn't succeeded. Not that he wants her back again, you understand; he is in love with my Flora right enough. I never saw a man so mad over a girl, but, naturally, if his wife's still alive, he wants to know it and arrange a divorce; and if the poor thing's dead, why, then I suppose he and Flora could marry right away. Not that I'm keen on it. I'd sooner my girl didn't marry a widower. But then,' added Mrs MacTavish, 'I don't suppose she'd be the first, even if he hadn't been married, if you know what I mean.'

'What's the man like?' asked Solange. 'What does he do? Is he a Frenchman?'

'No, he's an Englishman, though I will say he's a Scot on his mother's side. His name's Angus Martin, and he's a painter, and he's built a big house down on the shore near here. I don't know that he does anything in particular except paint. He's travelled a lot. He's very well-off, and they all say he's very clever. Designed this house himself and supervised the building of it, which goodness knows you need to do in these parts if your house is ever to get finished at all. But he's forty if he's a day, which I think is too old for Flora, though she's always liked men a good bit older than herself, and been bored with boys, so perhaps that doesn't matter much. Oh, no; it's not his age or even his being a widower that I mind. It's that we don't know if he's a widower or not, and I feel he ought to leave Flora alone until he's made sure of his position; but she's mad about him and won't listen to anything I say.'

'But what does she hope to do? Obviously they can't be married until they can find proof that his wife's dead.'

'Exactly, Miss Fontaine, and why I've told you about it is that, having got to know you has given Flora and Mr Martin an idea. In fact, when she told him you were here, he asked me to tell you all about it today. We are simple people, Miss Fontaine, and haven't mixed in what you might call the great world much, but we've heard of you and seen your name in the papers now and again. Mr Martin thinks that you will be able to find out whether his wife is alive or dead.'

'That's not my sort of work,' said Solange doubtfully. 'Do you know what there is to go on, Mrs MacTavish?'

'Very little, I believe. They had some kind of tiff. It appears they were quarrelling and she just went off one night. That's really all I know about it, but I expect he'll be able to tell you some more. Flora's going to ask him to come to dinner tonight.'

Solange had never met anyone who puzzled her so completely as did Angus Martin. Usually she either liked or disliked people, either responded warmly to all the good she felt in them, or was warned by that curious instinct of hers of some inherent evil which perhaps had remained undetected by anyone else for a lifetime.

Now she was at a loss and ruefully admitted it to herself. She could not say that she had with Angus Martin that overpowering awareness of something wrong which had so often warned her of a criminal, but neither did she feel the man was good and honest.

Angus was a tall, quiet, studious-looking individual, with a lean, interesting face. His dark grey eyes were deep-set, the eyes of a thinker, and would have been altogether pleasing had they not been set too close together. He had very beautiful hands, with long, finely shaped fingers, and his dark hair had that touch of silver at the temples which is supposed to be so fascinating to young women. Certainly Flora was fascinated, though whether by his distinguished personality or because she really knew some special fineness and goodness that was latent in his character, Solange could not guess.

Dinner might easily have been an awkward meal considering that all four of the diners knew of Angus Martin's invidious position, and of Mrs MacTavish's disapproval; and yet so charming in his quiet way—for there was nothing flamboyant about him—was Angus, so like a clear and flickering flame was Flora, that they both seemed to transcend any commonplace awkwardness that more ordinary people might have been unable to dispel.

There was no doubt, Solange admitted, that he was as madly in love with Flora as she with him. The complete round of the love emotion is a very rare thing. To find passion, mental sympathy, and physical suitability in one relationship is asking a good deal of life, but that Angus and Flora, despite the dissimilarity of their ages, had found it, it was impossible to doubt. Then why is it, Solange asked herself disgustedly, that I feel there is something wrong somewhere? It was to be many months before she was to find the answer to that question.

Not until dinner was over and they were taking their coffee under the bottle-palms in the garden, did Angus refer to the reason of the meeting, and then so simply and quietly that Solange found herself forced into admiration. Forced, she thought to herself, that's what's so funny. I resent liking and admiring him.

'I want you to know my story, Miss Fontaine,' he said, as he leant forward and lit her cigarette for her, 'because I am sure you are the person to help me.'

He smiled suddenly at Solange, and his smile was so charming in his ordinarily sombre face that in a flash Solange could see why it was that the fastidious Flora loved him.

'If you have finished your coffee,' he went on, 'perhaps you will come and walk through the gardens with me? I think it is easier to talk, don't you, when there are only two of you, and when you are moving about? Sitting still is all right for ordinary conversation, but it is no good for confidences.'

Solange drew her silk Chinese shawl round her shoulders, and, with a little smile of reassurance at Flora, obeyed his request.

His face became grave again when they were alone together amidst the pine trees. He told his story with the simplicity combined with attention to detail that shows a careful and acute mind.

He had married, when a young art student, a woman considerably older than himself, who had been his model. The marriage had not proved a happy one. He did not blame his wife in any way, he said; doubtless he was difficult to get on with, but the fact remained that they had been totally unsuited to each other. Things had not been so bad while they had been poor, but when some four or five years ago an unexpected legacy from a distant relation had made him a rich man, matters had gone from bad to worse. When she no longer had to do her own housework, Mrs Martin became thoroughly bored, and one of his reasons for completing his villa on this unfrequented part of the coast—for, a year ago, when he had been building, the place was practically undiscovered—had been that he preferred to keep his troubles to himself.

They moved into the villa when one wing of it was ready for occupation, and at first she had seemed pleased with her new home and had busied herself with putting it in order. However, one evening they had had a terrible quarrel:

'Really, Miss Fontaine, I can't remember what it was about. I know it started over something absurdly small. I hadn't admired a new hat she'd bought, or she thought a criticism I had made of the dinner was levelled at her instead of at the cook. You know how these things start—a few drops of bitterness trickle out which seem negligible, and

then suddenly one is overwhelmed by a dark and dreadful torrent.'
His face had paled, and for a moment he placed his long, sensitive
hand over his eyes.

'And then?' prompted Solange.

'Well, and then she went. It still seems incredible to me when I
think of it. I didn't expect to see her early next morning; she always
had breakfast in her room and never came downstairs till lunchtime. I
slept late myself, for I was tired and upset. I waited lunch for her, and
when she still didn't come I sent one of the maids up to her room. She
was not there, the bed had not been slept in, and some of her clothes
had gone.'

'Which clothes? The clothes she'd been wearing the night before?'

'Those and others as well. A travelling suit and a blouse and hat—
all the usual sort of things women travel in.'

'Had the car been taken out of the garage?'

'No, I think she must have left by one of the motor-buses that pass
my garden gate at frequent intervals. By that she could have got to
St Raphael and there boarded a train.'

'But surely,' said Solange, 'if she had left that morning one of the
servants would have seen her go out of the house?'

'The servants don't sleep in the villa, but in the *dépendance*.'

'The motor-buses don't run at night, do they?'

'No, but there's one very early in the morning.'

'Had anyone seen her on it?'

'No one could remember her, but the bus was very full of people
going in to market, and my wife spoke French perfectly. We had lived
many years in Paris.'

'Did she ever write to you? Or ask for money?'

'Yes, she wrote asking for money to be sent in English banknotes to
Poste Restante, Charing Cross. I sent her £100.'

'Did you take the numbers of the notes?'

'Yes, but you will be able to trace the transaction at the bank at
St Raphael. They got the notes for me.'

'Did she acknowledge them?'

'Yes, and a couple of months later I got a note from her written
from a house in Hereford Road, Bayswater, where she said she was
very ill in lodgings. I had by then just met Flora. You can see what she

is, Miss Fontaine, and won't be surprised to know that I loved her at once. I am not a man who has frittered himself away in light emotions, and I may say I had never loved before or realized in the least what it could be. I can only tell you that life will have no meaning for me if I can't marry Flora.

'When I got this letter from my wife I set off at once for the address she had given me, and arrived in London the following evening. I found my wife looking ill, but not desperately ill, though she had a nasty cough. I was sorry to see her so run down, and told her so. I offered to make, within reason, any settlement she liked if she would let me divorce her, or would divorce me. She promised to think it over and asked me to come again two days later. I trusted her, paid a lot of money—a thousand pounds—into her bank, and tried to possess my soul in patience for forty-eight hours.

'When I returned to Hereford Road she had gone, having closed her banking account and drawn all the money out of her bank. She must have bribed the landlady well, or won her sympathy in some way, for she refused to give me the slightest idea where she had gone; in fact, she said she didn't know, which may have been true, but my opinion is that landladies are invariably curious sort of people and study addresses on labels and that sort of thing. I went nearly distracted, and when I got back to my hotel I found a letter from my wife. It bore the Portsmouth postmark, and simply said she had no intention of doing me such a good turn as setting me free to marry another woman; the money I'd given her would last a nice time, and that when she wanted more she would communicate with me again.

'Well, I have lived in hopes that she would. I have more money than I know what to do with now that it's no good to me, but I have never heard from that day to this. That is my story, Miss Fontaine, and if you can prove that my wife is dead—which I think must be the case; or she'd have tried to get more money from me—you can name your own fee. If she is alive, perhaps she will consent to the divorce by now. Anyway, I want the matter settled one way or another. I can't go on like this.'

Solange studied him and saw that that was true. His face seemed to have set into lines of suffering, as he told his story, and his hand was shaking a little as he took a cigarette out of his case.

'But what do you want me to do?' she asked.

'I want you to go and see what you can get out of the landlady. I believe she knows something, and though *I* can't get it out of her, *you* might be able to. I need hardly tell you that the question of expense doesn't enter in. For Heaven's sake, find out where my wife is!'

They were walking slowly back towards the hotel by now, and already Solange could see Flora approaching them between the trees, her frock gleaming through the dusk. Solange glanced at Angus and saw that his eyes were fixed on Flora with such a look of hunger in them as startled her. It was so avid, so naked, so primitive in such a quiet and highly civilized being. She felt extremely interested in both him and Flora, and made up her mind swiftly.

'Give me the name and address of the landlady, and a description of your wife, and I can start tomorrow,' she said, not without a feeling of relief that she was going to have a respite from the hotel and its denizens.

Solange found the Hereford Road landlady less adamant than had Angus Martin. Perhaps this was because Solange represented herself as being Mrs Martin's niece, anxious to find her and do her best for her. Perhaps it was because of the two ten-pound notes that she crackled between her fingers alluringly, or perhaps it was because of the bottle of port that she sent out to fetch from the nearest public-house on making the discovery that the landlady, being a teetotaller, could only drink port.

'Poor lady,' observed Mrs Smithson pityingly, as she finished her third glass. 'If ever I saw death in any woman's face, it was in hers, miss. I don't need any doctors to tell me what I can see for myself. *I know*. Wasting away with consumption she was, and, of course, London wasn't the best place for her. "I'll never get better, Mrs Smithson", she says to me, for she treated me very friendly and like a sister, as you might say—"I'll never get better, and I'm bound to get worse, but at least I'm going to do it in the best surroundings", and so off she went, and I packed for her with my own hands. The boxes were labelled for Portsmouth, but more than that I couldn't tell the gentleman, because I didn't know any more, and I couldn't tell you any more either, miss, only that I had a postcard from her yesterday, and I think, perhaps, in spite of my having promised not to tell, I really ought to, for her own sake.'

Yesterday! Solange felt she was indeed in luck. Chance, without which a detective is so often powerless, seemed to be on her side.

'Indeed, I ought to know where my aunt is, Mrs Smithson,' she said smoothing out the ten-pound notes on her knee, and gazing at them reflectively. 'Perhaps you would let me have a look at the postcard and then you wouldn't feel you had broken your word.'

This compromise at once satisfied any scruples that Mrs Smithson might have had, and she handed over the postcard. It was addressed in an educated hand, the postmark was the Isle of Wight, and the picture represented children playing on the beach at Ventnor. Across the sky was written, *Just a little line to let you know I am comfortable, though much weaker, and to thank you again for all you did for me. I have a nice little bedroom facing south, with a balcony, and lie out on it in the sun whenever there is any. Yours affectionately, G. M.*

'No address, you see,' said Mrs Smithson, hastily pocketing the twenty pounds in case her information should be considered inadequate.

'That doesn't matter,' said Solange absently. She'll be easy enough to trace at Ventnor as she's living under her own name. Well, thank you very much, Mrs Smithson. I'll be sure and recommend your lodgings to anyone who wants rooms in London.'

'Thank you, dearie, and bless you,' said Mrs Smithson, whose tee-total liquor had begun to affect her tear-ducts, 'and I only hope you'll find the blessed angel a bit better.'

This pious wish was not to be fulfilled. The landlady had been right, and death was indeed stamped on the face of Gertrude Martin when Solange succeeded in finding her. She was lying out on a long chair on the balcony, and the pillow was hardly whiter than the face against it. She must have been a beautiful woman once. Her features, though wasted, still retained an exquisite fineness of contour. The great dark eyes, though sunken, were still brilliant. She did not hold out her hand to Solange after the latter had introduced herself, but lay looking at her with a whimsical smile on her pale mouth.

'I thought Angus would manage it,' she said. 'My congratulations to him. Of course, you come from him?'

'Yes,' replied Solange, 'I do. He'll be very sorry to hear you are like this.'

'Don't you believe it,' flashed the invalid. 'This is what he's been wanting. I'm only good for a few weeks more at the outside. Even the doctor admits that, and if you ask me I think it will be days. You're only just in time, Miss Fontaine'—she broke off and gave a little elfin chuckle. 'Oh, Lord, it would have upset Angus if he hadn't got his proofs. However, there's no need to worry about that. Here I am, and here you are. If you like to wait till I die, you can, and then go back and tell him all about it.'

She was interrupted by a fit of coughing, which left her shaken and exhausted. She motioned with her hand towards a medicine bottle half full of brandy standing on a little table. Solange poured some out and brought it to her. The sick woman's hand felt burning hot as it closed over hers round the tumbler.

Solange chatted with the landlady, a very much nicer woman than she of Hereford Road, and also went to see the invalid's doctor. He was a pleasant, straightforward, sensible man, and he told her candidly that Mrs Martin had very little longer to live.

Solange wired to Angus, although Gertrude Martin had told her that she would not see him, even were he to come over. Nevertheless, he came, as Solange felt that he would. Solange was as puzzled by the wife as by the husband. She had imagined from his account that she would find a vulgar, common woman, instead of which Gertrude was evidently possessed of a brilliant if caustic wit, and, so far as Solange could see, of a remarkably sound philosophy. It was hard to believe that this woman had ever ramped or raved over petty household details. But Solange knew from past experience that it is impossible for an outsider to gauge how hardly the presence of one human being in a house may press upon another. This woman, who showed traces of beauty and wit and now displayed such courage and philosophy, might indeed have raved like a vulgar termagant against her husband. Marriage was a relationship that did queer things to people.

What she and Angus said to each other Solange never knew. To all appearances, he was the devoted husband. He took up his quarters at the nearest hotel; every day he called to enquire, and sent her flowers and fruit and champagne. But Gertrude only saw him twice, once on his arrival and once a fortnight later, on the day she died. He made no pretence of affection in his talks with Solange, but he was obviously anxious to conform to all the decencies of life.

'What do you think of my husband?' Gertrude asked Solange abruptly one day. Solange hesitated. 'You don't know what to think, is that it?' asked the dying woman shrewdly.

'I feel I know him better than I did,' said Solange, 'but there's something about him that makes him very difficult for me to know. I don't think I can even explain what it is.'

'I suppose you mean that everything seems all right, and yet you have some sort of a feeling that it isn't?'

Solange had never in all her life felt so startled. She had been lying back in her chair, but now she sat up suddenly and stared at Gertrude. She went swiftly in her own mind over her acquaintanceship with Angus Martin. She had nothing against him. His conduct towards the dying woman, towards Flora, towards herself, was in every degree what it should be, yet somehow she liked Gertrude better than Angus. Indeed, it was for Gertrude's sake she had stayed on in Ventnor, a place she abominated, after the job she had contracted to do—the finding of Mrs Martin—was completed. The two women had a queer sort of liking and respect for each other, and to Solange there was the added fascination that Gertrude puzzled her. Why was there sometimes that odd look of compunction in Gertrude's eyes when she was talking to her?

'You're the only person who's made me feel mean over the whole business,' said Mrs Martin one day. Solange stared at her, uncomprehending. 'Oh, never mind. It doesn't matter. But you are good to me. I like you. We could have been friends. I haven't met many people as decent as you in my life. Ah, well, it can't be helped.'

That was the last day she spoke really sensibly. Next evening she was wandering in her talk, and repeated several times, 'I hope he'll play straight, as I have. Mind that he plays straight.' Twice she mentioned a name, but it was not that of Angus; it was 'Davie'. She lingered over her last pronunciation of the name very softly, and so died.

Solange stayed for the funeral, saw Angus give the order for the simple headstone: 'In memory of Gertrude Martin, wife of Angus

Martin. Died June 3rd, 1929', and then travelled with him as far as Paris, where she was going to stay. He thanked her very warmly when they parted.

It was odd, she told herself, completely unreasonable, that she should still have that little feeling of dissatisfaction. It's as though the pattern weren't quite right, somehow, she thought, and yet really the pattern is perfect. I found Gertrude Martin. She wanted to die. He, of course, wanted her to die, and dead she is. I've done my job successfully. I've got a nice cheque. Why aren't I quite pleased? I don't know. I suppose it's because, like Mrs MacTavish, I feel he doesn't really deserve Flora, although he loves her so devotedly. The funny thing is I feel he didn't quite deserve Gertrude, either. Oh well, it's none of my business any longer.

And that was where Solange made one of the many mistakes that she made in this particular case.

It was some six months later that Solange again met Angus and Flora. It was a rainy, stormy autumn for the South of France, and Solange, who was staying in her own little house in the mountains behind Cannes, was becoming thoroughly bored and was glad when an invitation came from Flora to go and stay at the Villa Sans-Souci.

The first evening passed happily enough. Solange arrived too late to see the garden, but the house itself was charming. Angus had been his own architect. He was a man of amazing versatility and, besides being a portrait painter, he was a brilliant musician and architect. The house, though built in the Provençal style, was not a slavish imitation. Solange thought she had never seen a more delightful room than the drawing-room, with it patiné walls of parchment colour, rubbed through with silver, the brilliant vermilion of its tiled floor, its silvery ceiling and beaten silver electric-light fittings. The furniture was of green lacquer, except for two rounded corner-cupboards of yellow Italian lacquer, and the curtains were of green and silver brocade. The whole house was at once gay and restful, and suited Flora marvellously well. She looked more like a Botticelli than ever, and just as virginal as when Solange had first met her.

She lay curled up, a mere wisp of silver, on the green divan, one of those rare creatures who could have had dozens of lovers and husbands, and yet remain in appearance the eternal virgin—the most fascinating type in the world, and one to which, strangely enough, sometimes the most depraved of women can belong.

The next day the storm that had raged all night had beaten itself out, and the sun was shining, although the sea still ran with crests of foam upon the little beach at the bottom of the big garden. They all bathed, for the sea was still warm with the stored heat of the summer. Angus and Flora stayed in longer than Solange, who ran up to the house, her towel wrapped round her, glowing with a sense of physical well-being. All was for the best. Angus was just one of those people who were rather difficult to know, but the nicest fellow in the world. Flora would always be radiantly happy, the house was perfection, and the garden a dream of loveliness with its cypresses and roses.

The short cut into the house for her room was, Flora had told her, through a pillared pergola covered with roses, and into a sort of garden room, whence a flight of stairs led up to the bedrooms. Towards this pergola ran Solange, singing happily as she went. She only sang when by herself; she had no ear whatever and could not sing two notes in tune, but she herself enjoyed the performance very much, and it was always with her a sign of high spirits.

The pergola was made of square concrete pillars, which, with the cross-beams above them, were painted the same soft jade green as the shutters of the house. A riot of late roses hung all about the pergola, which ran all along that wing of the building. That's the most effective thing in the whole house, thought Solange, as she moved towards it.

She was passing under the shadow-net thrown by the leaves, when suddenly she stopped. For a moment she thought she must be going to be ill. Perhaps she had swum too far in the rough sea. Her skin felt cold, her heart fluttered, and seemed to fade away in her breast, then started to race as though it would choke her. So sudden was the impact of the sensation that she stood still for half a minute, hoping she was not going to faint. Then she went on indoors and sat down in a deep garden chair, leaning her head back. The horrible sensation passed away in a few moments, and she went up to her room and dressed. When she left her room she came down again to the garden room, and, looking out, saw Angus and Flora just coming up from the beach. They were making for the ordinary entrance to the big hall when Flora caught sight of her and came towards her. Angus hesitated for a moment, then went on into the hall.

'Ready for a cocktail?' called Flora. She ran under the showering roses and came into the garden room. 'Angus will make them in a few minutes.'

'I'd love one. Where do you have them? Under the pergola?'

'Funnily enough, we never do. I don't know why. It's the nicest place of all to sit in, I think, but Angus never will. He says it's draughty. I love it, don't you? It's just the right mixture of sun and shade, and I love those great square pillars. But we always have drinks on the terrace when it's fine. I shan't be more than a few moments.' And she went on into the house. Solange stepped out into the pergola.

Curious—the heat seemed to have gone out of the sun; Angus must be right, and there must be a draught in the pergola. But it was not a draught that seemed to stir the hair of her bare head, or make her skin prickle as if she had gooseflesh. She did not feel physically ill as she had when passing through, but she shivered, nevertheless. She turned her head and looked suddenly over her shoulder. She had the absurd feeling that she was not alone, that something venomous was close to her. She recognized the sensation for that tingling sense of evil that some people gave her, and she stared down the length of the pergola either way, and peered into the garden. There was no one to be seen. Yet she was still cold, so cold that now her teeth actually chattered a little. I stayed in too long, that's it, she thought angrily. But she had not stayed in as long as Angus and Flora. She forced herself to remain where she was and looked about her more curiously, with an eye attentive to detail.

There were eight pillars in all, each about two and a half feet square and ten feet high. Red and pale yellow roses grew round them and clambered over the beams laid across their tops. One pillar had been newly repainted. She could see the paint on it glistening in the sun, and the roses, that looked sickly and drooping, had been cut away to allow of the paint being put on over a large surface. She went towards it and touched it. Yes, the paint was wet in a big patch.

And then the 'feeling' took Solange and shook her as never before. She stared wide-eyed, her heart beating fast in pure terror. For she had never had the 'feeling' in her life except for people. She had once had

it in the presence of the dead, when she had gone into the room where
the sinister Mr Brownlie lay smiling over his base secret, but never had
a place given it to her. I must ask if this house is haunted, she thought,
with a contemptuous absurd, but there it was.

'Had this piece of land any history, do you know, Flora?' she asked,
'before Angus built on it, I mean? Is there any ghost story connected
with it, or was a crime committed here?'

'Not that I have ever heard of,' said Flora. 'Of course, it must have
been a very lonely strip of shore until people began to build on it, so
I suppose anything might have happened here, but I never heard
that anything did. Why, Solange, you're shivering; don't you feel
well?'

'I believe Angus must be right,' said Solange, laughing; 'there must
be a draught here, or perhaps there's a spring underneath and the
damp strikes up, but it isn't a nice place to sit, somehow. Come on,
Flora, show me all over the house. You know you promised you'd
show me Angus's painting-room when he was away. I haven't seen any
of his work yet.'

'Angus hates showing people his work,' said Flora. 'It's been difficult to persuade him to have this show in Paris, but his things are so
good, he really ought to be better known. Come along, we'll go and
look now while the light's still good.'

Angus Martin's studio ran along the north side of the house at the
back. It was reached by an outside stairway of stone. In front of it, over
the bedrooms, was a flat, stone roof with a balustrade round it.

'He comes and walks about here when he's got really stuck in his
work,' explained Flora. 'I love the studio, but I very seldom go up
there because he has to be alone to paint, except, of course, for his
models.'

They went into the big, bare, empty room with its sloping north
light—obviously the room of a worker and not of an amateur. There
were none of the rich hangings, the divans, and the bronzes, so often
described as making up the studios of fashionable painters. At one end
of the room was a low, wooden, model throne. A lay figure sprawled
dejectedly in a chair, bald head lolling and still hands hanging down
towards the floor. An unfinished canvas was on the easel, a carefully
cleaned palette was on a scrubbed wooden table. There was a sink in

one corner of the room, and all round the wall the canvases were stacked with their backs to the room.

Solange glanced around her and felt she liked Angus Martin better than she ever had before. Then she stepped up to the canvas on the easel and stood looking at it. It was the picture of an old tramp, and if ever an evil and mean life showed in any man's face, it did in his. He was a bleary-eyed, sly, dissolute-looking old fellow, with a loose, cunning mouth, and long, dirty hands folded over the top of his stick. The picture was a brilliant piece of work, unfinished as it was.

'But how magnificent!' said Solange. 'Of course he ought to have a show if he can do things like this. But what a dreadful old man. I wonder you could bear to have him in the house.'

'Oh, but there's the outside staircase,' said Flora. 'So many of Angus's models are so terrible, you couldn't have them going through the house. He only seems to like doing very ugly and wicked-looking people. I think that old man has a dreadful face, don't you? He's an awful old man, called Matthieu, who is well known in the countryside here. He just wanders about and makes himself such a nuisance that people pay him money to get rid of him, and then he goes and spends it in an *estaminet*. Angus began that picture months ago, before he went to England, but he's never had him here since. I think they quarrelled.'

She began to pull out some of the canvases from the wall, so that Solange could see them. They were all brilliant, all interesting, but even in the landscapes, showing grim piles of rocks and distorted trees, Angus seemed unable to show anything but the repulsive side of Nature; something cruel and sad had left its impression on them. They looked the work of a man whose soul was sick. That's it, thought Solange, suddenly. I don't feel he's evil. I have never thought that, only that something's happened to him that's made him all wrong, somehow. His soul is sick.

She turned several more canvases to the light and studied them. They were all bold and cunning.

'Oh,' she said suddenly, turning towards the window the portrait of a woman; 'this is the most terrifying of the lot.'

The picture represented a woman of about fifty, with a thin shrew's face. Her greyish-sandy hair was unkempt about her peering eyes, her twisted mouth was indescribably bitter. Solange found herself flushing as she looked at the thing, it was so cruel, such an outrage on the privacies and decencies of Nature. It had been painted by sheer hate. She felt that, however foul the woman was, no man should, in common decency, have depicted her so brutally.

Flora was silent a moment. Then:

'It's hateful, isn't it?' she said. 'When I first found that, I almost felt I disliked Angus. Of course, I don't mean that really, but somehow it seemed so dreadful that, however awful she was, he should have shown her up like that. I think that's what they finally quarrelled about; she must have come up here and found it. I don't really blame her for running away after that, do you?'

The blood hummed in Solange's head, and she waited a moment to control her voice before she spoke.

'You haven't told me who it is,' she said at last.

'Oh, I thought you would recognize it. Don't you think it's like her, then? It's Gertrude, Angus's first wife. Was she very changed when she was dying?'

'Yes,' said Solange, 'yes, she was very changed . . .'

Gertrude Martin—what a gullible fool she had been—but how diabolically ingenious the plot that Angus had woven to obtain freedom to marry Flora! He couldn't be free to marry again unless he could prove his first wife's death. She ran her mind swiftly over the past year. She remembered how Angus had asked Flora to tell her the story of their frustrated love, how he had enlisted her help, how he had given her the clue of the London lodging-house. Clever, oh, how clever! So much better to let a third person discover the dying wife, instead of doing so himself! She understood now many sardonic phrases of the false Gertrude which had puzzled her at the time. Gertrude—she would always think of her by that name—what had her motive been? Money to die in comfort? Somehow, that didn't fit in with the stoical, philosophical woman she had grown to know so well, and for whom she had had such an admiration. And then there came to her in a flash the dying woman's last words, 'I hope he'll play straight, as I have . . .' And then, that softly breathed, 'Davie . . .' Yes, it was for someone else that she had lent herself to that carefully planned deception. It was to get money for somebody—a husband, perhaps, or a son.

Everything was accounted for—even her own feeling that all was not quite straight with Angus. Of course, it had been an awful situation for him! That woman in the picture would be quite capable of staying away without letting him know her whereabouts, or whether she were even alive or not, just because she knew he wanted to marry someone else. It was a jealous and vindictive, as well as a bestial, face.

And then there came to Solange, mechanically stacking canvases so as to keep her face turned away from Flora, another thought. Why had not a woman such as the one shown on the canvas turned up again since his remarriage? That was not the sort of woman to let him enjoy felicity with her successor. Only death could be keeping such a woman from disturbing his happiness. Had he heard of her death since her impersonator had died at Ventnor? Or—or had she died before? But then he would only have had to bring proofs of her death if he had known of it. *Unless her death had been such an one that it could not be revealed.* I mustn't leap to conclusions, she told herself; after all, it's always possible that she did die, but that he has never heard of it. She may have had an accident soon after she left him, or died of 'flu; anything may have happened, and he may never have been able to trace it. That is the only solution . . . that, or the other one . . .

The picture—why, in Heaven's name, had a man who had so carefully planned an elaborate fraud kept the one thing that betrayed him? Criminals—luckily for the police—nearly always did something of the sort. There are dozens of cases where they had carefully destroyed all the evidence against themselves, except the one fatal thing that, for sentiment's sake or by sheer oversight, they had kept. The vanity of the artist might have absolutely inhibited Angus Martin from destroying the most brilliant, if the most cruel, of all his works, or perhaps more strange and subtle motives had been at work. He might like to look at it and remind himself of what he had escaped, to add to his present happiness. Perhaps he was of that deep egoism that cannot bear to destroy relics of the past because, by so doing, something of himself would die.

Solange was startled to see whither her thoughts were leading her. True, the elaborate deception practised by Angus had been a crime of a sort, but she knew nothing worse of him. Yet she felt a deep unease in her heart.

When, a couple of days later, Angus returned from Paris in high spirits, having fixed up his show on very satisfactory terms, she tried to tell herself that any dark suspicions of him were unjustified. She had deliberated over her own duty in the matter and decided, with rather a feeling that she was being a coward, against any action. What could ensue but endless worry if she told Angus that she knew he had lied, that he had staged an elaborate comedy to deceive her? He would merely reply, Yes, I didn't know where my wife was; I thought she must be dead, but had no chance of ever proving it, and I was mad to marry Flora. I admit I did a wrong thing, but what do you propose to do about it? Tell Flora, and break her heart? What is there to be gained by it? Besides, between the two of us, she will probably believe me if I deny your whole story. And she will certainly stick to me, even if I admit it.

Yes, that would be true, Solange knew. Flora would feel that Angus had risked even his soul for her, and only love him the more. Passionate and very feminine women did not take very seriously a technical offence against the law. The best woman in the world didn't think she was doing any wrong in smuggling, or cheating the income-tax, and it would seem a small thing to Flora that, for love of her, Angus had deceived the registrar of deaths, especially as by so doing he had eased the last weeks of a dying woman.

But was that elaborate comedy of deception the extent of his criminality? Back and back to that nagging question Solange always came. But I know nothing, nothing; there has never been any hint of a worse crime, no suspicion of it in any quarter whatsoever. I must mind my own business, and just bring my visit to an end as soon as possible. A wire calling me to Paris . . .

The wire arrived. Flora bewailed it, but Angus, though he said everything that was charming and polite, did not seem too desolated. Solitude with his Flora was evidently enough for him. In reply to Flora's affectionate requests that she should stay one day longer, she at length acceded so much, and then, with a lighter heart, her decision taken, spent her last day but one happily enough in the winter sunlight amid the pine woods. Angus looked a little out of place at a picnic, but Flora shone with a new grace; she seemed the spirit of the woods incarnate, running like a child hither and thither, singing little snatches of song in her small, though true and bird-like voice.

She was a little tired when they returned, and went to her room to lie down till dinner, at the anxious solicitation of her husband. He himself went up to his studio, and Solange went down to the sea, regretting that she would so soon be exchanging it for the murky Seine. Soon the swift dusk of the South would fall, but the beach got the western sun, and she lay on the sand absorbing the last of the blessed warmth.

A dark figure came plodding noiselessly towards the little break-water, and only the sound of feet scrambling up its side made Solange sit up. A face was looking at her over the cement path that ran along the top of the breakwater, a dreadful face . . . where had she seen it before . . . that sly and brutal countenance with the sloppy mouth and rheumy eyes? Of course . . . the old model, the man whose portrait had been upon the easel the other day in the studio.

The old man stayed a moment, staring goatishly at her; then, in reply to her crisp and angry French, touched his decrepit hat and apologized. He was only on his way up to the studio of the English painter, he whined. With many smirks and would-be ingratiatory smiles, he shuffled past her and took the little path that led up to the side of the house and the outer stairway. Solange watched him go, her very flesh creeping with distaste. Here was a foul thing that crawled on the fair surface of the earth and made the daylight abominable. Odd that the fastidious Angus could bear him near him, even as a model, even granting that he apparently liked to paint the shocking secrets of base souls. And then she remembered that Flora had said Angus had quarrelled with the old man, had forbidden him the house. And Angus was not a man who changed his mind, whose emotions were brief and passing in quality.

Solange rose to her feet, and in her turn went up the path to the out-side stairway. At its foot she stood hesitating for a moment. What could she say if she were discovered spying? She did not even know quite why she was doing it herself. She only knew that in this house of strangeness her senses were on the alert, and that her senses had warned her of something very terrible in that old goatish man. Now, as she stood on the stairs, her every nerve warned her of danger, some dreadful danger that was imminent. Whom it threatened she did not know, or where evil lay, but that danger and evil were wrapped up in the very fabric of that house, she was at last certain. Softly, she went up the stairs in her soundless, string-soled shoes, and stood outside the door of the studio.

Low, angry, rapid French came to her ears; she bent nearer to the door and blessed Heaven that, in that land of scamped workmanship and wood not properly seasoned, the door had shrunk so that there was a gap between it and the post. As she listened her pale face grew paler; she realized that this was what, in the back of her mind, she had suspected ever since she had visited the studio three days ago.

Oh, what was the good of this old tramp thinking he could black-mail a man like Angus Martin, a man with his deadly determination, his powers of planning, his lack of scruples? You're signing your death warrant, she wanted to call to him. He was a foul old man—a blot on humanity, but it was not in Solange to treat any human life as without value, unsentimental as she was. This old man's life would be in danger now, in deadly and immediate danger. Fool, fool, fool, why did he threaten a man like Angus Martin?

The voice of Angus replied to the threats, calm, cold, but deadly.

'I will not have you coming here in the daytime. I've told you so. If you do this again, you shall not get one penny more from me. I have told you so once and I expect you to believe me. I'll give you the sum you want, but I shall have to get it first, and you will come here after dark or not at all.'

'After dark . . . after dark. I know the sort of thing you do here after dark!'

'Don't be a fool. The house is full of people now. It was empty that time you came before . . . and found me.'

'All the same, I'd rather you met me at the inn or at the harbour.'

'Thanks, and be seen by all the world handing money to a foul old brute like you, whom no one will touch. You will come here or not get it at all.'

'Well, I shall come in the daytime. Everyone knows you have painted me. No one will think anything if they see me coming here. They will only think I have come to sit to you again. I won't come in the dark. I'll tell the whole story to the police first.'

There was a little silence, then Martin's voice said flatly:

'Very well, as you will. Come at five o'clock tomorrow afternoon. I shall have to go into St Raphaël first to get the money.'

The footsteps of the old man began to shuffle towards the door, and Solange fled down the stairs. Without noticing where she was going, she ran on, only eager to get out of sight and, turning the corner of the house, took refuge in the pergola. She heard the footsteps of the old man move away through the pines; then there came to her ears a remote and muffled bang which she guessed was Angus shutting the door of the studio after his unwelcome guest.

The old man had gone, but was to return the next day at five o'clock. She herself was leaving on a train that drew out of St Raphaël at 4.08 p.m. The house would be free of her presence, but surely Flora would be there? No, for Flora would come in to see her off. But then she would be back soon after five. If Angus contemplated anything against the old tramp, surely it would not be with Flora in the house. Yet, knowing what she now knew, Solange would give very little for the chances of old Matthieu's life. No one went to the studio without the permission of Angus. A body could be concealed there till nightfall made its disposal possible. It was true that old Matthieu was a condoner of crime and a blackmailer—a breed of whom Solange thought worse than she necessarily did of murderers—but that did not allow her to leave him to his death without making an effort to save his worthless life.

The swift darkness had fallen as she stood thinking, and she felt very cold. She came to herself and to the present moment with a little shiver, and suddenly realized where she was—a sentence she had heard of Matthieu's came back to her. That was why she had felt that awful chill as from another clime in this spot; she knew now. And as she stood, less fearful now she knew all, it seemed to her that through the darkness came a little stuffless laugh, a dreadful laugh of enjoyment.

Did the mortal remains of Gertrude Martin, that sheath of flesh and bones that had housed so much malice in life, still hold its evil thoughts and sensation now that it was dead and corrupt and sealed within a painted pillar? Did what men called the soul, that quality or essence that neither Solange nor any explorer into the nature of man had ever located in the laboratory, cling about what had been its mortal habitation and spread its old accustomed influence, in this case such a malignant influence, around it? She was not afraid of poor Gertrude Martin, her thoughts were too occupied with practical questions, but her flesh revolted from the place where she stood, and she went out into the garden and thence into the house.

Angus made no attempt to go into St Raphaël next day to get money, which did not surprise Solange. It was not money that would be awaiting old Matthieu when he arrived at the studio that evening. Solange herself borrowed the car and spent the morning making artless but acute enquiries into the past of Matthieu—and heard enough to make her very pleased with her morning's work.

When the time came for her to leave to catch her train, Angus excused himself from accompanying her. Flora's lovely eyes showed a hurt surprise—Angus was going to let her have the dull drive back alone! But when he held her close and told her that he wanted to work, she gave him her lips sweetly, the gracious, yielding creature that she always was. No wonder, thought Solange, watching, that he loved Flora after having been married to Gertrude.

Flora had a lot of shopping to do in St Raphaël, things that Angus had asked her to buy, quite a long list of them. He doesn't mean her to get home until well after five o'clock, thought Solange. The problem was how she herself was to evade Flora and get back to Sans-Souci in time to spy upon or, if necessary, to show herself, at the interview with old Matthieu.

'Don't come and see me off, Flora darling,' she said, as the car ran down the steep hill between Fréjus and St Raphaël. 'I hate people hanging about on platforms to watch trains go out. It always seems hours. I don't care how fond you are of the person, there never seems anything to say.'

'Well, I *have* a lot of shopping to do,' said Flora, 'so if you're sure you don't mind . . .'

'Not a bit, I'd rather.'

She kissed Flora goodbye in the station entrance and waited till the car was out of sight, then she put her luggage in the cloakroom and went on foot to a little garage she knew of, where she had ordered a racing Bugatti to be ready for her. She tucked her little red felt hat down behind the seat, and pulled on a leather motoring helmet that she carried in her bag, complete with racing goggles. The red leather coat was reversible, being lined with dark blue leather. Solange now turned it inside out, and when the Bugatti a moment later started back for Sans-Souci, it would have been impossible to recognize the Solange who had left to catch the Paris train.

She did the distance in thirty minutes, and it was only a quarter to five when she ran the car over a rough cart track into the pine woods on the other side of the road from the villa. Still keeping on her goggles, she looked quite like a stranded lady motorist in need of help as she went through the trees by a circuitous way towards the outside staircase of Sans-Souci.

Under the staircase she knew there was a door opening into a place where garden tools were kept. She slipped through the door and kept it a crack open, so that she could watch for old Matthieu's appearance. After about ten minutes' wait in the stuffy darkness, she heard shuffling footsteps and, peering out cautiously, saw the old man reach the foot of the stairs. Then she heard his feet on the steps that sloped above her head. She waited a minute and then followed him up the staircase, and once again applied first her ear and then her eye to the gaping crack in the doorway.

She heard the voice of Angus, calm and unemotional, give the old man a brusque greeting, and then, as she peered through, she could see him point contemptuously to a wooden chair set just by the electric lamp, which was lit, for it was already dusk out of doors. Old Matthieu dropped into the chair with a grumbling remark about the steepness of the stairs.

'I never wanted you to come up them,' retorted Angus bitterly, 'and the sooner you go down them again, the better I shall be pleased, but as you won't go without your money, here it is.'

He was fumbling in a drawer in the bureau behind Matthieu's back, and Solange heard the rustling of notes. Angus had his back to her, and very gently she pushed the door a little way open. She saw Angus take a packet of notes in his left hand, and, with his right, take out of the drawer a heavy revolver. He held it by the barrel, so evidently it was unloaded and he meant to use it as a club.

'Here's your money,' he said abruptly, his voice rather strained and high. Old Matthieu swung round and held out his hand, but Angus threw the notes on to the table. 'Count them,' he ordered.

'But these are only fifty-franc notes,' cried Matthieu, bending to his task. 'There's nothing like enough here.'

'Go on,' said Angus. 'The thousand-franc notes are underneath,' and he pointed with his left hand over Matthieu's shoulder while bringing his right arm up to strike the blow.

'Angus!' said Solange sharply, stepping into the studio and flinging the door wide open.

Old Matthieu made a grab at the notes. Angus stood like a man turned to stone, his right hand still upraised and his left hand pointing; only his head moved and turned towards Solange. His face was so drained of colour that it seemed the face of a dead man.

'It's no good, Angus,' said Solange. 'You can't cover up one crime by another.'

'Shut the door,' ordered Angus sharply.

'I prefer it to remain open. I hate firearms as a rule, they always make me feel a fool, but I've got one with me now,' and she levelled her little revolver at him as she spoke. 'Yours isn't loaded, so you'd better keep where you are.'

'No, it's not loaded,' said Angus. 'May I put it down?'

'Yes, put it down, and I think you'd better go and sit on that chair the other side of the table. Matthieu, drop those notes. They're not for you.'

The man whose life she had saved was as angry as the man whom she had prevented in the commission of a crime. Matthieu snarled at her as he reluctantly withdrew his dirty, yellowish talons from the pile of notes. A filthy old man, she thought; a blackmailer and much better out of the way, but she had had to follow the law that says life must be saved, however vile it may be.

'Where's Flora?' asked Angus, in a shaking voice. 'For Heaven's sake, don't say Flora's come back with you?'

'No, that's all right. She doesn't know I've come back. I overheard you and Matthieu yesterday; I know all about it, how he came up to the studio just after you had killed your wife, and then hung round and saw you cementing her up in the pillar of the pergola that night. You can't go on paying blackmail, Angus; it's too stupid.'

'I know it is,' he answered grimly. 'That's why I was going to do this instead.'

'More stupid still!'

'As things are,' he admitted, 'if I'd known you knew—but you see, I didn't.'

'I suppose now,' remarked Solange, 'you want to kill me, but you can't go on for ever like this, you know, Angus. You're a very clever man, and I admit you lay your plans remarkably well, but there's a limit to what even you can do.'

'Oh, my God!' he groaned, suddenly breaking down and burying his haggard face in his hands. 'Don't I know it? You needn't think I should ever have been happy again if I had succeeded in knocking this old ruffian on the head. I was going to take his body out to sea to-night, in the canoe, and tip it overboard in the mouth of the gulf. Nobody'd have missed him, and it would have been a good riddance. But God knows I didn't want to kill him. He's brought it on himself, but I didn't want it. There wasn't anything else to be done.'

'Nothing else to suit your convenience, you mean. That's what the murderer always thinks. I suppose you killed your wife for the same reason?'

He looked up at that, and met her eyes squarely.

'I didn't kill her on purpose, that I swear to you! She came up here and found me working on a picture of her. We had an awful quarrel. She wanted me to destroy it, and I said it was the best thing I'd done, and I'd never destroy it. She made a dash at it and tried to get hold of it, and in getting it away from her, I knocked her over. She fell with her head against the radiator, and she never moved again. I was horribly frightened at first, I didn't mean it to happen, didn't want it. Then I began to be glad—I know it sounds horrible; why should I pretend? I had spent abominable years with her. I knew it would sound altogether too thin to tell the truth and say it was an accident. I'd been amusing myself working with the masons. We were building the pergola just then. I don't know if you know anything about building? No? Well, when you make concrete pillars, you build up a shuttering of wooden planks with thin, steel rods set just inside the shuttering.

'I waited till it was fairly dark—the moon was half-full that night—and then I went down to the pergola. There were no other houses anywhere near in those days, and I had only two servants, who slept in the *dépendance*, right away from the villa. I mixed a lot of concrete; it's made of gravel and sand and cement, and you make it with water on a platform on the ground. Then I went upstairs and fetched her; I carried her down over my shoulder. She was in a sort of evening wrap, but I got her travelling clothes and hat, because I wanted them to disappear as well.

'I climbed up the step-ladder and rammed her down between the steel rods in the shuttering. They gave a funny little clang; I remember how it startled me, as I jammed her in. And then I poured in the concrete. It was a hot night and the sweat ran off me. It seemed as if I were working for hours—and I was, too. I rammed the stuff down with the long-handled iron ram that the workmen had left, and then I found I hadn't enough concrete. I went down the ladder again, and found that, although I had gravel and cement, I hadn't any sand. I had to make some more as the stuff was only up to her shoulders in the pillar. I got the wheelbarrow and went down to the beach and brought it back full of sea-sand. That's why the pillar has never dried out properly, but what else could I do? I had to stand a lot of chaff from the workmen afterwards; they offered to do it again for me.

'Just as I was finishing, it was beginning to grow light with dawn, and I saw that one of her shoes, which must have fallen off, was lying on the ground. I went down the ladder to pick it up, and I suddenly heard a sneeze. It may sound quite funny to you now, but it was the most awful thing I ever heard in my life.'

The low voice paused, and Angus wiped the sweat from off his high, glistening forehead.

'It sounds more absurd still, but I thought it had come from inside the pillar. And then I saw the bushes behind the pergola move a little, and I dashed into them and dragged out this creature here. I nearly killed him on the spot; I wish I had, but he swore he would always keep my secret if I made him an allowance for the rest of his life. I didn't want to kill him. You won't believe me, I know, but I didn't— any more than I wanted to tonight, so I believed him and let him go. But first I made him take the shoe, and put it in the pillar and concrete it up himself. I wanted him to have a hand in it. I thought it might frighten him; he is afraid of the law and the police. Well, that's all. The first thing was an utter accident, and everything I have done since has been for Flora. Now, I suppose it's all no good and you'll give me up.'

'Wait,' said Solange. She kept her revolver pointed at the table mechanically, her hand alert, in case of any movement on the part of either man, but her brain busy thinking out the problem of her own conduct.

She felt sure that what Angus had told her was the truth. He was not a born killer. That was why she had never felt with him that overpowering sense of evil which she had always experienced at meeting a true killer. He was something almost as dangerous; he was a man of one passionately fixed idea, a man capable of any act for the furtherance of that idea, and his idea was Flora—Flora, and her happiness mingled with his own. He was, of course, the complete egoist and he had the ruthlessness of egoism, but he was not a predestined killer. Flora . . . What utter ruin this would bring into her life, how completely it would lay all waste about her.

Solange thought of the long-drawn-out months in a French prison, of a French trial, a trial of which anything might be the outcome. That dreadful night's work on the concrete pillar would damn him utterly, would show him to the world as a cold-blooded murderer, when he was, she felt convinced, merely a very level-headed man who had made the best of a horrible accident. That coolness of his, that iron determination, that cunning of mind and hand, were not amiable traits, but that was not her affair.

Still keeping the little revolver pointed at Angus, she turned her face towards old Matthieu and let loose upon him a flood of extremely scathing French. She told him of her connection with the police, she hinted at all the information she had gathered about him that morning, and implied that she knew a great deal more. Little matters of illicit business in the contraband line, a more serious affair when a traveller had been found stunned and robbed by the highway . . . There were quite a lot of little things with which she taunted Matthieu, and she ended up by assuring him that as he had kept silence all this time, and had helped with the concreting of the pillar, he would probably, if the whole story came out, spend his few remaining years in a convict prison.

Matthieu wilted in his chair, his loose mouth slobbered and quivered, his pale, rheumy eyes rolled afrightedly.

'At least,' he whined, 'I may take these with me?'

Lot's Wife

'Not a single fifty-franc note,' said Solange, 'and if ever you breathe a word of what you know, or come to this house again, your allowance will be stopped, and I will witness against you at your trial. Get out.'

She moved away from the door, and the old man, shuffling and panting, got past her as quickly as he could and went down the stairs. They could hear him drawing frightened, sobbing breaths, and Solange felt a twinge of pity. He was utterly base, but he had probably had no chance in life. She turned and looked at the man to whom many talents had been given, and her eyes were hard.

'How you're going to arrange your future life,' she said, 'I don't know. I shall have nothing to do with it. I shall have to give up my friendship with Flora, which will hurt her feelings very much, but it can't be helped. I warn you that if old Matthieu comes to any unnatural end, I shall investigate the affair myself, that's all.'

Angus raised his face from his hands and gazed at her.

'Of course, you're doing this for Flora,' he said, 'but I thank you all the same.'

'Chiefly for Flora, but not entirely. The lives of most human creatures are a bad mess, and unless the ends of justice are to be served, I don't see much point in making a worse mess of any one of them. If I were you, I should sell this house and go away.'

'I daren't. Do you think I haven't often wanted to? And then I imagine somebody getting to hate the sight of that pillar with its damnable patch of wet, and having the thing pulled down.' He broke off, shuddering.

'Well, that's your affair. You've got your punishment, whether you stay here or go away. There's one thing I should like to know: Who was *my* Gertrude Martin?'

'She'd been a fellow student of mine in Paris. She was a plucky girl, though she was delicate even then. Just before the . . . the accident happened to my wife, I had gone up to Paris and had run into her again by chance. She was dying of tuberculosis, but what was worrying her was that she was miserably poor. She had a little annuity which would stop with her death, and her son David was just growing up. After everything had happened here and after I had met Flora, I remembered her and I went again to Paris to see her. I'd tried to get her to take money before, but she was always proud, and said she couldn't take money when she could do nothing in return. I told her my wife had disappeared and that I wanted to marry again, and couldn't because I had no proof of her death. She agreed to my plan if I would start the boy off in life—if I would keep him at the 'Varsity and settle five thousand pounds on him.

'The rest you know. I did the thing thoroughly, with great attention to detail, and so did she. I wired her from here that she was to send the postcard to the Hereford Road lodgings. I had actually sent her the hundred pounds in banknotes, and paid into her account the three thousand pounds I told you of. I was determined that everything should be traceable.'

'She said,' remarked Solange, 'when she was dying: "I hope he'll play straight, as I have. Mind that he plays straight." Have you?'

Angus, a man who could work all night at walling up a woman, and who had planned the deliberate and cold-blooded murder of an old man, looked, and was, genuinely shocked.

'Of course I have,' he replied stiffly. 'I will send you my passbook if you like, or you can go to England and find David Grimshaw for yourself. He has just gone to Cambridge. He thinks his mother died on a sea-voyage and was buried at sea.'

Solange knew he was speaking the truth. It would have been impossible for Angus Martin to have cheated anyone of sixpence. She slipped the revolver into the pocket of the leather coat, and as she did so he heard the hoot of the horn as Flora's car came into the drive.

'That's Flora,' said Angus, starting up. Solange moved aside, and let him pass her.

At the head of the stairs he paused and looked round at her.

'I suppose you wouldn't . . .' he asked, and held out his hand.

'No, thank you,' said Solange.

The rebuff glanced off him and left him unhurt. He turned and ran swiftly down the stairs with no thought, Solange was sure, but that of relief and joy at meeting Flora in his mind.

Solange went through the trees, and when she was at a safe distance, turned and looked back at the house. A light had sprung up in the drawing-room, and she saw Angus and Flora standing together, his arms round her and their lips meeting. A very dangerous man, thought Solange. I'm sure his show in Paris will be a great success, but I don't envy him, all the same.

The picture of him and Flora clasped together in the lovely lighted drawing-room remained in her mind, but side by side with it was another picture—that of a damp-stained pillar. Flora might be happy in her ignorance, but for him there would always be a perpetual reminder—that pillar of salt in which the other woman stayed for ever, to nag and mock at him in death as she had done in life. In the warm and lighted house, Flora; but outside, in the dampness and the dark, there would always be, for his heart's undoing, the sly eyes and vindictive smile of his first wife.

11

GLADYS MITCHELL

A Light on Murder

THE BODY had been there for five days, and the men in the lighthouse could not get to it. Their relief was overdue, but before any of them looked southward for the welcome sight of their boat, he would first look to the west, to the black rocks against whose smooth-washed crevices the pale face and hands of the dead man showed up like pieces of paper.

They had no doubt of the identity of the corpse. They who had been four were now three. At night the great light, revolving its god-like eye, would pick out the form of their comrade, and then, as though to hide the sight from everything save the stars, it would sweep on until the next revolution again revealed the unthinkable thought—that Dick was dead.

'He must have jumped,' said Tom, the oldest and most experienced of the men. 'It's a bad thing for Maggie. Who's to tell her?'

'Funny how the sea picked him up and chucked him on the rocks and then never swept him off again,' said Dugald, the youngest man.

'It seems as if he'd been there a year,' said Walt, who was almost new to the lighthouse. 'I wonder what his trouble was? He never said anything, did he?'

'You don't need to have trouble to do a thing like that,' said old Tom. 'It takes fellows that way sometimes. You get browned-off on a light. Then you get to looking down at the sea from the gallery round the lamp, and then you do it. I knew a fellow once on the Dymballs —— But Dick never seemed that sort.'

The relief boat arrived two days later, and, in spite of a still-heavy swell, it took the dead man from the rocks. But when the captain looked at the body he refused to take anybody off the lighthouse. He returned to shore with poor Dick as fast as his boat could churn the seas. There was a knife between the dead man's shoulder-blades.

The police went out to the lighthouse and questioned the three keepers. It was soon proved that the knife had been the property of the dead man himself, but as it was impossible that he could have thrust it into his own back, there remained the question: which of his three companions had murdered him?

The fingerprints of all three men were taken but proved useless. There were no prints on the haft of the knife, and in the lamp-room and on the gallery (the only two places in which the murder was at all likely to have been committed unless more than one of the men had been concerned in it) there were the prints of all the keepers, the dead man himself included, on the railings and on the gear.

Kitbags, lockers, and clothes were minutely inspected for traces of blood, but the wound had not bled very much, and when no such traces were found nobody was particularly surprised.

Medical evidence at the inquest established that the man had been dead for eight or nine days. This coincided with the story of the keepers that about thirty-six hours after Dick had disappeared his body had been seen on the rocks and was there seven days. There was no other evidence worth considering, so the police decided to take the line that all three men were equally guilty of murder. No arrest was made, but the men were closely tailed and were not sent back to their duty.

'But, of course, they're not all guilty,' said the Inspector in charge of the case, 'and what we have got to do is to sort out the wheat from the chaff. The sooner the better, too. Trinity House don't like it that we've practically pinched three of their men. But we can't have them back on the light to destroy or to fake the evidence. But how to get at the truth——'

'We want a psychologist, sir,' said his bright young sergeant from Hendon. 'Why don't we brief Mrs Lestrange Bradley?'

'Mrs How-Much?'

'Lestrange Bradley, sir. The psychologist. Her speciality is solving murder cases.'

'Oh—her. Yes, well, it might be an idea. I don't like the thought of jugging an honest chap like a blinking prize turkey at a show.'

Mrs Bradley was interested in her new task. The men, at her instigation, were taken, one at a time, to revisit the lighthouse in her company. The fact that two police officers in plain clothes accompanied
each man was neither here nor there. Nothing was said on either side.

Mrs Bradley took the men in reverse order of age. She was anxious
to present old Tom (whom, privately and off the record, she did not
suspect of the murder) with the evidence of the other two as a guarantee of and a check upon their truthfulness. His long experience of
lighthouse work would be invaluable, she decided.

Young Dugald was her first victim. He was a red-haired, raw-
looking, chunky man of twenty-eight, married, with two children.
The dead man had been thirty-two, not very happily married, and
without children. As the keepers were relieved on a rota, there might
possibly have been trouble, Mrs Bradley thought, if Dick had known
Dugald's wife.

'We wass neffer relieved at the same time, Dick and myself,' said
Dugald, gazing out to sea with his warm, green hazel eyes, and speaking in the sing-song voice of West Scotland. 'But we wass friendly, for
all tha-at. I would not serve Dick a dirty turn, Cruachan, no! Not for
gold!'

'Well, if you didn't, who did?' Mrs Bradley enquired briskly, for she
dreaded a Highland lament for the dead man. Dugald turned his head
and looked thoughtfully at her. He saw a black-eyed, yellow-skinned,
elderly woman, not at all prepossessing to look at. Her appearance did
not seem to affect him. He had not a very high standard of physical
beauty.

'I will wish to be knowing that, myself,' he replied. 'You see, it was
this way.' He paused, collecting his thoughts. 'The pollissmen haff
put it all out of my head,' he said sadly. 'It wass so clear before all the
argument.'

Mrs Bradley could believe this. She waited patiently.

'You see, it wass this way,' Dugald repeated in his soft, sad tones.
'Dick wass on duty in the lamp-room, and the three of us, we wass in
the bunk-room. Dick wass on duty from daark until midnight, then I
wass to be on until two, Walt from two until four, and Tom from four
until daylight.' Mrs Bradley made a note of these times.

'But when I went up to relieve him, the poor man wass gone,' concluded Dugald. 'He wass not there. There wass no one.' So Dick had been killed before midnight. That was fact, unless contradicted later, Mrs Bradley noted.

'Yes, I see,' she said encouragingly. 'Did anything else happen that was out of the ordinary?'

'Well, you see, it wass a queer thing, so it wass, and I do not remember it happening effer before, but while Dick wass on duty that efening all of us, myself too, wass not feeling ferra well, and we went out from the bunk-room—but it is not manners I should be telling this to a lady.'

'But I understand perfectly,' Mrs Bradley assured him. 'You all had upset stomachs, and a need to leave the bunk-room. No explanation is necessary. You are telling me that, in your opinion, any one of you could have killed Dick. Were you all absent long enough for that?'

'You wouldn't watch the clock on such an occasion,' explained Dugald. 'You would be trying to sleep until you would need to go outside to be sick.'

Mrs Bradley nodded.

'And you were on duty immediately after Dick,' she remarked in an innocent tone. Dugald gave her a quick glance.

'That is so,' he replied. 'But, my sorrow! You must not be thinking I killed the poor man! Ochen, och, no! I would neffer haff been doing that! By Cruachan, no!'

Mrs Bradley accepted this denial with tolerant indifference, and Dugald was taken off. She spent the intervening time in drinking tea with the relief men—three instead of the usual four—and in being taken on an exhaustive tour of the lighthouse. She was shown the great lamp and received an explanation of its workings. She inspected the fog-signals apparatus, and did an immense amount of climbing up and down the spiral iron staircase and in gazing at the sea through unexpected windows which lit the upper floors of the tower.

She was particularly interested in the domestic side of the keepers' lonely lives. She saw the galley and received details of food, cooking, washing up, and laundering.

'You must all be a great comfort to your wives and mothers,' she remarked as she sat down on one of the bunks. The men grinned.

'Funny thing,' one of them remarked, 'but it's the single ones that are handiest at cooking the grub. It's the married chaps as does the chores.'

'I suppose it is understandable that the single men should be cooks,' Mrs Bradley observed. 'They are the ones who often have to fend for themselves on shore.'

One of the men agreed and the other one debated the point. The third man was on duty, for a watch had to be kept, and the log written up, by day as well as by night.

Soon the boat which had taken off Dugald returned with Walt. Mrs Bradley took him and his police escort up to the lamp-room again, as that seemed to her, as well as to the police, the most likely place for the murder. There was no doubt that the dead man had been on duty when he was killed; that is, if Dugald's evidence could be trusted; and it could easily be refuted by the others if he were lying. In any case, the gallery outside the lamp-room was easily the simplest place from which the body could have been tumbled into the sea. She looked forward to her interview with Walt.

Walt was a tough-looking six-foot man with fair hair and grey-blue eyes. He measured up the little old woman with a quick, sardonic stare, and shrugged his broad shoulders as he answered her first question offhandedly.

'Why, Duggie told us,' he said. 'He had to go on duty at twelve, but I reckon he took his time getting up there, because we all—well, p'raps he told you.'

'Yes, I've had that point put to me,' Mrs Bradley replied. 'You are about to tell me, I think, that although Dugald went to take over his watch before you were compelled to leave the bunk-room for the second or third time, you had returned to the bunk-room before he came down with the news that Dick was not to be found, and you thought him a long time gone.'

'No, it was the first time with me, but I reckon he wasn't gone as long as I thought. Besides, I don't blame him. It's no odds to anybody if a chap goes into the galley to see whether there's another cup of cocoa left in the jug, and hots it up before he goes on duty, and takes it up there with him.'

'So the mug was up there in the lamp-room when you and Tom went up?'

'I can't remember whether it was or not. What odds, anyway?'

'None, probably. How did the two men get on?'

'What, Duggie and Dick? All right, so far as I know. You *have* to get on with the other blokes on a light.'

'I should imagine so. Yet someone didn't hit it off with Dick.'

'I can't make it out,' said Walt.

The relief crew looked at the small elderly woman and the tall young man with some curiosity as they came back into the bunk-room with their escort. The plain-clothes officers then went off with Walt, took him ashore to the waiting police car and brought off old Tom to the light.

'Are you any forwarder, mam?' old Tom enquired when he had been disembarked at the lighthouse steps and had climbed to the galley for a mug of tea before Mrs Bradley questioned him.

'I shall be, by the time you go back,' she answered. 'No, none for me, Tom, thank you. I've already had some with the relief men.'

'I'll be glad to be back on here,' said old Tom wistfully. 'Rough on my missus, this is. She bears up well, but it's the disgrace. It'll get her down if things don't go right and I'm arrested. And one of us'll have to be, won't we?'

'It would interest me very much to know your opinion as to which one, Tom,' said Mrs Bradley. 'Who did it? Who committed the murder? You must have a pretty shrewd idea.'

But Tom was staunch. All three men had already been asked by the police (indirectly, of course, but sufficiently plainly) this very same question. None would give another away.

'Thinking ain't knowing,' said Tom. 'All I know is the one that *didn't* do it, and that there one is me. But all that's got to be proved.'

'Do you all carry knives around with you? Does a man have his knife with him all the time?'

'Yes, I reckon we always have a knife on us. It comes in handy, and a man don't always want to be climbing up and down them stairs, especially at my age.'

'I suppose not. What do you do with yourselves when you're off duty?'

'I dunno as we ever are off duty much in the daytime. On *and* off, as you might say. We don't reckon much on an eight-hour day, or anything of that kind, off here. We cooks and mends and washes and swabs up and plays cards and does knitting. I be the champion knitter and mender, and Dick, he were chief handyman. Dugald and him done the swabbing up, too, and Walt were main handy in the galley.'

'So Dugald and Dick were more often together on the job than either of you others?'

'Well,' said Tom, choosing his words, 'that might be so, but it weren't nothing to signify, and they always seemed to rub along all right.'

'Yes, I see. Now, Tom, there's one more thing. Dugald had to take over the duty from Dick at midnight.'

'Ay, that's right.'

'He went up to the lamp-room, found that Dick had disappeared—or so he says——'

'I reckon he meant it,' said Tom, in a tone of obstinacy. Mrs Bradley, having made the point, abandoned it.

'How long was he gone before he came down and told you two that Dick had disappeared?'

Tom searched her quick black eyes, but they told him nothing.

'I couldn't rightly say,' he replied. 'But I reckon he didn't go straight up. We'd often hot up a drink for ourselves and take the jug and two mugs up with us—one for the bloke on watch and the other for ourself, and drink it together before the watch came down to turn in.'

'Did you see a jug and two mugs up there in the lamp-room, Tom, when Dugald called you that night to say Dick had gone?'

'There was the jug, half full, and one mug, not used, mam.'

'Looks bad for Dugald, doesn't it?' said Mrs Bradley pleasantly. 'It looks as though he didn't *expect* to find anybody else up there. How much do the mugs hold?'

'Best part of three-quarters of a pint,' said Tom hoarsely, 'but young Dugald——'

'And the jug?'

'It's a two-pint size.'

'Were you surprised to see the body thrown up on the rocks, Tom?'

Tom stared, astonished at the sudden change of ground.

'No,' he said. 'Of course not. The way these currents run it was bound to be like that. The chap as chucked Dick overboard was a fool.'

'No. Ignorant. Murderers often are. How many times did you have to leave your bunk that night, Tom?'

'Three times, and Dugald twice and Walt twice. They got stronger stomachs than me. Sick as toads we was, all three of us.'

'You can arrest Walt for the murder,' said Mrs Bradley, later, astonishing the Inspector by her satisfied, confident tone.

'But how do you know?' he enquired.

'Tom knew the body would be washed up on to the rocks. Therefore I suggest that Tom is innocent.'

'We've thought that all along. It was rough on the old fellow we had to mix the sheep and the goats. But what about Dugald? Your point about the jug and the mug struck my men as pointing to his guilt. They thought you'd got him properly there.'

'I think not. Had there been more cocoa in the jug I might agree. What Dugald did was to take up one mug only—with the idea of dividing the rather inconsiderable amount of cocoa between himself and Dick, one having the mug and the other what remained in the jug. Did you ever know a man wash up an extra utensil when he need not? *I* never did.'

'I believe you. But how do you pin it on Walt? I agree you've eliminated the others, but will all this convince a jury?'

'Yes, when you've found the woman in the case—Dick's wife, I should rather imagine. Meanwhile, here is your evidence. Something had upset the men's stomachs that night—and lighthouse keepers don't have queasy insides. Each man had to leave the bunk-room from time to time during the early part of the night. You'll be able to find out what they had to eat. The point is that Walt was the cook. He could, and you'll find that he did, doctor the suppers of Dugald and Tom. He would not have doctored his own, but he made the same excuse as they did, to leave the bunk-room. What's more, I'm sure he's lying when he says he only went out once. The first time he went out he killed Dick, and the second time he tumbled the body over the gallery rail. He did not dare to risk staying away long enough to do both deeds at one time. His mistake was that he had not studied the tides. He was almost new to that lighthouse.'

12

HENRY CECIL

On Principle

I AM a young lady lying in bed in an hotel. I am not a very good young lady, but, then again, I am not a very bad young lady. I think you would find me a satisfactory mixture. I'm sure you find really good young people terribly boring and really bad ones almost worse. I am tantalizingly between the two and I think we should get on very well together—provided, of course, that you are also neither one thing nor the other, and provided, too, that you have pleasant manners and are quite good looking. I am talking naturally to young men. Young women will not be interested in me.

Ever since I was a child the good and bad in me have taken it in turns. For instance, when I was naughty in the morning I would try to make up for it in the afternoon by being particularly good. I did the same at school. If I was admonished for making a noise while we were supposed to be working, I would try to do a specially good exercise afterwards. I would really take trouble over it. So, again, when I took my first job, if I arrived at the office after nine o'clock in the morning I would stay on during the lunch-hour or go home late. Always I have felt the necessity for making up for what I had done wrong. You will probably call it conscience. I don't care for that word but prefer to talk of my behaviour as acting in accordance with my principles.

The other evening I, this not very good and not very bad young lady, was lying in bed, just as I am now, glancing at a book and wondering whether I should be happier at the dance downstairs. Suddenly the door of my room opened and a man came in quickly, shutting the door behind him very quietly. As soon as he saw me he took out a revolver. Then he spoke: 'Please not to make scream. I not speak

English well, but this' (and he indicated the revolver) 'speak for me in each language.'

'Nonsense,' I said, 'you speak perfect English. I heard you in the 'bus this afternoon. And do put down that ridiculous thing.'

'Oh—all right,' he said, 'I didn't know we'd met before.'

'We haven't,' I said, 'but I recognized you from seeing you in the 'bus this afternoon. Do put it down. I am a poor defenceless girl. You don't need a revolver to deal with me.'

'Suppose you ring the bell?' he said.

'Well, there is that, I admit,' I answered, 'but I'll promise not to ring it for ten minutes if you'll put that away. It makes you look so hideous. I must say you looked quite nice in the 'bus—from the short glance I took at you.'

'Very well,' he said, and put the revolver in his pocket.

'Good,' I said, 'now would you like to tell me why you are honouring me with a visit? But do sit down first.'

He sat down in a chair and gave a sigh. 'I'm just a hotel thief.'

'Well, I'm afraid I haven't very much for you. Now I believe the lady next door . . .'

He interrupted. 'I didn't come to get anything from you. A porter was after me and I slipped in here instead of going downstairs. I've got what I want. I don't know why I'm telling you all this.'

'I asked you why you came here,' I reminded him. 'Do you like being a hotel thief?' I went on.

'No,' he answered, 'but I've got to do something. I've tried almost everything honest from a city clerk down to a gigolo—but I couldn't get on at anything.'

'Poor boy,' I said. Now that he had put his revolver away he certainly looked very handsome. He ought to have succeeded as a gigolo. I suppose he was too independent. I like men to be independent. He was well made, too, rather like a Guards Officer, not that I know terribly much about Guards Officers.

'Would you like a drink?' I said, 'You'll find a bottle of whisky over there. You can give me one, too, if you like. I think I can do with it. The reaction, you know. I hate revolvers.'

'It's very kind of you.' He got up and, having found the whisky, poured out two glasses and handed me one. 'Neat?' he asked.

'A little water—please.'

He gave it to me and I noticed that he had very lovely eyes. I could have done with a pair like his myself—though my own are quite passable.

'Well, here's fun,' I said, and added, 'but I'm not quite sure that fun is the right word in the circumstances. Have you been to prison before?' He started at that—and put his hand quickly to his pocket. Then, when he saw that I hadn't reached for the bell, he withdrew it rather sheepishly.

'The ten minutes isn't up,' I assured him.

'Why did you mention prison then?'

'Oh—I just wondered if you'd been inside. I've never had a chat like this with anyone who has.'

'No—I haven't yet.'

'Well, I shouldn't go, if I were you. I'm told it's most unpleasant.'

'I'm not going, if I can help it.'

'Then why do you take such risks? You're bound to be caught sooner or later.'

'What else can I do? I must live. I tell you, I've tried everything of which I'm capable—and I simply can't make the grade in honest jobs. I'm a fool, I suppose. It was the same at school. I got all the colours for games you could think of—but they wouldn't make me a prefect because I couldn't get higher than the lower fourth.'

'What did you do after school?'

'The war started soon after I left. So that was all right for six years. Then I went into the City, but I was so stupid that I lost job after job. The time came when I couldn't even get a reference. D'you know, I've even tried selling newspapers and I couldn't make a success of that.'

'You certainly have tried,' I said, 'and you are very good looking.'

'Well—I tried to cash in on that too, but I could never get going. I suppose I didn't have enough capital to turn myself out well enough at the start. Then, even when I did get a stroke of luck, I was rude to the customers.'

'Oh—that's fatal,' I said, 'but I admire you for it.'

'Finally I took to this. I haven't done too badly so far, but I'm so stupid that I'm bound to be caught soon—in spite of what I said.'

'I think it's a shame that anyone looking like you should be reduced to this,' I said. 'I really am terribly sorry for you. I'd like to help.'

'What can you do? What can anyone do? If someone could remove the sheep's brains from inside my head and substitute something a bit higher up the scale, that might help. I can't think of anything else.'

'It's dreadful,' I said. 'Stand up, and let me have a look at you.' He got up slowly and came towards me. He really was a young Apollo. I hadn't realized as much in the 'bus. He was quite the most attractive young man I had ever seen. He seemed to read my thoughts.

'You're not too bad yourself,' he said. 'You see,' he added, 'that's the clumsy way I used to talk to customers. I could never pay them graceful compliments. Now, if you'd been a customer, I shouldn't have had any difficulty.'

'I am a customer,' I said.

Two hours later I rang the bell and gave him in charge. He hadn't done anything to annoy me—oh no, not at all—but I'm the hotel detective and you'll remember my principles.

NOTES

1

Anon. **W. S. Hayward**, to whom this story is attributed, was the author of some ten novels published from the 1860s to the 1880s.

2

Catherine Louisa Pirkis (1839–1910, UK) published fourteen novels between 1877 and 1894, after which she gave up writing fiction and devoted most of her time to campaigning for the then unfashionable cause of animal rights. Together with her husband, she founded the National Canine Defence League, which is still an active charity. Her last novel, *The Experiences of Loveday Brooke* (1893) was her only venture into detective fiction.

3

Fergusson Wright Hume (1859–1932, UK) wrote the nineteenth-century best-seller, *The Mystery of a Hansom Cab* (1886), which he published at his own expense after it was rejected by a major publisher. Although the book sold over half a million copies, Hume made little profit, having sold the copyright for £50. *Hagar of the Pawnshop* (1898) features beautiful gypsy detective Hagar Stanley, who runs a pawnshop in the Lambeth slums.

4

Charles Grant Blairfindie Allen (1848–99, UK) achieved notoriety with *The Woman Who Did* (1895) the story of a woman with feminist objections to marriage who chooses to live 'in sin' with her lover and bear his illegitimate child. Allen's two female detectives, Lois Cayley and Hilda Wade, appeared in the *Strand Magazine* in 1897–9. Allen died before completing the final episode of *Hilda Wade*, which was finished by Sir Arthur Conan Doyle.

5

Robert Eustace was the pseudonym of **Dr Eustace Robert Barton** (1868–1943, UK), a medical expert who collaborated with several distinguished crime novelists, most notably with Dorothy L. Sayers on *The Documents in the Case*.

Elizabeth ('Lillie') Thomasina Meade Smith (1854–1914, UK) wrote over 280 books, most of which were aimed specifically at a female audience. Best known for school stories, she was also a successful crime writer, journalist, and advocate of women's rights.

6

Baroness Emma Magdalena Rosalia Maria Josefa Barbara Orczy (1865–1947, UK) was a Hungarian aristocrat whose parents were forced into exile after a peasant uprising. Educated in Brussels, Paris, and London, she was a moderately successful artist before turning to writing in the 1890s. Best known for *The Scarlet Pimpernel*, she also wrote collections of detective stories, notably *The Old Man in the Corner* (1909) and *Lady Molly of Scotland Yard* (1910).

7

Hugh C. Weir (1884–1934, USA) founded an advertising agency and was editorial director of a New York magazine, but still found time to write over 300 movie scenarios. His only work of detective fiction, *Madelyn Mack, Detective* (1914) appeared simultaneously with a film of the same name. He dedicated the book to Mary Holland 'woman detective of real life', telling her that 'the stories told me from your own notebook of men's knavery' provided his inspiration.

8

Anna Katharine Green Rohlfs (1846–1935, USA) became famous as the author of *The Leavenworth Case* (1878), arguably the first detective novel written by a woman. She later said that she had written it as preparation for a career as a poet, but she abandoned her poetic aspirations and continued to write mysteries, which proved widely popular. *The Golden Slipper and Other Problems for Violet Strange* first appeared in 1915.

9

Arthur B. Reeve (1880–1936, USA) trained as a lawyer but never practised. In his time he was famous as creator of Professor Craig Kennedy, 'the American Sherlock Holmes', whose exploits featured in many novels and film serials. Constance Dunlap, a criminal turned detective, first appeared in 1913. Reeve later turned to real-life crime prevention, and, during the First World War, was involved in setting up the world's first scientific crime laboratory in the USA.

10

Friniwyd Marsh Tennyson Jesse (1888–1958, UK) was one of the First World War's few female war correspondents. After the war she became a playwright and novelist, and edited several volumes of the 'Notable British Trials' series. Her best-known novel is *A Pin to See the Peepshow* (1934), a fictional re-working of the 1922 Thompson-Bywaters murder case. *The Solange Stories* (1931) aimed to explore the gender-specific capabilities of a woman detective.

11

Gladys Mitchell (1901–1983, UK) became one of the most popular authors of the 'Golden Age' of detective fiction, writing under the pseudonyms Stephen Hockaby and Malcolm Torrie as well as in her own name. Despite her success as a writer, she continued to work as a schoolteacher until she was 60. She is best known for stories featuring Dame Beatrice Adela Lestrange Bradley, an eccentric psychiatrist and keen amateur detective.

12

Henry Cecil Leon (1902–76, UK) gave up a lucrative career as a barrister when his wife was diagnosed as having terminal cancer. In order to spend more time with her, he took the less well-paid post of county court judge and supplemented his income by writing fiction under the pseudonym Henry Cecil. His first book, *Full Circle*, was published in 1948 and marked the beginning of a successful writing career which included twenty-four novels, several plays, and a TV series.

SOURCE ACKNOWLEDGEMENTS

Anon. (attrib. Hayward). 'The Mysterious Countess' in *Revelations of a Lady Detective* (*c*.1864), by permission of The British Library, 1455 h 37.

Catherine Louisa Pirkis, 'Drawn Daggers' (*The Ludgate Monthly*, June 1893) in *The Experiences of Loveday Brooke, Lady Detective*, reprinted Dover Publications, New York, 1986.

Fergus Hume, 'The First Customer and the Florentine Dante' ch. 2 of *Hagar of the Pawn-Shop: The Gypsy Detective* (1897), reprinted Greenhill Books, 1985.

Grant Allen, 'The Adventure of the Cantankerous Old Lady' Part 1 of *Miss Cayley's Adventures* (*Strand Magazine*, vol. xv, 1898).

L. T. Meade and Robert Eustace, 'Mr Bovey's Unexpected Will' in *The Harmsworth Magazine*.

Baroness Orczy, 'The Man in the Inverness Hat' in *Lady Molly of Scotland Yard* (London, Cassell, 1910), reproduced by permission of A. P. Watt, London, on behalf of Sara Orczy-Barstow Brown. Copyright Baroness Orczy 1910.

Hugh C. Weir, 'The Man with Nine Lives', ch. 1 of *Miss Madelyn Mack, Detective* (Boston, The Page Company, 1914), by permission of The British Library, BL NN 2094.

Anna Katharine Green, 'An Intangible Clue', Problem III of *The Golden Slipper* (G. P. Putnam's Sons, Knickerbocker Press, 1915), by permission of The British Library, BL NN 3255.

Arthur B. Reeve, 'The Clairvoyants', ch. vi of *Constance Dunlap* (London, Hodder and Stoughton, 1916), reproduced by permission of Hodder and Stoughton Limited, London.

F. Tennyson Jesse, 'Lot's Wife', ch. iv of *The Solange Stories* (London, Heinemann, 1931), reproduced by kind permission of the author's estate.

Gladys Mitchell, 'A Light on Murder' in *The Evening Standard Detective Book* (Gollancz, 1950) reproduced by permission of Curtis Brown Limited, London, on behalf of the Trustees of the estate of Gladys Mitchell. Copyright Gladys Mitchell 1950.

Henry Cecil, 'On Principle', in *Full Circle* (London, Chapman and Hall, 1948) reproduced with permission of Curtis Brown Ltd., London, on behalf of The Estate of Henry Cecil. Copyright Henry Cecil 1948.